LOVE IS IN THE AIR

A hilarious friends-to-lovers romantic comedy

JACKIE LADBURY

Love is in the Air Book 1

Choc Lit

A JOFFE BOOKS COMPANY

Choc Lit
A Joffe Books company
www.choc-lit.com

First published in Great Britain in 2024

Cover art by Jarmila Takač

ISBN: 978-1781897461

To all my airline friends from over the years —
I just might have drawn inspiration from you.

x

CHAPTER ONE

The trim woman sporting a beautifully fitted navy Celestial Air uniform with shiny gold buttons on the jacket stepped out of the interview room. Ruby, more anxious than a turkey at Christmas, had barely uttered a coherent sentence as she was grilled about her suitability to become 'one of the team'. She had given them her heart and soul on a plate, while sweating profusely underneath her borrowed suit.

She gazed longingly after the woman as she crossed the floor and pulled open another door, flicking her neat, ash-blonde plait over her shoulder. She paused, shooting Ruby, sitting uncomfortably in the corridor, the briefest flash of a smile that softened her frazzled expression as she disappeared through the door.

Ruby had been told to wait in the corridor, and wait she would do, desperately praying her all-consuming nerves hadn't jeopardised her chance at the position she'd coveted for years.

She'd spotted the Celestial Air advert a month or so ago and her stomach had done a little dance all of its own. The small but thriving local airline was opening more routes and was recruiting. She had applied before but with no luck. Finally she would fit the bill having dragged herself to evening classes for a whole year to brush up on her schoolgirl Spanish.

The minimum height thing would be fine too. She was definitely a really tall five foot three, which — sod it — was five foot four by anyone's standards.

And so, without a second thought, she had tackled the online form as adrenaline rushed through her body. Finally life was moving forward.

She could barely believe she'd been invited for a second interview and yet here she was, sitting on a hard wooden chair trying to look like a lady, feet drawn neatly together as she pinned her hands down under her thighs to stop from biting her nails — waiting.

And it was excruciating, so desperate was she to land the job that was everything she'd ever wanted. She longed to wear the red shoes with the equally red soles that contrasted perfectly with the navy uniform and red-trim collar, although that was only part of the story, of course. She couldn't help but wonder if the shoes were real Louboutins though, even as she chided herself for her superficial thoughts.

The wait stretched out, and her stomach tied itself in knots. She muttered a plea: 'Say yes. Please, say yes,' before catching herself and rearranging her smile; talking to oneself was not a desirable quality. She squared her shoulders and inhaled then exhaled quiet as a mouse, praying she wouldn't be crushed by the next sentence she heard.

Biting the inside of her cheek she caught herself again and focused, although there was not much to focus on, apart from photos of various aircraft on the white walls, their livery blazing in blue, red and gold. They hung, mid-flight, on impossibly clear skies, their registration number written on a small plaque underneath each picture. She had no idea how an aircraft was allocated its registration number and was glad it hadn't been one of the questions asked at her interview.

She sighed resignedly. There was no way they were going to give her the job. She hadn't even known what the phonetic alphabet was, and they had laughed when she'd hazarded a guess and replied that D was for dog and F was for fish. She'd giggled too — guffawed really — realising the silly mistake she'd made. Not good.

She groaned audibly, clicking her heels smartly together as the woman returned and kicked the door behind her: the foot flashing a glimpse of the coveted red shoes.

The woman smiled. 'Ruby Hansen, isn't it?' she asked without preamble as she thrust a pile of magazines into Ruby's hands. 'Welcome to Celestial Air.'

Ruby jumped up, almost standing to attention, spine stretched tall, eyes straight ahead. 'Ma'am?' She gazed down at the pile of glossy magazines, taking them automatically, wondering what she was supposed to do with them as they slithered in her hands with a life of their own.

'Stick 'em in the VIP lounge, will you?' The woman nodded over to a door to the left of her. 'The place is awash with free magazines of posing celebrities no one cares about, and amazing houses that no one can afford in a month of Sundays. Gets on my nerves, if I'm honest, although the publishers think they're doing us a great favour by sending us freebies.'

Ruby concentrated hard on the woman's outpouring, not wanting to miss a word in case it was relevant to her interview. She rushed through the indicated door, slammed the magazines down on a side table, marshalled them into a straight pile to stop them from sliding to the floor and speed-walked out again.

'Okay?' the woman said, distractedly scrolling through her mobile phone.

'Yes, ma'am,' Ruby said, her shoulders square, chin jutting upwards. She almost saluted, hand half raised, but then thought better of it and lowered it slowly.

The lady threw her a bemused smile. 'We're not the air force, you know. Fiona will do. Senior cabin crew, if you want to know my title. Welcome to the madhouse.'

Her words filtered through Ruby's fizzing brain. Had they made a decision, then? She could barely contain her excitement. Bug-eyed, hardly daring to breathe, she asked, 'Does that mean I'm in?'

'Sure does. We like a girl with a sense of humour — you'll need it, working here.' Fiona winked and gave Ruby a smart salute. 'Three-week training course starting end of the month?'

'Absolutely.' Ruby breathed in, barely containing a huge grin. 'Thank you *so* much.'

And just like that Ruby was in, vowing there and then that she would sell her soul for this lady and would never, ever let the airline down.

A month later the problems started to surface.

CHAPTER TWO

'I get it, okay. You're not happy that I'm working for Celestial Air.' Ruby sighed at the double whammy of the crappy weather and yet another early morning disagreement with her boyfriend, Richie, who lounged across the bed looking nothing like the Adonis she'd fallen for three years ago. He seemed to be going for the vagrant look now: dull hair needing a good cut, stubble that no way looked designer, and a stained off-white tee shirt complementing the grey joggers bagging at the knees. Maybe she'd only noticed since she'd started at Celestial Air, where everyone was smart — even the engineers' overalls were pristine white.

Ruby turned away from him and manoeuvred around their bed towards the window, where her make-up bag overflowed across the windowsill. The tiny bedroom wasn't meant for a full-sized double bed, although the images online when they'd snapped it up showed it in a different light: one with space to walk in, for starters. It was impossible to open the window without a fair amount of her precious make-up being jettisoned to the ground outside. Once, a passing Canadian goose, drifting in off the stream at the bottom of their communal garden, snapped up her lipstick before realising it wasn't a delicious morsel.

She glanced upwards at the low rolling clouds and across at the swollen stream just yards away. The tinkling water had been the clincher in the summer when they'd first moved in together, but now it was just a torrent of dirty water flowing over churned up mud and clattering pebbles. The greyness of it all was depressing. To top it off, the squally wind rattling the windows and the rain tattooing a monotonous rhythm confirmed that it would be another bad hair day. Well, it was January; she could expect nothing else really. She sighed resignedly, took out her phone, angled it carefully out of the window and snapped a picture of the brooding clouds. She captioned it — *Bad hair day guaranteed* — and posted it to her Instagram page.

Reaching for her hair serum, she pumped out a glob, hoping to tame her wild locks while peering at her washed-out reflection in the mirror. Ruby's mum said they were descended from the Vikings somewhere along the line, and that was where her auburn curls came from. She'd loved that idea, had loved her hair until she met Richie. He had quickly dissuaded her of the belief that it was auburn, or that it was spun from a million sunbeams as her lovely grandmother had suggested. Neither did it cast her favourably as Ophelia floating on the river, said hair spread out as the Victorians *oohed* and *aahed* at the pale freckled Pre-Raphaelite beauty.

Nope, definitely none of the delicious compliments uttered in the past were true, according to Richie, and Richie, she had discovered, was *always* right.

If there was a perfect doppelganger for Anne of Green Gables, Ruby, with her pale complexion, annoying freckles and *dreaded frizz* would be first in line, of that she was guaranteed. Accordingly, she had revised her opinion of her hair — now known affectionately by Richie, as *labradoodle hair*.

She peered closer at the newly added pale green tints. Her hairdresser, Jayden, had promised a deep aubergine balayage, but as usual, anything she tried to better her *glorious tresses* — as Jayden ambitiously called them — ultimately backfired. She'd already posted pictures of the greenish tints giving off a luminous glow like something out of *Dr Who*. Many, many commiserations had come her way on Instagram, although the occasional fanciful person posted that they *loved, loved, loved*, her hair. Yeah, right.

Richie, thank goodness, clearly hadn't noticed the new green streaks as he hadn't said a word.

She glanced over at him reluctantly, trying not to catch his eye as she gauged his mood. The dark eyes fringed with long lashes that had once pierced her heart were hooded by angry eyebrows, and the full yet petulant lips turned down in disapproval.

She should, of course, be paying attention to his words — words that were as manna from heaven in their wisdom, in Richie's eyes at least, even though most of his mantras were filched from the internet.

By the time she realised Richie was a control freak, and to be cruelly honest, a bit of a fake, their finances were entangled and he had seamlessly taken over the majority of the day-to-day running of their modest apartment — and most of the day-to-day running of her life. She hadn't minded too much at first, but couldn't she just occasionally make a decision on her own without wondering what the backlash would be? Sometimes the urge to click her heels and shout, 'Sir, yes sir,' was too tempting, but of course that would cause another argument, one of many that wore her down, month by month.

But that was in the past. This was a new beginning. She would prove herself to be equal to the task and not be cowed by Richie and his *I'm only joking* remarks. She was ready for him and had already taken her new role as an ambassador for Celestial Air to heart. Two weeks in and she was still going strong. If only Richie would soften a bit. She crossed her fingers praying that today wouldn't be the day she failed.

'You seem to be getting awfully dressed up for someone who's just putting out fires.' Richie watched her from his prone position, his sardonic smile unnerving her.

'I'm representing the company, and they don't expect you to turn up in your trackie bottoms with bed hair, whatever the job in hand. They have standards, you know?'

'Right.' Richie looked her up and down as if she'd already failed the test. 'I thought you had to be tall and pretty to be an air stewardess.' His eyes reverted to his iPad.

The insult was as water off a duck's back, so used was she to Richie's little endearments. '*Flight attendant*, Richie, or *cabin crew* — *air crew* at a push,' she corrected, having learned quite quickly that *air stewardess* was an outdated title.

'Whatever. You don't fit the bill for any of them. Although, if I had to hazard a guess, you'd do for the cabin crew.'

She was already jittery about the day ahead and didn't need to get riled by him. 'Thanks,' was all she said. She really couldn't be arsed to explain that it was all the same job with varying titles. What did he think, that a flight attendant cavorted in a minidress with her boobs hanging out, while the industrious *cabin crew* scrubbed the aircraft on their hands and knees?

Ruby, trying to ignore him, squirted at wayward strands of her hair, the chokingly chemical smell of hairspray filling her nostrils. She spun around towards Richie, aerosol poised, the urge to blast him so tempting. Nuking him like a cockroach would be so satisfying, but she quickly checked herself and instead settled for a glare in the mirror, hexing him silently.

Richie sipped at the tea from his favourite Arsenal mug, the one that Ruby had set on his bedside table in an effort to prove that nothing would change once she started flying in earnest. She would still make the tea in the mornings and she would always be there for him. Except that she knew she wouldn't, not with the flight times and shift patterns — and Richie, having been in denial for so long, finally seemed to have cottoned on to it too.

He sniffed and reached for the digestive biscuit Ruby had placed next to his mug. 'I'm not sure I can cope with this, Rubes.' He crunched annoyingly on his biscuit.

'You have some thinking to do, then, don't you?' She tried to keep the quivering anger from her voice. Ordinarily, she was not one to snap, but now was really not the time to discuss her new career path.

In reality, he'd been grumping around ever since she'd had her first interview with Celestial Air and he'd looked positively sour when she was invited for a second. 'Bloody hell, I'll bet that was a surprise,' he'd said sincerely, the nastiness of his comment completely passing him by.

She was upset that he had such little faith in her but was not going to let his opinion sway her, not this time. She continued running the straighteners through her hair and squirting the spray, until her hair was practically solid; no drizzly rain would sneak past her defences today.

'You're telling me that you won't make a choice?' The tone of Richie's voice was vaguely threatening and he clearly wasn't going to let the subject drop.

Here we go, Ruby thought. Three years they'd been together, and now it was choose him or the job? Was he seriously asking the question? She didn't honestly know which way she would sway and hoped to deflect it for another day when she wasn't, quite frankly, in a raging hurry. She slammed down her hairspray can and faced him. 'Rich, I've wanted to do this job for, like, *ever* — and you've known that. How can you want to stop me? If you really loved me, you'd be happy for me.'

'You know what they say,' Richie said softly, placing his mug carefully back on the bedside table.

'What who says?' She'd noted the crack in his voice. Now she was pretty sure his eyes were filling with tears, which was seriously weird. 'What are you on about?' His mood swing was confusing but she really didn't have the time or inclination to pander to him. Not this morning.

'If you love someone, set them free.'

'Really? What stupid arse thought that one up?'

'Sting?' Richie paused. 'And maybe me?'

'What?' But to Ruby's ears it was already a statement, written in stone. A statement to be concerned about? She gaped at him. She knew he was a jealous man, knew it the day she'd met him when his first words were, 'I want you — all to myself.' She'd been flattered, of course, but as time went by his possessiveness became more of a pain in the arse than proof of his devotion. Control, not adoration.

'This is because you think I'll run off with a pilot, isn't it?'

'No, I just miss you when you're not around.'

That was the first she'd heard of it. Her own lips twisted in disbelief, but she said, 'It'll be fantastic for you. You'll finally be able to start on all those hobbies I've apparently stopped you from pursuing.'

'Maybe I don't want to do them anymore — not on my own, anyway.'

'And what if I don't want to do them with you, either way?' Around and around their silly spats went.

The mug of tea was picked up again and Richie held on tight, knuckles white, as if he wanted to strangle it. Angrily he kicked off the duvet in case Ruby hadn't grasped how pissed off he was. 'My hobbies, or lack thereof, are not really the issue here, are they?'

'Are they not?' Ruby sighed, watching his face contort to outrage and then harden to suppressed anger. She could view his little temper tantrums dispassionately now and knew he could carry on for hours until she gave in, but this time she wouldn't — couldn't. She'd invested too many hours into her new career, not to mention her income — or the lack of it, should she mess up. Obviously, flying around Europe for a small regional airline wasn't as exotic as flying around the world, but it was a start. And everyone was so friendly; she was made to feel like she belonged the moment Fiona dumped the pile of magazines on her and saluted.

She smiled at the memory even as her hands trembled at the thought of the day ahead. She hoped so much to deliver her promise to never let Celestial Air down, or herself, but today was going to be a real challenge. The last two weeks had been a breeze compared with what she faced today. The firefighting challenge had finally arrived.

Ruby had suffered a fear of fires since she and her best friend Charlotte accidently set the scrubland behind her house on fire when she was twelve. Her older brother had told her the thick grass reeds that grew by the pond could be smoked like a cigarette and it had made her want to try it. She'd snuck a box of matches out of the kitchen drawer and trekked out to the slimy green pond with her friend, giggling as they waded into the gunky mud in their wellies, picking out the stubby reeds to try and smoke by the side of the pond once they had dried out. In the sunshine she could still recall the acrid taste of burning in her throat as she'd foolishly lit and then sucked on a red-hot reed, dropping it as it burned her fingers and lips. The dry grass under her feet had begun to spit and crackle, flames leaping up out of nowhere, quickly eating up the brittle bracken. An inferno rapidly snaked across the field, thick black smoke billowing upwards, filling her nose and mouth, stinging her eyes and making her cry out in fear.

The terror stayed with her, and even now the sound of a fire engine triggered an irrational prickling of the skin, tears springing unbidden, to be blinked away. She and Charlotte were lucky to get away with their lives, the fireman had said as they arrived back home, soot-stained, coughing and fearful of the inescapable dressing down from their parents.

She shook her head, dismissing the memory, needing to conquer her fear. Maybe learning about fire extinguishers and their uses would go some way towards helping her, but she still had to get through the practical exam, which loomed like a huge beast waiting to pounce.

Trying to escape from the blackened shell of a burnt-out aircraft, spraying foam on to purpose-built fires, wearing a full-face mask and heavy padded coat did not seem the way forward, and she feared it would end up being another nightmare that would follow her to the grave after she inevitably failed to carry out any of her duties.

She swallowed down the fear. If she didn't manage to complete the course today she was out, no second chances — and no rent money. Richie's sullen face today would be a breeze compared to his fury if she got kicked off the course and couldn't contribute her fair share of the bills. And he would gloat for ever that she'd had the temerity to think she could succeed at something other than a dead-end council job, shuffling bits of paper around and listening to batty Mrs Roberts in Human Resources telling the same old noisy-neighbour stories week after week.

She finished dressing, couldn't face any breakfast and left early, no longer willing to jolly along Richie, who turned his thunderous face away from her as she tried to kiss him goodbye. She gave her hair one last blast of hairspray as if it would cement her future as well as her hair, and set off for the airport.

CHAPTER THREE

Ruby manoeuvred her car into a space and took a deep breath before stepping out, as an invisible wraith of mizzle misted her hair. 'Bugger,' she muttered, holding her mobile phone over her head — as if that would help. It was as useless as a Christmas paper crown for keeping the rain off, so she gave in and decided to put it to better use. She scrolled down to find her new partner in crime's number. She texted: *Hi Lucy, I'm here, are you?*

Yeah, I'll see you by the coffee machine in the crew room.

Lucy was also a newbie and they'd bonded together over Resusci Annie, the rubber resuscitation doll whose face was remarkably serene considering the pulverising she endured on a regular basis. Ruby had breathed air into Annie's rubber mouth while Lucy pumped at her plastic heart, fake red blood lighting up around her track-suited body. They'd both rolled their eyes at the ridiculousness of what they were doing, even as they knew it was important to pass that part of the test, and they'd stifled giggles as Lucy stuck out her top teeth like a vampire and pretended to bite Annie's neck. Ruby had taken hold of the rubber hand and pronounced her *very ill indeed*, earning a mock glare from the first-aider while everyone laughed. Learning how to resuscitate was the easy part, Ruby now realised; they were being eased in gently.

Walking hesitantly to the building that she already viewed as her new workplace, she mentally prepared herself for the ordeal ahead. She reached the swing door to the crew room and took a deep steadying breath. She was finally *in*, after years of dreaming — and she was among new friends. She was not going to mess up just because of a stupid fire that she caused when she was a kid.

She shivered as she remembered the video they'd all been obliged to watch the day before, of an aircraft bursting into flames on landing and the mostly successful deploying of the slides as people threw themselves out of the doors, eyes wide with fear.

'Eighty people out of one hundred and eighty got out of that one alive,' Fiona had said solemnly. 'A fire started on board and one of the crew used the wrong extinguisher and exacerbated the fire.' She reached under the desk and flourished a red fire extinguisher. 'With the right training and equipment the damage of an on-board fire can be minimal. Indeed, there have been many recorded incidences of survivals simply because the appropriate equipment was used.' She reached under the desk again. 'With the wrong equipment you can make the situation worse.' She brought out a bottle of water and gave it a shake. 'Water doesn't always save the day.'

Everyone nodded. They had learned that much already.

Ruby *so* wished she hadn't seen that video.

'Steely core, steely core,' she repeated as she pushed open the double doors, bumping into someone standing on the other side.

'Steely who?' A pair of amused eyes looked at her, the rest of his face falling very nicely into focus as he sipped at steaming liquid from a cardboard cup. Smiling, he raised his pilot's cap. 'Welcome, Steely.'

'No . . . no, that's not my name,' she said, swivelling swiftly to rescue her arm as the doors almost swung shut on it.

The man feigned confusion, tilting his head to one side. 'That's a shame, I do like an interesting name. Mine's Milo — not very interesting, I suppose, but both arms intact.' He placed his drink on top of the coffee machine, raised his arms and shimmied his fingers like jazz hands, smiling cheekily.

Ruby, bemused, wondered what he was going on about and didn't smile in return.

Her bewilderment must have showed as Milo added, 'Unlike my namesake, *Venus de Milo*? No arms?'

The penny dropped. She had visited the Louvre on a school trip and remembered seeing the beautiful statue. It had given her a brief but intense interest in the Greek gods. 'Don't tell me, you were conceived in Paris.'

'Bingo. My mother was, and still is, an incurable romantic.'

Ruby shrugged. 'Could have been worse, they could have called you David, after Michelangelo's statue. He had a notoriously small, err, appendage, I believe, or you could have been named Hermaphroditus, who had a bit of both.'

'I like it, a girl who knows her Greek gods, and you didn't even mention that Venus de Milo was actually a woman. Very polite.' The cheeky smile returned and suddenly she knew who she was talking to. This was First Officer Fraser, who all the newbies gushed over — the straights *and* the gays — all silently praying that he would fall in love with them. His family owned a stately pile and a billion sheep on a trillion hectares of land, or something crazy like that, and by the looks of him, his good fortune also included a body and face straight out of a fashion magazine. She smiled tightly, understanding what the fuss was about, but not prepared to play the game.

'Hi, Milo, nice to meet you.' If she could do one thing right today it would be to keep resolutely away from this man and his high opinion of himself, and his non-witty banter.

In the interest of her Instagram account she determined to take a blatant snap of him, but only because the sun, showing its face for a second, reflected off a wetly glistening aircraft wing in the background, sending up a glittering shard of light. 'Say cheese,' she said. 'Oh, and also, say *yes*.'

'Yes?' he agreed, turning around to follow her line of sight, looking amused.

'Thanks.' She smiled, and before he had time to blink she'd put his cute face on her Instagram account. *Cool guy alert — with epaulettes. #Plymouthairport!* It was a sneaky way of asking his permission, but his face was in shadow anyway, so it wasn't clear who he was.

She gave him a quick smile of dismissal and walked over to the coffee machine to distance herself, but to her surprise he followed right behind her.

'Where are you going?' he asked.

'What's it to you?' It came out sharper than she meant, but all in all, that was a good thing. He needed to know she wouldn't be taken in by a pair of summer-sky-blue eyes.

'You're my partner for the day. You should be buttering me up, not running away.'

'Sorry?'

'I was just messing around — you know, the Steely Core bit. I know you're Ruby and you've been partnered with me — on the firefighting thing. They try to pair a newbie with someone who's been through this bollocks before.' He indicated a list of names on a sheet of paper stuck to a cork board. He turned, paused and peered at her, clearly waiting for her slow thought processes to catch up. His smile almost faltered and he blanched at her horrified expression. Nevertheless, he rallied. 'It's not all bad, you get to hold my hand — so we don't lose each other in the mock-up cabin.' He winked again and held out his hand.

As if she'd been hypnotised, and although she had no idea what he was talking about, Ruby reached out and took it.

'There we go, that wasn't too bad, was it?' Milo asked, trying to reassure her with a gentle smile.

On the contrary, a shot of electricity rushed up her arm and a flush of heat rose up from her chest to her neck, as if Milo had secreted a hand buzzer in his palm. The urge to distance herself from him was overwhelming and she lurched away from his grasp as if stung. As luck would have it, Lucy sauntered through the door exactly on cue and Ruby launched herself at her new friend like a pet dog being reunited with its owner after months in the wilderness.

'Lucy, here you are,' she gushed.

Lucy took a step backwards, deflecting Ruby's embrace. 'What's up?' She disentangled her friend's arm from around her shoulders, glancing quickly at Ruby's companion.

Ruby shrugged. 'I'm just pleased to see you.' She knew it sounded lame but she held on to Lucy like an alcoholic glued to her last glass of wine.

Lucy shot her a puzzled look and glanced at Milo. 'Hi, Milo, what have you done to my friend?'

'Just getting acquainted.' Milo seemed bemused again and Ruby cringed inwardly, wishing Lucy hadn't asked the question.

It was no surprise that Lucy knew Milo. Unlike herself, Lucy seemed to know everyone and everything about them, regardless of the fact that she and Ruby joined the airline at the same time. Lucy mixed with the *beautiful people* as Ruby called them: the ones who waltzed into VIP nightclubs without a nervous glance that they might be hauled out by their collars, and whose Instagram accounts managed to bag 20,000 followers simply by posting pictures of themselves in tiny outfits that they threw on and nearly missed, pursing their lips like suckerfish.

She looked through the full-length window that showed the apron, which she had learned was the weird name for the area where the aircraft sat on the tarmac. A large seagull perched itself on the wing of a plane, its feathers blowing in the wind and Ruby groped for her phone, being easily distracted by anything Instagrammable.

Surreptitiously, she snapped the image and slipped her phone back in her pocket. If she could make it look as if the aircraft was flying, the seagull's feathers ruffling on the wing, it would be a fun snap. Suitable captions ran through her head. *Another bad hair day*, maybe?

She caught Milo's curious glance but he turned away as their eyes met and she was grateful she didn't have to explain about Instagram and how much her followers meant to her. Still, she felt her cheeks burning at his attention. Never before had she felt such a strong attraction to someone, let alone within minutes of meeting them. Never.

It would not do. Normally she shied away from anyone remotely good-looking, knowing that she would never measure up in their eyes. She had considered herself lucky to bag Richie, an eight-out-of-ten sort of guy with a reasonable body and fine jawline, even if his eyes narrowed a bit when she talked about her new job. But no mistaking, he was the man for her, the only one she wanted, and their future was guaranteed. *They were entwined together like two palm trees*, she thought, vaguely remembering someone famous using that daft analogy.

But still she watched surreptitiously as Milo spun away at the sound of his name and was soon engrossed in conversation with another crew member.

'Why is he on our course if he's a qualified pilot?' she asked Lucy when they were out of earshot.

'You have to renew your fire training every third year, just like the first-aid qualification.'

Ruby's heart sank. 'We have to go through this again? How come I didn't know that?'

''Cos you're in a world of your own with your photos and your blogging.'

'Am I?' Hurriedly she pulled her phone out of her pocket and shoved it into her bag. 'Don't say that, I don't want Celestial Air to think I'm not giving one hundred per cent.'

'Don't worry, your secret is safe with me.' Lucy turned around and raised her hands to grab attention. 'Hey, everyone, Ruby's on Insta if you want to follow her. She takes fabulous photos and is writing about Celestial Air.'

'Lucy!' Ruby elbowed her friend.

Lucy laughed. 'No one cares, look.'

It was true. Half the newbies were engrossed in their own phones, and the rest didn't even glance up until a fireman, unmistakeable from his high-vis jacket that announced FIRE CREW on the front, called them to attention.

'Okay, listen up, you guys. My name is John and I'm the chief fire officer here.' He stood, legs apart, his chest puffed out as if he thought he was on the set of a reality TV programme.

Someone giggled and he glared at them. 'It *is* time for some serious fun. And by that, I mean *this*.' He adopted a sly grin and tapped his clipboard. 'But there is no reason why *that*—' he pointed in the direction of the window — 'shouldn't also be fun.'

Everyone looked confused. 'What's he rabbiting on about?' Lucy hissed.

'The fire is roaring,' he added ominously, confirming that his ranting was firefighting related.

All eyes swivelled towards the window, where the rain that had recently stopped decided to unleash itself over their particular part of the world again. The sky was a bruised navy and steel grey and a brutal wind scattered raindrops like bullets against the window. A loud crack of thunder made everyone jump as lightning lit up the blackening sky.

'Good luck with keeping a fire going in *that*,' Ruby hissed.

'Most people take something positive away from this day,' John shouted over the din of an aeroplane coming in to land, its engines whining as it shut down, adding to the cacophony caused by the weather outside. 'As I said,' he shouted, 'you should come away with something from this training session, even if it's only superficial burns and pinkeye from the ashes.' He raised his hands, laughing. 'I'm joking.'

'Wanker,' someone muttered, and Ruby held her breath praying John hadn't heard. He *was* full of his own importance, but he probably had cause to be: extinguishing aircraft fires was a pretty impressive job.

'So, grab some insulated gloves, a heat-resistant coat and follow me,' John finished with a smile.

Everyone shuffled around a bit looking lost until the first brave soul took the initiative and walked over to the line of yellow coats, unhooked one and struggled into it.

By the time Ruby had trooped along with the queue of people, there were only extra-large coats left and reluctantly she heaved one on. It weighed a ton and she giggled as she drooped under its weight. Grabbing a pair of bright orange gloves from the dwindling pile, she grimaced as she dragged them over her cold hands. The gloves looked as if they had had a long and successful career in digging gardens and the middle finger on the left hand had been chewed off — by a rodent, or maybe a very anxious firefighter. Sighing, she followed the others along the corridor and out of the door, imagining how a mediaeval knight must have felt weighed down by chainmail and the certainty of their fate.

Following the others blindly, she arrived at a huge square of tarmac dotted with sunken pits, where a series of slightly pathetic fires struggled to stay alight, valiantly throwing a plume of thin ash up every few seconds. This she could handle, she thought . . . Then John poured something on the fires and they perked up no end, roaring into the air like flamethrowers — the bastards.

Now it was real.

She squared her shoulders; it was make-or-break time.

CHAPTER FOUR

The fireproof coat not only weighed a ton, making her knees sag, but the zip chafed at her throat and the baggy sleeves fell past her fingers, and to compound her misery, rain dripped icily down the back of her neck like Chinese water torture. She wondered what part of this John had in mind when he'd described it as 'fun'.

To make matters worse, each person had to put out the fires individually and it took an age as everyone waited in line in the rain, freezing their bums off. To Ruby's mind the fires were like those birthday candles that reignite every time they're blown out. Ruby wondered what on earth John kept pouring on to the wood that burned so robustly. No eco-friendly worries for this man, clearly.

Everyone huddled underneath the corrugated-iron shelter to keep out of the rain — rain that slanted in anyway, so it was a pretty pointless exercise in trying to keep dry. By the time it was her turn she was rigid with apprehension and numb with cold. John continued to pour his flammable liquid on the fires at random intervals, and bright yellow and blue flames leaped obligingly to attention, sizzling as raindrops doused them momentarily.

Milo gave her big, sympathetic eyes as he joined her side. 'You look freezing, and why are you wearing King Kong's coat?'

'Hmm?' She tried to speak but her lips were frozen together — or they might as well have been. She rubbed at them until sensation came back. 'King Kong? Oh, that old gorilla never comes out in the rain, so he didn't need it.' She could barely raise a smile at her own joke, though; it wasn't just the coat that was weighing her down.

'Such a lightweight,' Milo agreed. 'Unlike his coat,' he added, clearly prepared for some light-hearted banter.

When she didn't reply, his smile faded. 'You okay?' he asked.

'I'm fine.' She didn't dare elaborate, as vocalising her fears would make her bolt for her car. She gave a tight smile to a fireman as she accepted an extinguisher, nodding as he reiterated its uses.

'Class A, B and C extinguisher, okay? Electrics, grease and general fires. Right?'

'Yep. Got it.' The extinguisher was the size of a small dog and bloody heavy considering it was filled mostly with foam, but she hoisted it on to her shoulder and gave a good impression of someone ready to do battle. Inching towards the fire, she batted at the burning flakes of ash that blew in crazy whorls around her face, a whirling dervish taunting her in a game of tag she would never win.

She looked bleakly at Milo.

'Ladies first,' he said, taking a few steps backwards.

'Thanks.' She sighed heavily, glowered at the fire, and in a moment of madness shouted, 'Geronimo!' intending to take it by storm. Sadly, it roared up ferociously as if accepting the challenge and she bottled it, coming to an abrupt standstill. 'I think it's alive,' she whimpered, trying to stare it down, but it didn't care and carried on being ferocious and bright and hot. She waited a minute, drawing strength from the scant reserves left in her body, breathing in and out raggedly as she tried to quell her fear.

Coming to a decision, she could either walk away and lose, or fight and win. She decided to win. Heaving the extinguisher to a vertical position, she inched forward and squeezed the trigger, but her fingers, numb with cold inside the insulated gloves, would not move. She grimaced as she threw all of her might into it, fleetingly wondering what the hell she thought she was playing at, giving up her sensible job and upsetting Richie to the point where she might not even have a boyfriend anymore, to do *this*.

Smoke caught in her throat, soot clogged her eyes and the rain turned the ash into slush to settle on her cheeks as she closed her stinging eyes and squeezed even harder on the trigger. Any thoughts of stealing a quick Instagram picture to remember this most miserable of times disappeared. A whooshing sound emanated from the extinguisher as her eyes widened in surprise and a jet of white foam burst forth and landed on the seething flames.

The immediate rush of satisfaction soon dissolved when John raised the megaphone to his lips and shouted, 'The fire is not out!' indicating Ruby and her treacherous, still-burning fire.

John was safely tucked up in his Portakabin, she noticed, and couldn't help but feel resentful. She resisted the urge to throw the fire extinguisher at the cabin and storm off.

'Aim the extinguisher at the base of the fire,' he enunciated clearly as if she was an idiot, which she clearly was as she couldn't put out a simple fire.

Gritting her teeth, she gave the fire another blast of foam, hitching the unwieldy coat back over her shoulders before it managed to drag her trousers down with the sheer weight of it. The fire disappeared as if it had never been there — now a soggy pile of grey matter apart from a few bits of ash floating half-heartedly in the air before being quickly attacked by the rain.

Proud as punch, she stood there relishing this small achievement while muttering insults at the dead fire as if they'd had a fight, until a fireman took her extinguisher from her and guided her away — before she could take a photo of the wind whipping up the pile of smouldering ash into a whirlwind, which she suddenly knew would have been the very best photo in the world. Damn.

But she'd done it! With a grin she couldn't contain, she almost hopped, skipped and jumped back to her colleagues, who were chatting casually as if the most momentous event in the world hadn't just taken place, right in front of them.

'This is the very last time I do this refresher course,' one of the old-timers shouted over the din of an aeroplane coming in to land, its massive form blotting out the light as it skimmed the line of trees and thundered on to the runway, causing the tarmac to vibrate.

'You say that every time,' someone else said with a laugh.

'Old John won't let us go until our eyes bleed or we disappear into that wreck of an aircraft, never to be seen again,' a captain replied, reminding Ruby that she might have won one battle but there was worse yet to come.

Tugging at her lumpy yellow coat once more, she shoved her hair out of her eyes and wiped ineffectually at her itchy, grimy cheeks, thanking God that at least Milo — *with the arms* — was nowhere to be seen.

'Hey, I have a good idea, why don't we just stand here and wait for the rain to finish the job?' A tall man she'd never seen before grinned at her as water dripped off his nose.

She nodded and smiled politely, not really wanting to engage in conversation, and turned her attention once more to John, who had dispensed with his megaphone and was shouting into the wind, tapping his clipboard again. 'Let's get a move on and then we can all have a well-deserved cup of tea.'

Lucy sniffed loudly. 'Tea? That's a bloody joke, surely.' She wiped a hand across her forehead, trying to clear her eyes of wayward strands of hair, leaving a smear of soot behind. Ruby thought it probably wasn't worth telling her about it; they probably all looked as if they'd been sweeping the insides of a chimney with their faces.

'Why don't we just piss off to the pub and then get our-selves a sensible job in Marks and Sparks?' someone else said.

To Ruby this seemed like an excellent idea but no one took it any further, and she suspected that in reality they all loved their jobs as much as she knew she was going to. They wouldn't leave for all the tea in China.

Ineffectually, Ruby retied her hair as the wind whipped it up in twisty curls, plastering it to her cheeks and forehead, random wisps waving in the air as if she'd stuck her fingers in an electricity socket. 'Please tell me that this is the worst it gets?' she said to no one in particular, staring up at the sky and the relentless rain.

Lucy sniffed again. 'Get myself all tarted up, don't I, so I don't let the side down and hope I might find a tasty fireman, and then they stand us out in the freezing bloody rain and heap fire and brimstone down on us. I tell you, they're taking the piss.'

Lucy hammed up her role as a wronged woman, while Ruby enjoyed the camaraderie that surrounded her. She felt a moment of pure happiness and joy that she'd been given this opportunity in life. This was where she belonged, and no amount of disapproval from Richie would dampen her enthu-siasm — although the rain was making a pretty good fist of it.

John clapped his hands to get everyone's attention and Ruby's stomach looped the loop.

'Right, gather round, we're going to do the aircraft cabin fire next, so get your smoke hoods ready and split up into twos — your names were paired in the crew room, I believe.'

Ruby heard the dreaded words, 'smoke hood' and the horror of every nightmare she'd ever had returned. *Smoke filled her mouth and nose, her eyes . . . she couldn't see. She was being taken by a creature made of slime and smoke.*

It had been a recurring dream for years after the Day of the Unfortunate Torching, as she now called it.

To put out a raging fire was bad enough, but doing it in a tunnel wearing what amounted to a space helmet was just wrong. She took a deep breath. If ever she needed her steely core, it was now.

As if he sensed her fear, Milo was suddenly by her side. He clearly knew what was heading their way, whereas she could only imagine the horror to come.

'Hi, I'm Milo, and I'll be right here, to make all your dreams come true,' he said in a terrible American accent, his mouth set in a rictus grin like a ventriloquist's dummy.

Ruby wasn't sure what style he was going for, but the incongruity of it made her laugh.

'Yes, this is *just* the right place to make all my dreams come true.'

He shrugged. 'I'm lying, clearly.'

She laughed again, the tension in her body easing.

'It's just a mock-up — a smoke-filled, burnt-out shell of an old aircraft.' He narrowed his eyes as he glanced over the hulk of an aircraft in the near distance, menacing and brooding like a submarine surfacing in a sea of grey. 'It's no big deal. We just stroll in, drag out the body and come out to the fresh air.' He raised his hands, palms up, to show that when he said *fresh air*, he really meant wind and rain.

'Smoke-filled? As in *full* of smoke?' she asked.

'Doesn't sound *that* bad, does it?' he added, looking doubtful.

She swallowed hard, fighting back nausea. Like hell, it didn't.

'Cheer up, you get to hold my hand, remember? You can squeeze as hard as you like. I'm well 'ard.' He grinned as he flexed his pecs.

'No offence, but even holding Harry Styles' hand as he sang that he adored me would not be enough compensation for this.' But she had to admit that holding Milo's hand was sensible; at least he could lead her through the cabin. But she wasn't impressed and it was all she could do not to harrumph loudly in disgust, like her grandad did when Boris Johnson came on the telly. She wondered if Milo would be quite so jaunty in half an hour's time if he failed the course because of her.

Milo was gearing up to say something with his rictus ventriloquist smile when he was interrupted by John shouting through his megaphone again.

'Most of you know the drill for this, but for the benefit of the new crew, here's what happens.' He glanced at the latest recruits. 'You enter the aircraft cabin here.' He pointed at a gaping hole in the blackened hull. 'The aircraft will be full of smoke, obscuring your view, and your job is to find and retrieve the dead body. For a bit of extra fun we've thrown in a few random fires at various points inside the aircraft. So, extinguish the fires and rescue the body, which, for the squeamish and so we don't get sued, is a dummy. Ha-ha, what a surprise.' He waited for the laughter that didn't materialise, although a few people tittered thinly.

He went on. 'You drag your body out of the aircraft, keeping your smoke hood on at all times or else you *will* fail this course. Are we all clear on this?' His look was comically ferocious and everyone nodded meekly.

'The dummies are mostly filled with sand — stops 'em burning up — and they can be very heavy, so make sure you don't lose your partner as you'll need four hands to carry it.' He beamed at them as if he was offering them a real treat. 'So, who wants to go first?'

Lucy twisted her hair on top of her head and picked up one of the ugly smoke hoods from a waiting fireman. Grinning with a Wallace and Gromit kind of smile, she grabbed a pilot named Giles by the arm and said, 'I'll start, and I'll take this dummy with me — save me having to find one.'

Giles laughed good-naturedly as he reached for a smoke hood. 'Thanks very much.'

Ruby stared in fascination. Was the woman mad? Surely she wasn't actually considering going into that thing?

But Lucy pulled the hideous hood over her head, shoved an escaping strand of hair into it, gave a thumbs up and disappeared along with Giles, who lumbered into the forbidding black chasm after her.

Ruby watched tight-lipped, hardly breathing as she waited for Lucy and Giles to reappear from the monstrous maw, convinced that she would never see her friend again. They would burn to death, or at the very least be murdered by the dark forces that surely lived inside that shadowy den. She bit her lip, blood throbbing in her head as she stared at the gaping hole, waiting. She closed her eyes and held her breath, until a whoop of jubilation split the air.

She let out her breath. Lucy had made it. Ruby's smile of relief was quickly replaced by a frown as whatever lurked inside that dark heap of junk would now be waiting for her.

With a measured, determined gait, two other crew members entered the shell of the aircraft, smoke hoods pulled tight, dark silhouettes against a smoggy sky, as if they were entering a spaceship in some kind of catastrophe film where the sad victims boldly go where no one with any sense would go, never to return. They always died, that much they had in common — even if the pet cat was rescued.

Ruby fumbled under her layers to locate her phone, dragged it out and snapped half a dozen images before shoving it back into her jeans pocket, unsure if it was appropriate to Instagram this, even though she knew she could make it look even more moody and mysterious than it already was.

She waited fearfully until they too lurched out from the hull of the aircraft. The woman was slapping at her hair as she wrenched the hood from her head, and Ruby, panicked, looked around for help, convinced her colleague's hair was on fire. She ran towards the woman, slowing to a standstill when she realised she was simply shaking her hair out of its rubber band. Feeling slightly silly, she confronted the burnt-out aircraft close up and her legs started to wobble along with her bottom lip. She really was a hopeless case.

Tears of anger filled her eyes and she turned around to hide her face, heading away from the goings-on. She sat down heavily on a low wall, hunching into her vast waterproof coat, fighting to keep full-on tears at bay. It would be too mortifying to let herself blub in public, but she honestly didn't think she could enter that thing wearing a suffocating smoke hood, or even have the courage to enter it at all. She had failed, she knew it, pathetically and catastrophically — and it was utterly expected, according to Richie.

She bowed her head when a pair of feet planted themselves directly in front of her. The man, who she wished was wearing a suit of armour and riding a white stallion, was actually just Milo and his stupid jazz hands. So she was surprised at the overwhelming urge to throw herself into his arms and weep, having to sit on her hands to prevent her doing so.

'Come on, we're almost at the finishing point.' Milo sounded positively cheerful but then he peered closer. 'You're shivering, is it the cold?'

'No, it's because we're both going to die in that thing.' She flung her arm out in the direction of the brooding aircraft and dashed away rogue tears that leaked out of her eyes, hoping that they would look like errant raindrops flinging themselves dramatically on to her cheeks.

'Die? Why are we going to die?'

'The Dark Angels will smite us — or the Gorgoraths that are right now twirling their axes over their heads in readiness to send us to the edge of darkness. One of them will get us, that's for sure,' she said, gabbling with the certainty of it.

Milo laughed. 'Someone has an overactive imagination, I think, and I don't recall ever using the word *smite* in my life. This isn't a video game, you know. Demons won't magically appear when you produce your gold tokens.'

'Tell that to the Gorgoraths and see where it gets you.' Her eyes were wide and her hands shook. She was only half-joking, and she was such a coward — and she hated herself for it.

Milo stooped down, concern in his eyes as he held her gaze. He reached out a hand, and for a nanosecond she thought he was going to tuck a strand of escaped hair behind her ear, like they did in the movies, a prerequisite to a love declaration. He'd probably get his fingers entangled in the mess and a huge black spider would pop out from behind her ear and bite his finger off. She smiled at the thought.

Milo withdrew his hand as if reading her thoughts, and mistaking the reason for her unlikely grin, said, 'That's better.'

Unfortunately, the panicky feeling, instead of diminishing, rose in her throat and she fought to steady her breathing. 'It's the smoke, and the hood — I'm terrified of it. And I *hate* the dark. I just . . . can't . . .' She shrugged helplessly and felt her mouth twist with the effort of holding back tears all over again. 'Sorry you got lumbered with me.'

'Hey, it's going to be fine. Captain Courageous to the rescue.' He flexed his muscles again and grimaced as he squeezed his biceps. 'Oh dear, flatter than a hedgehog run over by a tractor.'

She smiled, even as she disagreed with him. His muscles were perfectly formed and his arms were actually quite beefy, but she attempted a laugh anyway, because it was expected of her. 'Anyway, you're not a captain, you're a first officer.'

'Mere detail.' He waved the comment away, paused and seemed to arrive at a decision. 'You know what, you *can* do this and I'm going to make sure you do.' He took hold of one hand and then the other, cocooning them inside his own, and fixed a gimlet eye on Ruby's face. They stared at each other wordlessly. Ruby didn't know if he was warming her up or transmitting courage in a weird, silent way, but somehow it did manage to calm her, and the drowning feeling abated.

'Okay?' he asked. 'Breathe with me for a minute or two.'

Hands and eyes locked, they stared at each other as they breathed steadily in and out in unison. 'Just believe that you can do this.' Milo rubbed his thumb over her wrist.

After a gulp or two and some very heavy breathing, where she debated the possibility that she was hyperventilating and needed a paper bag to breathe into, she nodded. 'Yes, I believe I can.' She didn't believe it for one minute.

They stayed in position, Milo's warm hands still embracing hers — and she was sad when it all too quickly ended.

'I do this with some of my cows when they're stressed — and occasionally the sheep too.'

She smiled wanly as Milo pulled her to her feet.

'You have cows?' She was completely flummoxed. 'You hold their hands and gaze into their eyes?'

He waggled his head. 'Yes . . . well, kind of. I look into their eyes and they trust me.'

'That's weird.'

'Is it?'

'Probably. I really have no idea.'

'They need comfort as much as the next, err, cow. Makes perfect sense.'

'Does it?' she dead-panned.

'Hmm, well, let's just focus on you for now. Steely Core, yes?'

'That's the one,' she agreed, glancing down at his hands, still holding hers from when he pulled her up.

He let go rather too abruptly, she thought, when one of the firemen strolled up to them, and although she didn't blame him — the gossip machine cranked up here as much as anywhere — it would have been nice if their solidarity had lasted just that bit longer.

.

CHAPTER FIVE

Ruby faced her biggest challenge head on as the waiting fireman passed her and Milo each a smoke hood.

She tried not to whimper.

Steely core, steely core. The mantra ran through her head and strengthened her resolve.

Milo glanced at her. 'I promise that I'll stay close to you, and if you get too scared it doesn't matter, we'll just get out ASAP. It's not that important. Okay?'

'At least we'll get out of the rain for a minute, right?' she offered up weakly as they walked towards the black and broken hull of the aircraft.

Milo squeezed her hand. 'Good gal. Deep breath and off we go.'

She nodded briefly, pulled the hood over her head and fastened the cords tight around her neck.

Milo gave her a thumbs-up, took her hand and squeezed her fingers as they entered the silent tomb of the aircraft.

To Ruby's mind, it was as if they were actually in a computer game, waiting for the monsters to leap out at them with their Knives of Chaos or the infamous Devil's Claw. She knew what devastation they could cause, had seen it on Richie's computer screen. She thought she saw movement to her left and gave a squeal of terror that sounded laughable when it whined out through the microphone in her smoke hood like a strangled kazoo.

Milo whirled around and, convinced that he'd seen it too, Ruby started to make a run for it.

Milo stepped in front of her, barring her way, and as she lashed out, he grabbed her arms and pulled her towards him, holding her tightly. 'Stop, just stop. Slow down.'

'I can't . . . I can't breathe. Please let me go. I'm so sorry.' She pushed against his chest but he held her all the more tightly. 'Hush now, it's fine. Just take a moment to get used to the surroundings. Look, there are lights in the roof.'

She glanced upwards, having to move her whole head because of the restrictive hood. He was right. Dimmed lights, dotted around the cabin, gave off a wash of light so pale that wispy, ethereal shadows hovered around their heads from the residual smoke. Ruby watched as the smoke dissipated, clearly will-o'-the-wisps ready to disorientate her. It was better than having a Gorgorath bearing down on her, she supposed.

Milo picked up a fire extinguisher and passed it to her. 'Here, take this, and for God's sake *use* it.'

She bristled, not expecting him to be so sharp. 'I was planning on doing just that.'

'Good. We need to get the job done and get you out of here, okay?'

Ruby didn't believe that a solitary fire extinguisher would do the trick, unless she coshed the monsters over the head with it, but she took it from him and readied it in two hands, like a sword.

'Don't hold it like that,' Milo said, his voice sounding mechanical through the microphone.

'You do you, and I'll do me, okay?' She grimaced as she gripped the extinguisher and whirled around, determined to catch the monsters unawares. But there were no monsters breathing down her neck, nor any about to splice her with their weapons. The noise of her own breath inside the hood

33

was frightening enough — rasping and laboured, echoing in her ears as her heart raced. But now she had a fire extinguisher between herself and the world, she managed to calm down — just enough to see that she was, in fact, behaving like a deranged teenager. 'Okay, no monsters here, move along now, nothing to see,' she muttered, almost convinced.

Milo let go of her hand and pointed at the toilet cubicle, and as her eyes adjusted she made out a thick swirl of smoke coming from under the door. Despite her misgivings, she smiled. They had found their first fire.

She approached the door, took off one of her thick wadded gloves and rested the back of her hand on the top of the door, working her way to the bottom, her professionalism finally kicking in. 'The heat is only at the bottom, so it's obviously not raging. We'll be safe to open it, just a little,' she shouted, belatedly realising that she didn't need to raise her voice so much.

She cracked the door open a fraction of an inch as Milo dived in, extinguisher at the ready, preparing to empty it into the cubicle.

'It's in the waste bin,' he said, cracking open the lid and sending up a plume of billowing smoke. 'This should do it.' He squirted the contents of the extinguisher into it. With a loud hiss of the foam, the fire instantly died and Milo gave a thumbs-up. Shuffling out of the toilet, they headed on through the ominous-looking grey smoke, the floor underneath them squelching with years of water and fire-aged debris.

Another fire smouldered under a passenger seat, and with a quick shot of foam it fizzled out with a satisfying hiss.

Milo rubbed his hands together. 'Atta girl. Now for the body.'

'You're actually enjoying this, aren't you?' She glimpsed the fire officer at the end of the tunnel waiting for them to finish. Literally the light at the end of the tunnel, she mused, wanting to run towards it and embrace the fireman.

They found the sackcloth body to the left of the main door when Ruby almost fell over it, walking backwards, holding out her fire extinguisher like she was toting a gun. She almost cried with relief. It was over.

Emerging into the daylight blinking and dazed, she was elated. The general disinterest in her achievement, however, was woeful. Considering what she'd been through, they should be clapping, singing a congratulatory song and dancing a happy jig, but she supposed she was the only one who knew how huge an achievement it was.

No one cared.

But, by God, she had done it.

Milo dragged the sand-filled body behind him, dumped it at Ruby's feet like a cat presenting a dead bird as a present, and it was all Ruby could do to stop herself thanking him sotto voce. *Good boy, well done.*

Instead, she struggled out of her smoke hood and lifted her face up to the rain. She knew she looked a total wreck. Her hair was plastered to her scalp — apart from the bits that stuck out like a coiled spring — and her cheeks felt tight and burned, as if she'd left a face pack on for longer than suggested. But she had never felt better as she gulped in air, happy to be alive, having escaped from nameless creatures and unnatural disasters.

'Exterminated,' Milo said, Dalek-voiced.

Ruby laughed. 'Exactly.' She dragged the body across the ground and presented it to John, with as much of a flourish as she could manage, considering it was a bag of sand dressed in striped pyjamas.

John simply glanced down at it and went back to his clipboard, which was a bit underwhelming, considering Ruby thought she was in line for a bravery award at the very least.

'Whatever,' she said despondently. *Stuff him*, she thought, turning around, hand raised in preparation to high-five anyone in close proximity. She was saddened to find a surprising lack of takers — in fact, there were none. 'Oh,' she said as disappointment washed over her. Her colleagues, huddled in the Nissen hut rather than braving the elements, were all wrapped up in their own little worlds and trying to make the best of a miserable situation. She deflated some more, but suddenly, comforting arms wrapped around her in a bear hug and the ground shifted from under her feet.

Milo had come up behind her and now swung her around in the air. 'You did splendidly,' he said. 'Proud of you.'

She laughed at his enthusiasm. 'Yes, we did it,' she agreed.

He set her on the ground and beamed down into her face.

They had a *moment* together as their eyes met, but it quickly passed as the rain threatened to defeat their flash of unity, but *something* had passed between them, for sure.

They made their way to the Nissen hut to find that their colleagues were now heading back to the crew room to spruce themselves up and obliterate all signs of the arduous morning.

Ruby, as usual, felt slightly disadvantaged, not being one for slapping on make-up and titivating — she wore the necessary basics, but she didn't really care as she was with Milo, plus she'd fought her demons and won. Okay, they were mostly imaginary demons, but still, she'd got the better of them. 'The Gorgoraths have been vanquished,' she heard herself say.

'Another one of those weird *Ruby* words,' Milo muttered.

John broke the moment. 'Quiet, everyone. Now, the good news is that you've all passed and the even better news is that I'm buying the ladies a drink at the Four Ashes. That's the pub over the road. Tea, apparently, is not sufficiently reviving. Follow me.'

Everyone cheered and John beamed. Ruby felt her heart going out to him. He was a decent chap who probably had the rough end of the deal trying to tame an unruly crowd of people who were more likely to take the piss than take him seriously.

'Sexist,' Lucy said, 'but who cares if he's buying the drinks.' Checking her face in the camera app on her phone, she grimaced. 'What a fright.' She smoothed down her hair and wiped a hand over her cheeks, although how that was supposed to improve her looks was anyone's guess.

'You are coming, aren't you?' Lucy looked from Ruby to Milo, her eyes narrowing as if they were trying to hide something from her, maybe planning their own celebration.

Ruby threw a questioning look at Milo, suddenly aware that it mattered to her that he'd want to spend more time with her.

'Yeah, I'll have a quick one. I have to get changed first, though, give me a minute or two.' He pulled his mobile out of his pocket and scrolled, frowning. He seemed rather distracted compared with a few minutes earlier, and Ruby's euphoric mood cooled.

Turning on his heel, he stepped away and Ruby followed him with her eyes as he spoke quietly into his phone. She shook herself out of her trance. She had Richie and it didn't matter who Milo spoke to but, even so, she glanced at him furtively. She knew it had to be a woman, the way his face lit up: what else would bring that kind of animation to a man's face? Maybe football would do it? Football was the only thing that animated Richie these days. But anyway, Milo was nothing to her, just a new friend and colleague, and she needed to remember that.

CHAPTER SIX

Lucy breezed into the pub as if she had been drinking there all her life, while Ruby lagged behind self-consciously entering a room composed of mainly male, off-duty airport workers. She was used to taking a back seat, never expecting or getting much attention, always ready to apologise and move out of the way. The same intuition now engulfed her, as if she expected someone to say, 'What, that little dumpy one with the frightful hair, she flies for Celestial?'

Case in point, one of the firemen on the course had passed her a black bin bag and asked her to start clearing up the debris left behind as they were all leaving.

Being Ruby, she had automatically taken the bag, her eyebrows raised in query.

'Oh, sorry, I thought you were a . . . erm . . .' He trailed off, looking frantically around until he spotted a woman in a red overall with a brush in her hand.

'You thought I was the cleaner?'

'Yes. No, of course not.'

But of course, *yes*. And she didn't know why he would think she was any different from the others, but clearly she didn't have the right look about her — whatever that was.

Lucy on the other hand was blonde, lithe and tall with a wide, wide smile, and every man she bestowed it upon immediately wanted to marry her — or do something with less good intentions. She was the perfect woman for the job.

She sat down next to Lucy, waiting for the drink they'd been promised. Ruby assumed it was a bit of a custom and she'd be churlish to turn it down, but she was uncomfortable that John was buying their drinks for doing no more than his job.

Lucy had no qualms, though, oozing with the confidence of a beautiful woman who expected to be bestowed with gifts, as she stared at her own reflection in the mirror behind the bar and fluffed up her hair.

'I don't suppose you had much of a struggle to be taken on by Celestial?' Ruby asked, watching her friend. 'I've applied three times in the past and this is the first time I was even given an interview.'

Lucy looked surprised. 'I can't imagine why, you have every quality they ask for — and yes, I did have to go through the same degree of torture that you did. Good cop, bad cop has nothing on that bunch of thugs, believe me.'

Ruby laughed. 'Sorry, didn't mean anything by it, I'm still pinching myself that they want me to grace their aisles. I'm guessing it's partly to do with learning Spanish.'

Lucy again looked puzzled. 'Why do you say that, with your pale skin, haunting eyes and hair to die for? You're gorgeous.'

It was all Ruby could do not to snort with derision. 'Did someone pay you to say that?' she scoffed.

'Of course not, and it's not about looks anyway, it's about being competent and having compassion, which anyone can see you have in shedloads.'

'Thank you.' Ruby was genuinely touched at her new friend's words. 'Once I found a ten-pound note blowing in the wind and gave it to a homeless guy huddled in a blanket against a wall. Richie still goes on about it now. Admittedly, I snapped a picture and posted his gappy smile on Instagram as he clutched the money in his hand, so it wasn't a completely altruistic move. He said it was an easy swap, if someone was daft enough to pay a tenner for a picture of his ugly mug.'

'I'd smile at anyone for a tenner.' Lucy laughed. 'There's a difference between being a mug and being compassionate, though. Sometimes I'm not sure you know where to draw the line.'

'What makes you say that?' Ruby asked, perplexed.

'Just some things you say about your boyfriend.' She shrugged. 'I dunno, I'm probably way off the mark.'

But the throwaway comment gave Ruby pause for thought. Her mum had always said Ruby was too desperate to be liked and tended to get walked over. She was also ninety per cent sure that her mum didn't like Richie, although she would be far too polite to say so.

But none of that mattered right then. She was where she wanted to be, in the job of her dreams and nothing and no one could change that. Richie's failings, or her own, were not about to be scrutinised.

'It's not quite the glamour job it's made out to be, though, is it?' Lucy was inspecting her hair again and sliding tiny bits of ash down the length of it, which she dropped on the floor with an easy carelessness. 'Yep, the days of doing little more than looking beautiful and speaking with a plum in your mouth are long gone, but today it might just have its advantages.'

Lucy winked as a tallow-haired, bronzed fireman walked through the door studying Lucy with interest. 'Seriously, though, the shifts look tougher than I thought, but I'm going to give it my best shot, even if I look like Hagrid after the Battle of Hogwarts by the end of the day.' She sighed. 'I have to report at four thirty for my first flight. That's four thirty in the morning, by the way. There shouldn't even be a four thirty in the working world.'

'I know what you mean,' Ruby agreed, thinking about her first shift where she landed at eleven thirty at night. Richie was *not* going to like that kind of timetable.

They fell silent as Giles and Milo walked over, sat down and placed their drinks on the table. 'Do you mind?' Giles asked politely, taking a seat anyway.

Milo sat next to Ruby, and a purr of contentment mixed with a bewildering sensation of possessiveness claimed her. Sure, he wasn't hers to be possessive about, she knew that, but he had looked out for her — and he had hugged her — so in her book they were now firm friends.

She glanced at him in his jeans and crisp blue-linen shirt, which suited his colouring. It looked expensive too, with double stitching and covered buttons. Sure enough, there was a little logo on the sleeve, to show the people 'who knew', she assumed, that it was quality. She peered at the logo but couldn't work out what it was: a Loch Ness monster, a shark? She wondered at his organisational skills to have brought a change of clothing with him.

If their shoes and their teeth are clean, you can't go wrong, her mother always said, and Ruby surreptitiously peeked under the table to check, but his trainers gave nothing away. Still, she would bet her last Quality Street that his *good* leather shoes were polished up and waiting in a box somewhere for when the occasion arose.

'Have you lost something?' Milo stuck his head under the table.

She shook her head. 'No, I was looking for my bag.' She reprimanded herself again; what did the state of his shoes matter to her?

Milo peered under the table. 'It's on the chair,' he whispered conspiratorially.

'Oh, erm, silly me,' she hissed back, feeling foolish.

In reply, he gave her a huge wink. *Your secret is safe with me.*

She coloured up, feeling that he knew exactly what she was doing. Maybe everyone's mother gave out such words of wisdom, to check out boyfriend or girlfriend material. Guiltily, she changed the direction of her thoughts. Richie was at home waiting for her, although an image of him sulking into his tea didn't exactly inspire her to loyalty.

She glanced at Milo, who seemed unsettled now, checking his phone, twisting around to stare out of the window, wiping the glass with his arm to clear the condensation. He sat down again and gulped back his drink, immediately standing up at the sound of an engine reverberating through the pub and shaking its ancient timbers.

The purring grew and filled the pub, and many sets of eyes swivelled towards the car park as an ice-blue sports car pulled up with a squeal of brakes and a shower of gravel. A glamorous woman, all pouty red lips and piled-up blonde hair pushed her sunglasses on to her head, climbed languorously out of the car and inclined her sun-tanned face in the direction of the pub window, assured that whoever she was looking for would be ready and waiting.

'Eyes right, Milo,' Giles said, looking over at the door to the pub.

'Look at the body on that,' one of the firemen said loudly. 'The car! I meant the car! E-Type Jag, if I'm not mistaken. Pristine condition.' He laughed, his friends joining in the joke. 'How the hell has she got herself one of those?' Giles asked Milo, who looked uncomfortable as he shrugged innocently.

Ruby knew nothing about cars but did know about glamorous women and quickly put two and two together. *Of course. How stupid am I? Why would any man have a change of clothing with him unless he was about to go on a date?* She instantly disliked the woman and her pretentious sunglasses. Why the hell would she need sunglasses in January — in the rain?

Beside her, Milo picked up his glass, took a sip and pushed his chair away. He looked for all the world like he was steeling himself for battle, Ruby thought.

She watched as he picked up his phone, shoved it into his pocket and muttered a hurried goodbye. He looked decidedly shifty, although heaven knew why, he had clearly bagged one of the world's most beautiful women. Pausing, he turned, nodded at Ruby and said, 'Until the next time.' He deposited his empty glass back on the bar top, winked at her and added, 'Your secrets are safe with me.' And with that, he was gone.

'That's reassuring,' was all Ruby had time to say as he disappeared out the door. Watching him climb into the sleek car actually made her heart ache. It was as bad as the time she was bought an ice cream that toppled off its cone before she'd even taken one lick. Traumas like that are not easily forgotten.

She had truly felt as if something magical was happening with Milo, and now it was as if the tide had gone out just as she was getting ready for a paddle. She blinked as the passenger car door of the Jaguar slammed.

'What a beauty,' Giles muttered into his drink.

Ruby gave him a sour look.

'The car, of course,' he said hurriedly. 'Although let's be fair, the driver was pretty stunning.' His gaze was wistful.

Ruby, who didn't need to look twice, still found herself glancing out of the window to see the back of a blonde head and a wisp of exhaust smoke dissipating in the ether. 'Bloody hell,' she mumbled, staring glumly into her drink. Yep, Milo was definitely falling into the loving arms of someone far more worthy than she was. It was the order of the world, she knew, but still she didn't like it.

'Look, but don't touch.' Lucy side-eyed Ruby, shoving her with her shoulder. 'Your face, honestly, if looks could kill.'

Ruby took a minute to adjust her *sucking a lemon* and *righteous indignation* expression into one of benevolent love of all Barbie doll bimbos who showed up and took the wind out of her sails. 'Not at all. I'm spoken for, remember?' She smiled her indifference, but inside she was upset that, of course, someone like Milo would not only have a girlfriend, but she would, of course, be beautiful and most likely rich. The warm feelings she'd carried around faded and she came over all weary. She was exhausted, and all she wanted to do was to go home, put on her pyjamas and veg out.

'But you still want to know the *goss* on him, I'll bet.' Lucy sipped at her drink, eyes bright with something akin to fervour and unwilling to relinquish her upper hand.

Ruby shook her head. 'I can't see that it's any of my business.' She knew all she needed to know about Milo and the sooner she forgot about him the better. 'Richie, remember?' she stated, but wasn't sure if she was reminding herself or informing Lucy of her coupled status.

But Lucy threw her a look that said *yeah, right*, and continued, 'Milo, the man with everything, including the face of a God along with confidence the size of a small planet.' She only paused to draw breath. 'Loretta, if you can believe the name, is a low-key model, but posh, and I think does the promotional stuff for Milo's family, which is probably how she managed to snare him.'

'Of *course* she's a model,' Ruby muttered into her wine.

'Although in my opinion she's not all *that*, you know? Anyone can dye their hair yellow and wear *screw me* red lipstick.'

'If I dyed my hair yellow I'd look more like a Minion than Barbie,' Ruby scoffed.

Lucy laughed but looked pensive. 'Being a model's not all about looks, is it? A bit like being airline staff.'

'True, but the odds on me ever getting to strut along a catwalk on the strength of my compassion and competency are negligible to nil.'

Lucy smiled at that. 'And my knees still knock together when I walk, so that's me out too,' she agreed.

They brooded for a moment on their failings.

'Anyway,' Lucy rallied, 'he's twenty-seven, lives in a crumbling pile in Scotland, old money, good stock and all that, will probably marry said Loretta Long Legs, who has *connections*.' She sniffed as she waved a hand towards the car park. 'She, of course, after a brief *pseudo* career will produce a couple of sprogs to carry on the family name without a hint of personality to get in the way. Not to mention the dosh she'll bring with her.'

'That's very sexist,' Ruby said but she thought, *Scotland? What on earth is he doing here in Devon, then?*

'Maybe, but true.' Lucy shrugged. 'Either way, he's out of your league, I'm afraid. I could get you one of those nice little firemen over there, if you want.' She waved her glass in the direction of a couple of men playing darts in the bar.

Ruby's eyes widened. 'God, no.' She shook her head. 'I have Richie, don't I? I was intrigued, that's all. On which note, I need to go home to get some abuse hurled at me before I start putting a positive spin on myself for getting through the day without setting my hair on fire or blinding a fireman with my extinguisher crazy foam.' She drained her drink and picked up her bag. On seeing Lucy's horrified reaction, she added, 'It's only banter — light-hearted abuse.'

'Hey, abuse in any form is still abuse.'

'I'm joking — Richie's lovely,' she said, but her smile was wan and her heart heavy. As she drove home her traitorous mind kept drifting towards Milo. He had poise and a gentlemanly air about him which fitted Lucy's description of his upbringing. His voice sounded like a dulcet melody played out on a clarinet, melodious and lilting, and his eyes gave off a vibe of consideration and sensitivity. And his confidence came with his good looks and old money, but he didn't come across as big-headed, maybe a little cocksure, but that again probably came with old money and an automatic assurance of his place in life. Plus, he seemed to like her — that was always a bonus.

She shook her head at her foolishness. Enough. The bloke was probably ruthless in his charm offensive when he felt like doling it out. Probably just practising out his moves on her, she mused morosely, knowing that she was foolish enough to be taken in. But if only Richie was a little more gentlemanly in his ways — more considerate of her personal space and emotions. She tried hard to be a caring person, it was the way she'd been brought up, but he didn't return the favour in any way, and it was becoming harder to play the game. She sighed, remembering when they'd first met and he bought her flowers every weekend and really listened to every word she said instead of having his eyes glued to his computer or his phone. Still, she supposed, she wasn't an angel either, and individuality was what made the world go around so she shouldn't grumble. She sighed heavily as she picked up her car keys and left the pub.

CHAPTER SEVEN

Richie was home when she let herself in, and she couldn't decide if she was happy at that, until he declared that he'd cooked dinner.

'Wow, impressed,' she said, lifting the lid of a delicious-smelling dish. She was genuinely taken aback and felt guilty about her earlier traitorous thoughts.

'It's only a packet mix poured over chicken bits and veg,' Richie said, but even so, it meant she didn't have to cook and for that she was grateful.

'You have a bath and I'll sort this out.' He smiled and rubbed her back affectionately.

She raised her eyebrows, doubly surprised at this new turnaround. He must feel bad about being grumpy earlier, she decided, but she didn't need to be asked twice, and disappeared into the bathroom. It was at times like this when she remembered why she loved him. She ran a bath and poured reviving bath oil into it, sinking into the water gratefully, luxuriating in the easing of her muscles after the arduous day.

She was relieved that their relationship was back on an even keel after their disagreement over her new job. She hadn't given Richie much attention these last few weeks, her mind mostly full of exams, flight drills and the use of safety equipment. It was all so bloody hard, and if anyone ever tried to undermine the importance of her job she would give them what for.

Celestial Air had, however, opened up a new life for her. Some of the cabin crew had colourful love lives and unusual friends, and Ruby looked forward to hearing the latest episode about who had fallen out with whom, or who'd had a cheeky one-night stand, dragging themselves, half dead with tiredness, into work the next day. They were mostly fun people with zany personalities and she would often laugh her way through the day.

They also seemed to like her company, which was more than she could say for Richie, but maybe she'd got him wrong. He was certainly trying his hardest tonight, judging by the aroma wafting through the air. She determined to be nicer. After all, it took two to make a relationship.

She climbed out of the bath and changed into her leggings and a sweatshirt and sauntered back into the sitting room. 'Richie?' she called. After a moment or two, assuming he was in the kitchen, she poked her head inside. Nope. Finally, at a loss to where he could be, she opened the front door, peering into the gloom of the night. 'Richie?' she shouted tentatively. Something was going on out there but she couldn't really see what. He was talking to someone in a van, which was kind of weird, but probably nothing more than a dodgy sale of Xbox games going down. Unconcerned, she closed the front door to keep the heat in and checked on dinner.

After a while he came back in, slamming the front door, dusting down his hands.

'Ah, there you are. Shall we eat? What were you doing out there?' Ruby asked, not really expecting an answer.

'I'll tell you in a minute,' he said, disappearing into the bedroom.

She thought no more of it as she dished up the food and asked how his day had been — as the new Ruby would endeavour to do every day from then on in.

Richie worked from home, selling unnecessary insurance on white goods to poor saps who knew no better, so she didn't expect a riveting conversation. She waited for him to ask about her day, but he didn't, merely grinned and nodded to himself as he wolfed down his food.

Ruby, knowing him from old, was used to his wheeler-dealer ways and knew something was brewing. Prickles of anxiety ran up and down her arms and she swallowed with difficulty as an unspecified worry started to gnaw at her. The air was thick with unspoken words. Something was up, for sure.

He fidgeted, legs jiggling, fingers tapping on the table, sliding his hand towards his phone before hesitating and ignoring it. He glanced over at her too many times as if he was on the verge of confessing something: *It's a fair cop, I murdered him*, or something similar.

'I do have some news actually,' he said, surprising her mid-mouthful.

'Oh?' Ruby tried to put enthusiasm into her voice as her stomach clenched.

'I bought you a present.'

'Really?' This was *not* expected — a rarity, or at least it was since they'd rented a place they couldn't really afford.

'It's outside. Take a look.'

Intrigued, she abandoned her dinner and pushed the curtain aside. 'I can't see anything.' She thought maybe a new plant for their tiny courtyard garden or a barbeque, which would be bizarre in winter, but Richie was all about a bargain.

'It's right in front of you, the yellow moped.'

'The what?' She peered past the garden and, sure enough, a moped sat there, squat and banana yellow, glowing in the light of the acid-orange lamplight.

She turned to him in confusion, brow furrowed. 'But why? What am I supposed to do with a moped?'

'Get to work.'

'But we have a car — and I have to wear a uniform.'

Richie's lip curled. 'You saying you're too good for a moped?'

'Of course not, it's just that I assumed I'd take the car.'

'You assumed wrong, then.'

'What?' She couldn't understand his logic. 'But you work from home.'

'Exactly.'

Ruby wasn't sure how this proved his point, but as if he'd clinched the deal he fumbled under the table and produced a pink crash helmet, thrusting it at her.

'It's brand new, so take good care of it.'

Ruby looked down at the candy-pink helmet and up at him, aghast. He genuinely seemed proud of himself, smiling as if he truly expected her to be over the moon at this unexpected development.

She sat down at the dining table, crash helmet in her hands, trying to work out why on earth he would buy her a moped, and bizarrely, why a pink helmet when the bike was yellow? Worst colour match ever. Completely irrelevant, but still. 'Are you joking? You do know that I have the bank loan for the car, so in theory it is *my* car.'

'Yes, but don't forget the insurance and log book is in my name.'

Ruby balked. 'And?'

'That means I can dispose of it, if I want.'

'No, you can't.' But she was unsure of her ground here. 'And why would you want to?'

'I've bought another car,' Richie said, puffing up like a proud peacock.

'What? Why?'

'You know how you kept saying your new job would enable me to have a hobby? Well, that's what I've done. I've bought an old classic car to do up.'

'But you don't know anything about cars!'

'I've joined the local classic car club.'

'Oh.' She was speechless for a moment. Classic cars in her mind were euphemisms for knackered old wrecks that needed shedloads of money throwing at them. She felt sick with apprehension. 'And they'll help you with this *classic car* when it breaks down?' Ruby's face heated up. She had a terrible premonition about this. 'What kind of car is it?'

49

'It's a Porsche, a very old one and it was a massive bargain.'

Ruby's eyes boggled. 'A Porsche? A freaking Porsche? What the hell?' She stared at him disbelievingly, waiting, praying for him to tell her it was all a bad joke.

'It's Auratium green — quite a rare colour, named after a Japanese lily. I read about it on Google.' His tone was muted, though, as if he was also re-evaluating his purchase and questioning the wisdom of it. But he finally grabbed his phone and scrolled through it before shoving a picture of an old grey-looking car at her; it didn't much look like any kind of lily she'd ever seen.

Ruby barely glanced at it, simply shook her head in disbelief. There was no point in asking why he'd done it, that wouldn't get them anywhere, and anyway she knew why. He had to prove he had the upper hand and could do what he liked, but what the hell was he thinking? Her mind was racing. They could barely afford the car they had, let alone one that needed work doing on it. 'Just . . . why?' She couldn't keep the incredulity from her voice.

He shrugged. 'Why not?'

'Why not?' She flicked at her fingers. 'Number one, we're saving for a house. Number two, we can't afford the car we have. Did you ever in your wildest dreams think about buying a Porsche? Has it *ever* occurred to you before?'

'Who wouldn't want a Porsche?'

She floundered. 'Yes!' she yelled. 'If it was a pristine, brand-new number that was free, won in a raffle or something, but not a rundown heap that's going to cost shitloads of money.' She didn't care that she was shouting. 'Number three, we don't have the money to maintain a Porsche. How much does it do to the litre? How much is the insurance, how much is the tax?'

'Oh, if that's all you're worried about, don't be. It's not even roadworthy yet. It's going to live in a barn — that's where it is now, and the guy's happy for me to tinker around with it there.'

Ruby was thrown. 'Erm, I suppose that's a different matter.' She sighed heavily, a million questions buzzing around her head. 'At least we still have a car that works.' She narrowed her eyes as Richie shuffled around a bit, rubbed at his nose, leaned against the wall looking decidedly shifty.

'Don't we?' She did not like the look on his face. He looked like a bear caught with his paw in the honey jar.

Richie eyed her. 'The thing is.' He rubbed at his chin and looked haunted.

Ruby knew that look. She narrowed her eyes.

'The thing is, I part-exchanged our car.'

Ruby shot up so quickly she hit her knees on the table and the chair flew backwards, crashing to the floor. 'You what?'

Richie winced and had the grace to look sheepish. 'I'm working from home and it seemed a bit of an extravagance to have both. You should be pleased I'm saving us money.'

Ruby gaped at his ridiculous logic. She composed herself, placed her hands on the table and glared at him, though he didn't seem particularly bothered by her death stare. 'I'm the one who needs a car and the one with the bank loan for that car — and that makes it my freaking car.'

'In theory.'

Ruby was steaming. In truth, she'd never felt as if the car was hers, even though she'd been paying for it since the day it had arrived outside their house. Richie always had first dibs on it. 'It's illegal to sell a car with finance on it,' she threw at him even though she was unsure of her ground there.

'That's okay. The guy said that he would arrange that it was a write-off, so you could still pay off the loan and it wouldn't be listed to the creditors when he sold it on.'

Ruby thought she was going to be sick. Never in her wildest dreams would she have thought Richie could be so stupid — and devious. 'That's fraud, isn't it? Anyway, I won't let you take the car.'

'It's already gone.'

'Gone where?' she asked. It was outside ten minutes ago. Her blood ran cold and she raced back over to the window. There was no car.

'I don't know, he just drove it off.' He shrugged as if it was no big deal.

'Jesus Christ,' Ruby spluttered, balling her hands. 'Not only have you done the stupidest thing ever, you've also broken the bloody law.'

Richie seemed to think about that for a moment and then he brightened. 'Think, though, when the Porsche is done up we'll look the business cruising along the coast road, won't we?'

Ruby unclenched her fists, slowing her breathing. 'There are no words, Richie, none that are suitable for our neighbours to hear, anyway.' She could barely look at him. How could he be so selfish?

She turned on her heel. There was no point in doing anything else, apart from committing murder, and even though she could easily strangle him, she would be the one to end up in jail — and a knackered Porsche and crap boyfriend weren't worth a lifetime in jail.

'It's more fun than buying a house.'

That stopped her in her tracks.

'A house that I'd probably spend my free time doing up. Me in overalls up a ladder, getting a crick in my neck, while you swan off around Europe looking glamorous and living it up.'

The adrenaline drained out of her body in seconds as she stood by the bedroom door. Was this what it was all about? Her job? It seemed to be so. He wanted a posh car to feel — what, equal to her? She laughed hollowly but she was also desperately sad at the way things were panning out. 'Oh, Richie, what have I done to you?'

'Don't you worry about me. I'm fine.' He glared at her, a belligerent expression on his face, and she knew that they were close to meltdown. It was too late in the evening and they were both too fired up. She simply would not let him ruin her new career. She would continue even if she had to cycle to work — on a unicycle, with a clown's hat on rather than a helmet.

Reluctant even to share a bed with this man she was beginning to think she didn't even know, let alone like, she simply stared at him. If she had the enthusiasm and wasn't so knackered she would walk out. Her mouth twisted wryly; she couldn't even drive away because she no longer had a car.

Huffing, she rummaged in her drawers and pulled out a flannel, long-sleeved nightdress that she saved for when she had one of her bouts of tonsillitis, alternatively shivering and sweating throughout the night. As she slipped it over her head she was aware that her relationship with Richie was on seriously rocky ground, and the sad thing was, she wasn't sure she cared anymore.

'Goodnight, Richie,' she shouted through the open door. It was all she could muster. She wondered when their relationship had started to sour. They used to have such fun together, just going for long walks and sharing a bottle of wine, discussing their rosy future. It was probably too much responsibility that had done him in, and that was on her, pushing him to share a flat and save every spare penny towards buying their own home.

He had looked like a little boy ready for a fight back there, fists clenched, lip jutting, and she was overwhelmed with sadness that she had made him behave in such a way. Maybe buying a Porsche was a cry for help. She sighed loudly. She was too tired to fight and had to get up early in the morning. When the course was over she would have a long chat with him — if she hadn't brained him first. She climbed into bed and blotted the world out.

CHAPTER EIGHT

Ruby was irritable and sleep-deprived the next day but was aware that she couldn't take personal issues to work. She simply couldn't believe Richie had been so irresponsible, and she was now stuck with a yellow moped as her only form of transport — for the time being, anyway.

The bloody man was clearly punishing her for having the nerve to apply for a job without getting his approval first. Maybe his endgame was to jeopardise her career, but no way was he going to manage it. She was determined to be one of Celestial Air's outstanding crew members.

She glared at Richie as she left the house and then glared at the moped sitting there looking pristine and shiny and all pleased with itself. Bloody thing! She wanted to kick the ludicrous vehicle over and stomp on it, wishing it was Richie's head.

She'd had to order a taxi, which pissed her off because it was money she could barely afford, but she could hardly ride a moped for the first time all the way to work.

Luckily she was only five miles from the airport, so it wouldn't be too arduous a journey when she finally learned how to ride it. It was all the palaver that went with it that was the pain in the arse. The bloody crash helmet that would give her helmet hair, as if her hair wasn't already enough trouble. Plus she'd now have to allow at least fifteen minutes extra to get changed and tart herself up in the cloakrooms.

She soon forgot her bad mood. Her new friends, as she had come to view her work colleagues, were all in high spirits, taking their place around a huge mahogany table to decide, in order of importance, how to identify dangerous items taken on an aircraft and how best to dispose of them. They scoured the table, inspecting the weird objects clustered in the middle with interest.

'Now, which one out of this lot of weird and wonderful creations might be an explosive and why?' Fiona, immaculately turned out as usual, was taking the class today and Ruby, still so grateful that she took a chance on her, was anxious to please her.

She picked up a used sick bag. It was fixed to a lollipop stick with something like red dental floss hanging down and a grey lump of chewed gum inside. 'This one,' she said, picking up the article with thumb and forefinger, trying to keep the distaste from her voice.

'Urgh, is it a used tampon?' Lucy blurted out, wrinkling her nose in disgust.

The room went quiet as all eyes, wide with horror, swivelled to stare at her and then at the item in Ruby's hand. Ruby fought the urge to drop it back on the table.

Lucy coloured up instantly. 'Sorry, no, of course it isn't. Why would anyone take out a tampon while sitting down . . . Oh, God, what am I saying?' She turned to Ruby. 'Kill me now.' She trailed off, her hands to her cheeks, her eyes round in dismay.

'It's a home-made bomb,' Ruby said, putting her hand over Lucy's to comfort and silence her as she spoke.

'Okay. Good call. Why do you say that?' Fiona asked smoothly, ignoring Lucy's remark, although her eyes had glinted with something akin to amusement.

Ruby shrugged. Even though it was glaringly obvious to her, she wasn't sure why. 'I think it's the stick — reminds me of a firework.' She made a rocket noise and did a flying motion with her hand. 'Whoosh.'

Everyone laughed, the relief in the room palpable after Lucy's faux pas.

'That's right, and it would have indeed gone off like a rocket had it not been found in time,' Fiona agreed. 'It's a replica of a bomb that was found in the seat pocket of a 737, halfway over the Mediterranean. Luckily one of the cabin crew spotted it when she checked the seats for rubbish. It was timed to go off three hours later on its return to the UK and would have detonated in the air, blowing the aircraft — well, sky high.'

The silence was palpable as the class processed this piece of information, the importance of their job hitting them. They could literally save a planeload of people — or not, if they were negligent.

Next up was a man's shoe, probably one of the most famous bombing devices to headline the news some twenty-odd years ago. The guy sitting next to Lucy picked it up, inspected it, pulled away the heel and grinned, pleased with himself. It was chock-full of putty — purporting to be Semtex.

Fiona took the shoe from the guy and held it aloft. 'The year 2001. A United Airlines Boeing 767 flight. A terrorist tried to hide plastic explosives in his shoes.' She put the shoe back on the table. 'This was the catalyst that started the airline checks that passengers have to endure today. A double-edged sword, as we are all grateful that we are kept safe, even as we moan about queues and delays.'

Slowly, Ruby and the others discovered that all of the items on the table hid a bomb or had the ability to create a bomb when combined with other materials. A baby's bottle, innocuous enough, but not when full of liquid explosive; an expensive box of chocolates with the bottom layer replaced by a detonator; a bouquet of flowers given as a leaving present with a slim explosive and timer interweaved with the intricate florist wire keeping the bouquet together. That people would go to such lengths to kill fellow humans was a sobering lesson learned.

Fiona continued with an invective of real-life situations, from someone phoning up an airline to say there was a bomb on board — hoping to delay the flight because they were running late — to a mentally unstable steward leaving a threatening message on the toilet mirror for no discernible reason.

'So, if you think that one of your crew is acting weirdly, there might well be a serious reason for it. Do *not* hesitate to report them to the higher authorities.' Her hand slammed on to the table with a *thwack*, making several people jump. 'That goes for drugs or excessive drinking — turning up for a flight intoxicated is a jailable offence. It happens more often than you would think.' She looked around the room. 'I'll bet none of you here knew that you could go to prison for such a thing?'

Most of the classroom shook their heads in fright. Ruby imagined the shame of being arrested for being drunk on duty.

'After that sobering thought — excuse the pun,' she said, 'let's go out to the aircraft and I'll show you the safest place to secure a bomb should one be found mid-flight. And then the fun bit — sliding down the emergency chute.'

As one, they obediently stood up and walked to the hangar, where an engineer was in the process of preparing to deploy the emergency slide. The aircraft was dark and perishingly cold, until an engineer put the lights on and shoved the 'caterpillar' through the doorway, and the long rubber tube whooshed out heat at a furious rate.

'It costs a bit to inflate a slide so we only want to do this once. Pay attention as you might one day have to go through the same procedure. If one of you punctures the slide on your way down, say goodbye to your colleagues as you leave the building — make sure you drop your ID off at reception.' She pulled a sad face. 'A puncture renders the slide as much use as a very large slug, so take your shoes off before you jump.' She took her own shoes off and threw them out of the aircraft door, where they landed with a clatter.

Ruby gasped in virtual pain and vowed she would never treat her beautiful airline shoes so carelessly.

'Fold your arms and jump. What do we do before we jump?' Fiona shouted.

'Take our shoes off and fold our arms,' everyone shouted in unison. Liam, one of the stewards, grabbed the crash axe from the flight deck to take with him, but was told to put it back in no uncertain terms.

'I thought I could use it to take on a shark if we landed in the water,' he said, a grin on his face.

Fiona shook her head, smiling. 'There's always one joker.' She relieved the man of the axe and nodded at the engineer to fix it back into position in the flight deck.

'Okay, let's do it!' Fiona shouted. She grabbed a loud-hailer and became a different person, shouting, 'Move it! Go, go, go!' She pushed people who dithered down the slide. 'Shoes off, fold arms, jump!' she shouted over and over again.

'Shoes off, shoes off.' The chant was shouted at regular intervals, just in case it hadn't been rammed home enough, as everyone slid down the slide, arms folded, shoes most definitely thrown on the tarmac before doing so.

Ruby's adrenaline kicked in and it was as real as any emergency by the time she stood up on the tarmac after slithering down the slide, exhilarated and proud as punch that she had completed another task. She was nearly there.

CHAPTER NINE

Having initially brushed aside the problem of getting to work, Ruby had a rude awakening when she finally used Bananarama, the yellow moped she'd named in a fit of optimism and Instagram musings. The shine of arriving to work in a taxi every day quickly wore off as the expense of it grew: she still had a bank loan on a car she no longer owned and no spare money to buy another one. Richie, unbelievably, still couldn't understand the enormity of his actions, buying a bloody Porsche that was probably good for little more than boosting his ego. Graciously he'd informed her that she wouldn't be in trouble regarding the bank loan as she hadn't specifically said it was for a car when she took it out, so should be in the clear to carry on paying for it, even though she had no idea where it now was.

Yeah, cheers for that.

Had he done this to make life difficult for her? Or was he a typical man whose head was turned by a fast car? Either way, a yellow moped was currently the only form of transport she had to rely on, apart from a pushbike with a flat tyre and rusty wheels. The only way forward was to make the most of it and turn it into an adventure. At first she wobbled horribly, terrified that she would fall off, but she quickly learned how to whizz along the roads, keeping an eye out for the many potholes and sunken drains that threatened to topple her by the minute.

The ungainliness of sitting on a moped wearing a skirt was an unpleasant first, as it kept flying up past her thighs and she couldn't keep letting go of the handlebars to pull it down. Also, the backpack she had overstuffed with paraphernalia and carelessly thrown over her shoulder kept falling off with a weighty *thunk*, making her sway precariously. Realising how vulnerable her body would be if she came off, she quickly took to wearing jeans, and just as quickly invested in a pair of waterproof overtrousers after a miserable journey in the rain, spending two hours in the classroom with damp, cold legs. Who would have known that riding a moped could be so complicated — and so expensive? When she had to turn up in her uniform looking polished and pristine, things would undoubtedly become even more problematic.

The phrase 'Bloody Richie' was more often on her lips than not.

She had braved the weather once more for another day in the classroom at Celestial Air, this time for more drills: oxygen, crash axe and pilot incapacitation.

At the end of the day, Ruby climbed wearily on to her moped, having pulled out her crash helmet from the top box — another expense she could ill afford — and plonked the helmet on her head with a huge sigh of both relief and resentment. The sky was overcast and a light haze of rain misted the air, but she had plenty of time to get home before nightfall. She was not looking forward to the ride home, but at least her crash helmet had a face visor. Thank Richie for small mercies.

'*Wipe all lipstick from mouth, ensure oxygen is turned on and flowing before fitting mask to passenger's mouth and nose,*' she muttered, to check out loud that she had correctly answered the drill examinations she'd just sat. She would know it by rote eventually, but at the moment it didn't come easily.

She was just about to start the moped when a man wearing a green waterproof jacket and an old-fashioned fedora hat at a jaunty angle sauntered up to her, a determined smile on his face. She pulled off her helmet. 'Hello?'

'Jerry Millett from the *Devon Chronicle*.' He flashed a badge and his smile widened.

Ruby took in his craggy features and red-veined nose that signalled a lifetime of boozy nights. He was a stereotype of a journalist and even advertised the fact, as his hat had a little tag pushed into the brim that read, *Press*.

'Pretty brave of you to come out on that, given the weather.' He indicated her moped and looked up at the forbidding grey clouds gathering overhead, the droplets threatening to become a deluge.

'Pretty brave of you to wear that hat in any weather.' She pointed to his battered felt hat, intrigued.

'One of my little quirks.' He pushed it down on his head. 'It belonged to the founder of the *Chronicle* and it brings me good luck.'

'It's cool.' She fidgeted to find her phone, itching to take a photo for Instagram. The hat was patchy in places, green felt rubbed away to leave balding, grey marks. It reminded her of her nan's ancient stoles that had moulted and left big gaps in between the fur. She would hazard a guess that it smelled pretty ancient too. It looked as if it would be happier retired somewhere — preferably in a bin.

'You one of Celestial's newbies?' he asked.

'Yes, just recently joined.' She was deliberately vague, slightly wary about giving out information to the press.

'I'm writing an article about Celestial Air's routes and its new breath of life; it being our own home-grown airline, we're keen to promote it.' He lifted a camera slung around his neck as if explaining why he was hovering around the airport.

'Oh, brilliant.' That was a good thing, right? She gawped at his camera: a Nikon that she would die for. 'I'm a rookie photographer,' she explained, having ogled the camera for a beat too long. 'I'd love to do more, although I tend to use my iPhone for photos these days — so much quicker. But I already have enough photographs of Celestial Air to keep my Instagram page loaded for years.'

Her smile dimmed as she lifted her hand, palm upwards, feeling the first drops of rain. Bugger, she hated riding in the rain. Maybe a windshield would have to be next on her list. For now, though, she was happy talking to a fellow photography enthusiast.

'What do you do at Celestial Air?' Jerry asked.

'Hmm?' She refocused, pushing her hand into her pocket, feeling for her phone. 'Oh, I'm in training still, I've just recently started — as cabin crew, not as a pilot,' she added hastily. 'I think possibly I got the job because I've learned a bit of Spanish in the last year. *Juan come manzanas*. That means "Juan eats apples."'

Jerry's mouth twitched. 'Very handy for the fruit course of your meal service.'

Ruby giggled. 'Yeah, terrible example — what am I thinking? When I learn to say, "Our aircraft has perfect aerodynamics," or something awesome, I'll be sure to let you know.'

She liked the twinkle in Jerry's eyes as they took in the measure of each other. The rain suddenly picked up speed and became the downpour it had threatened.

Ruby hastily wiped rain water from her face. 'You need to save your hat from the rain. I'm sure it would disintegrate given the slightest encouragement.' She knew she was being cheeky but he seemed the sort to take it.

Jerry smiled and nodded. 'Can't say it copes well in the rain, which rather defeats the point of a hat, I know.' He raised an eyebrow. 'Would you have time for a coffee, maybe? I'd like to have a chat about your job — it would make the article a bit more substantial?'

'Oh, err, I guess. There's a small café inside.' She wasn't in a hurry to get home and could wait out the rain chatting to this man who had all the makings of being interesting.

He gestured for her to lead the way and she headed back into the airport that she'd only just left, belatedly remembering her pink crash helmet was still tucked under her arm.

They settled in at a table with a view of the runway, and she placed her pink helmet at her feet while Jerry plucked his ancient hat off his head and placed it on a spare chair, patting it like a treasured pet.

Jerry indicated for drinks to be brought to the table from the hovering waitress, while showing no sign of whipping out a notebook or shoving an oversized microphone in Ruby's face. He had an earnest look about him, though, like a school-teacher who really wanted to award her top marks for inter-esting content. His eyes fixed on her face. 'So, how was your training?' he asked, confirming the teacher vibe.

And Ruby told him everything, coming to a breathless stop after declaring that the emergency life-raft training was the last thing to complete, but she wasn't worried because she was a strong swimmer — and then they would be done. She wondered out loud that maybe he could come and take a photo of everyone being awarded their wings, and he agreed enthusiastically, finally producing a mobile phone and tap-ping into it.

She also told him that a moped wasn't her desired mode of transport, but that for now she was making the best of it. He seemed intrigued at the juxtaposition of a young woman turning up in jeans, on a moped, to a supposedly glamorous job. He could make a story about it, if she didn't mind?

'Can I get a picture of you on the moped before you go?' he asked as their conversation wound down.

The sun had peeked out from behind a cloud and the rain slowed to an occasional smattering, although it looked just as likely to whip up into another torrent. Ruby, not one to take a lull in the weather for granted, wanted to ride home as quickly as she could.

'Sure, but I'm not allowed to wear my uniform yet, so it would be a bit pointless.'

'True. Maybe you'll allow me to come back when you've finished your training?'

Ruby was thinking she should check with Fiona about chatting to a journalist, when out of the corner of her eye she saw a couple of pilots passing by. One of them peeled away and headed for their table.

Milo stopped, paused and said, 'Jerry, it *is* you. How you doing, mate?'

'Milo, my man.' Jerry jumped up, almost knocking his chair over and reached out a hand. Ruby gaped in surprise as Milo grasped Jerry's hand and pumped it up and down while Jerry clapped him on the back as if they were long-lost relatives. They finally let their hands drop and stood beaming at each other.

'So, how's Daisy?' Jerry asked, still grinning, clearly thrilled at bumping into Milo.

'She's grand. I swear she thinks she's a star since you did that photo shoot. Expects to be treated better than the others.'

'She is quite special, though, isn't she?'

Milo nodded and, to Ruby's eyes, gave a secret smile as if conjuring up fond memories of *Daisy*, whoever she was with her *special* attributes.

Suppressing a stab of jealousy, she nevertheless pricked up her ears. Wasn't his girlfriend named Loretta? And who were *the others*? She had clearly underestimated his talent for attracting women, and although her heart rate had picked up, she determined to remain indifferent.

He hadn't even acknowledged her presence, which was pretty galling. Tucking her chin into her neck to try and make herself invisible, she wished she could slide her pink crash helmet on her head and slink away. Clearly she wasn't memorable enough to be recognised, which was, to be fair, quite insulting, but maybe the smoke hood, sooty face and oversized yellow jacket was all he remembered — the finer details, such as they were, lost from his mind already.

Alarm bells rang when he said, 'Hey, come and take some decent photos airside. I can clear it with the owner, he's cool. Bring your apprentice with you.' Finally he looked at Ruby.

'You what?' Ruby spluttered, bristling and jumping to her feet in surprise as much as outrage. He really didn't remember her; she couldn't believe it. She wanted to laugh out loud and imagined recounting the story to Lucy later. Richie would love it, if she was ever stupid enough to tell him.

'Oh, she's one of yours,' Jerry said, forcing Ruby to raise her head to give Milo a tight smile.

To her amazement his eyes lit up. 'Steely Core, is it really you? When did you start working for the *Devon Chronicle*?'

'Ha-ha,' she said, although she was quietly pleased that he did, after all, remember her.

'Sorry, didn't recognise you with all that . . . hair. Wow.'

Ruby smiled tightly at the comment. Did he hate her hair? It had been tied up tightly as recommended by Fiona for the firefighting course, which was just as well or else she most definitely would have set fire to herself. Milo didn't dwell on her hair, though, for which she was grateful.

'Come on,' he said, 'let's give Jerry some decent photos of our aircraft, shall we?' He held out his hand and she flinched, resisting the inevitable tingle shooting up her arm at his touch.

But he didn't notice her reticence, just had eyes for Jerry as he tugged her to her feet. 'I'll get clearance from Ops, shouldn't take a minute.' He pulled out his mobile phone and tapped in some numbers, and within seconds they were heading through security and were airside, Ruby with her pink helmet once again tucked under her arm.

They climbed up the steps to the aircraft and Ruby tried not to be overawed by Milo smiling cheekily as he climbed into the pilot's seat with confidence. For a minute she thought they were going to fly the aircraft but thankfully not.

Jerry snapped away and she took out her iPhone and took some of her own photos as the sun glinted off the badge of Milo's cap, and again when a dark cloud turned the whole flight deck into a moody collage of stripes and raindrops. The weather really couldn't make up its mind and Ruby loved it — from a photographer's point of view, not as a moped driver.

At first she felt like an uninvited guest to the party, tagging along like a spare part, but when Milo took Jerry through to the flight deck and demonstrated the controls, simulating flying by making silly *vroom, vroom* noises, it set herself and Jerry laughing like a couple of kids and she relaxed.

Eventually Milo climbed out of the flight deck and answered Jerry's questions about the new routes — answers that Ruby had no idea about, and she listened in with interest. Milo was clearly in the know about so much more than the average worker at Celestial Air and she understood, with a pang, that he had merely acted in a professional manner towards her on the firefighting day, and she wasn't special to him in any way.

She wasn't, and would never be, Daisy or Loretta or any of the others, whoever they were. His magnetism was real and it came down to his genial personality and interest in his fellow man. He had also been endowed with the best traits God had to offer, which certainly helped. The vibes he gave off were like sunshine and spring rain restoring a dark, parched field.

She wished she could remain detached or view him the way Lucy did — an entitled brat with a big ego — but she had seen past that, or was she just being all *fan girl* over him? It was as if he had waved a magic wand and bewitched her. Unwittingly she had compared him to Richie and wasn't surprised when Richie came up lacking.

Jerry took a few photos of herself and Milo posing against the aircraft wing, elbows leaning on the huge engines. She smiled when told to, but froze like an ice statue when Milo casually slung his arm around her. Surely it was inappropriate, but she did like the solidity of his weight on her shoulders, which was probably inappropriate too, so what the hell; they were both doomed.

'Great stuff — I think I have all I need,' Jerry said, finally letting his camera dangle on his chest. They trooped back through to the terminal and stood by the main entrance, watching the dusk creep in as the rain eased. Jerry finally took his leave after giving her his card and she promised, with a wry smile, that she would send him her Instagram username so that he could follow her.

So Milo and Ruby were left standing together staring at Jerry's back as he retreated, hat once more sitting jauntily on his head.

Milo drew in an audible breath. 'Fancy a coffee — or something stronger?'

She did, would have loved to, but she knew it wasn't wise. Milo was just being friendly and she couldn't risk it. She needed to go home and analyse how a switch had flicked so suddenly in her brain to make her view Milo with wistful longing. Lust? She hoped not.

Richie would probably be waiting and she really didn't want to be much later.

She sighed and prepared to turn him down. 'I would love to, but I don't like riding in the dark, especially when the roads are slippery.'

Milo looked deflated. 'That moped really is yours, then? I've been wondering about it, every time I see it in the car park.' His forehead crinkled as if he was puzzled but too polite to question *why*.

'Yep, Bananarama is really mine.'

Milo broke into a smile. 'That's awesome — good for you.'

She loved him for those words alone. *Yes!* A moped was a good thing, Milo had said so and that made it the truth.

'You should take your motorbike test, though, or at least have some lessons in advanced riding,' he continued. 'A motorbike rider has to have the eyes and ears of all the other drivers, 'cos they sure as hell won't notice you, yellow or not.'

'That's not a bad idea, actually.' She'd had a few near misses in the gloomy weather and could probably learn a thing or two if she had proper guidance.

'I wouldn't want that beautiful face of yours to get damaged,' he said.

Ruby blinked in surprise. Had he really just said what she thought he said?

They locked eyes just for a second before Milo broke the spell. 'Sure I can't persuade you into a cheeky latte?'

She hesitated, so tempted to spend time with him, but still she shook her head. It didn't seem right when she had Richie and he had Loretta — and she certainly wouldn't want to be part of his harem, along with Daisy and the nameless *others*. Her already bruised heart deserved better than that, and such a path would be emotional suicide. She told herself once again that the less she saw of Milo the better. She almost convinced herself that it was true as she turned to leave, pushing her helmet firmly on her head so as not to allow her mind to be changed, or her eyes to follow him.

CHAPTER TEN

The training course was almost at an end but there was one last thing to do before sitting the exams: the aircraft crash-landing on the sea, and the ultimate rescue of drowning passengers immersed in a thrashing, shark-infested sea. Thankfully this fictional scenario took place in the local swimming pool. Not one frantic shark cresting gigantic waves, or one aeroplane, crashed or otherwise, to disturb the calm surface of the water. Just a rubber dinghy and a man testing the chlorine levels in the pool with a test tube.

It was an easy task in Ruby's eyes as she enjoyed swimming, but she worried about her hair going frizzy and the chlorine turning her balayage highlights greener than they already were. *First-world problems indeed*, she thought wryly, debating whether to try out the swimming cap that she'd rolled up in her towel along with the pyjamas that were recommended as they were light and roomy. 'Do you think I'd look stupid — maybe get away with wearing it ironically?' she asked Lucy as she swung the white rubber swimming cap with pink roses around on her fingers, dreading the thought of tackling her hair either way.

'Hmm, can't you just make your neck a bit longer to keep your head out of the water?' Lucy asked with mock seriousness.

Ruby tried it out, pulling back her shoulders and stretching her neck. It didn't work remarkably well and she inadvertently pulled a weird face with the effort, causing them both to giggle.

'Big fail, but . . . I'd lose the cap, to be honest,' Lucy suggested.

Ruby had to agree and tried stretching her neck again by pulling her shoulders back and holding her head high as she watched the others line up on the side of the pool. She noticed that she was the only one wearing pristine new pyjamas, creases still visible where they'd just been taken out of the packet. Most wore washed-out affairs, baggy and thin, while some wore leggings and tee shirts — she wished she'd had the courage to do that. Distracted, she tried to work out if they'd all borrowed their dad's pyjamas. Was she the only woman who went to bed done up in a silk nightdress with a slit practically up to her navel because her boyfriend wanted it that way? So distracted was she that it took a moment or two to realise, to her horror, that everyone was also wearing a swimsuit underneath their pyjamas rather than underwear. It literally hadn't occurred to her to put on a swimsuit as she was so focused on the silky nightdress versus pyjama conundrum.

Her cheeks reddened with mortification as she ran through her options, quickly accepting that there were none, apart from crying off — and she hadn't come this far to fail at the last hurdle.

But when she thought about it, it wasn't such a problem. She could bluff her way if necessary and it wasn't as if they had to get undressed in the water. She could summon up her steely core if needed. She smiled at the conjured image of Milo.

She hadn't seen him since the meeting at the café, but she was aware that her thoughts strayed to their past meetings more than was strictly necessary. She idly wondered if she'd fabricated the affectionate familiarity that they shared and the, not strictly professional, comment about her pretty face. She stopped her thoughts in their tracks. *Enough.* Keep temptation, in the form of Milo Fraser, firmly out of the way.

The day continued regardless of her abstract thoughts, as they took it in turns to sit in the dinghy alternatively shouting orders and jumping into the water, pretending to drown and waiting to be rescued. It was all quite mediocre and it took a long time for each person to take a turn. When it was Ruby's turn she obligingly used her loudhailer to save her drowning colleagues, directing them to the dinghy and blowing her whistle.

Someone shouted, 'Look out, shark!' and everyone instinctively swam faster towards the boat, laughing.

'Rocks ahead. Quick, get in the boat!' Lucy shouted.

'Land ahoy, everybody. We're saved!' shouted another.

Things were a bit more lively now, and she began to enjoy herself until it was her turn to be rescued. She slipped into the pool with a surge of confidence, and even though she had to pretend she was drowning she managed to keep her hair above the waterline as she flailed around a bit, camping it up for effect. She allowed herself to go limp as she was cupped under the chin by her rescuer, who dragged her back to the dinghy, dunking her face repeatedly under the water as he kicked his legs underneath her. *There goes my hair*, she thought ruefully as he deposited her, coughing and waterlogged, at the side of the dinghy.

She clung on to the rope that hung over the sides as surprisingly big waves washed over her and for the first time, from her new perspective, she wondered how she would manage to climb back into the dinghy, the sides being smooth and a lot higher than her body. No one else seemed to have had a problem but it didn't look easy. Spluttering a bit, she swiped the water out of her eyes and, spotting a bit of a commotion further down the pool, focused keenly on one of the other swimmers waiting to be rescued.

Abbey, a slight, shy girl, was near the edge of the pool but flailing around a bit as her head disappeared under the water. She was acting the part a bit too well, Ruby thought as she peered closer. Abbey disappeared in a flurry of displaced water and barely audible shouts for help — and didn't reappear. Ruby blinked hard and waited, automatically holding her breath. 'Oh, my God, it's real.' She took a deep breath and pushed off from the side of the dinghy, shouting as she swam with all her might. 'Help . . . Abbey . . . someone,' she managed as she thrashed though the water. She reached Abbey in seconds, still not quite believing that she really was drowning. She'd expected her to resurface, but she was still under the waterline.

'Help, help!' Ruby yelled as she took another deep breath and dived under the water to reach Abbey, whose eyes were wide with terror, her head looking ready to burst, eyes bulging, cheeks bright red.

Ruby had to get them both above the waterline before Abbey was compelled to ingest the chlorinated water. Ruby managed to grab her and pulled with all her might, kicking her legs ferociously, swimming upwards. For a slight girl, Abbey was surprisingly heavy, but they both surfaced with an enormous splash and a huge intake of breath.

The lifeguard, finally seeing what had transpired, dove in and took over, keeping Abbey's face above the water as he swam safely to the poolside with Abbey in his arms. Ruby powered to the side of the pool and clung on, heaving in great gasps of air and fighting tremors in her arms and legs.

Fiona, who'd been watching from the sidelines, rushed over to Ruby and hunkered down, touching her arm and peering into her face as she held on to the side of the pool. 'Are you okay?' Her voice was gentle and concerned and it made Ruby's bottom lip quiver.

'I think so. I do feel a bit shaken, though,' she said, trying to control her trembling.

'Do you want to get out? We can call a halt to this, if you like.'

'Oh no, I'll be fine, really. I need to finish this and get back into the life raft.' And to prove it — and before she capitulated and climbed out — she pushed herself away from the side and swam towards the dinghy.

Which was all well and good, her little bit of bravado giving her courage, except she couldn't climb back into the boat. She swung one shaking leg up on to the rubber sides, but her feet couldn't get a purchase, not even by curling her toes around the top. A moment of sheer panic hit her, as if a shark really was bearing down on her. Pulling hard on the rope that hung down the sides, she tried to pull her body up; it looked easy enough in the films, but her arms began to tremble and she fell with a splash back into the water. The tears that had threatened now began to fall and her reserves of energy had all but drained away. If she didn't manage to get back in, would she fail the test? She wasn't sure.

'Can someone help me?' she shouted as the dinghy rocked precariously, sending more waves into her face.

Matthew, a smiling young steward, peered over the edge. 'Oh, hello down there. Need a hand?'

'Just a bit.' She tried out a smile, failing badly.

Matthew leaned over and without another word unceremoniously grabbed her by the neck of her pyjama top and the leg of her bottoms. She felt herself being hauled upwards, but just as she was almost to safety she caught her bottoms on the rope and promptly became detached from them, her legs slithering out in one smooth motion, revealing her knickers and pale legs. Matthew was left holding Ruby's arm as the bottoms slid over the side and floated for a minute or two before sinking gently to the bottom of the pool.

She stared, mortified, at her white legs and then at her fellow boatmen, willing someone to help. She deliberated diving down there — but how much more of a spectacle could she make of herself? Absolutely all eyes would be on her. With horror she realised her knickers were the red Christmas ones that her friend Pippa had bought her for a laugh and — oh, God! — they had a huge exploding Christmas cracker with 'BOOM' written in big black letters across her bottom.

She stared at the sunken pyjamas, the legs undulating as the water rippled, and wondered how weird she would seem if she just left them there, faking indifference as they waved gently at everyone from the bottom of the pool for all eternity.

But as she deliberated, a bored-looking lifeguard unhooked a long pole from the wall and lazily dunked it in the water, flicking the ill-fated bottoms on to the side of the pool.

'Thank you,' Ruby shouted, giving the young man a thumbs-up and a watery smile.

The nightmare wasn't over though as Fiona shouted for them all to swim to the side while the dinghy was partially deflated in the water. Realising she had no choice, she slid over the side, praying that her embarrassment would soon be over. This sort of thing was written in the stars for some people; they were destined to go through so much more humiliation than others, just for being who they were.

She would have to get out of the pool in her Christmas knickers — showing her ghostly white winter legs and bikini line that she *sooo* should have waxed. She swam slower than a sloth and waited until everyone else had climbed out and disappeared into the changing rooms. Hurrying up the pool steps, intending to make a grab for her pyjama bottoms on the way, she decided to check on Abbey, have a shower and go home to curl up in a ball with a hot water bottle and wait for sleep to come.

She lunged for her bottoms and spun around as a single slow clap started up. She couldn't see anyone at first but more clapping followed, growing into a crescendo, as every single one of her colleagues came out of the changing rooms and lined up against the wall clapping.

She backed away, her eyes round and horrified.

'Boom!' someone shouted, and she wanted to die at the judgement of these people she thought were her friends. It was as if she was back in the school cloakroom, where the boys would swipe her school bag off her shoulder and throw it around. She winced and clutched her pyjamas to her chest, her eyes darting to see the quickest way out of the building, absolutely intending to make a run for it, winter legs or not.

Even Lucy was smiling and clapping like a mad sea lion. Why would she do that?

Then Fiona appeared and she too was grinning and clapping. Abbey, huddled up in a towel next to her, walked over and hugged Ruby with all her might. 'You saved me. I was so stupid to pretend I could swim. I'd convinced myself I would be okay, because I could tread water for a bit, but then I lost the rhythm and felt myself sinking.'

'Oh.' That was all Ruby could say, as she understood that her colleagues weren't belittling her but genuinely cheering her. She hugged Abbey in return and clapped her hand to her mouth as tears of relief spilled over her eyelashes. 'I need to get changed,' she said, releasing Abbey and lowering her face so no one could see how upset she had been.

Lucy bounded over, throwing an arm around her friend's shoulders. 'Come on,' she said, 'I'm going to buy you the biggest glass of wine — a pint of wine, in fact. Name your colour.'

Ruby nodded slowly. Wine with her new friend was exactly what she needed right then. 'To be honest, I think I need the help of an alcoholic haze to blot today out. I never want to remember anything that happened, ever again.'

'Rubbish, you're a hero. Come on, you need a hot shower and lots of wine. And don't worry about your Christmas cracker knickers — put a picture of 'em on your pert little bum on Instagram and they'll be selling in their thousands come Christmas.'

Lucy grinned and Ruby followed suit. 'That's not a bad idea actually, I could get hold of the distributor and pitch the idea to them.'

'There you go, then, every cloud and all that.' Lucy punched her friend playfully on the arm.

'Ow.' Ruby rubbed her arm, feigning injury. But she laughed, relieved that everything was okay with the world once more.

They were ensconced in the pub a little while later and Ruby had already returned to the subject she'd determined to avoid. 'Tell me the truth. Do you think everyone focused on my bikini line? Why didn't I wax before I came out?' she wailed.

'No one noticed. I'm sure they were too busy staring at your knickers.' Lucy tried not to giggle. 'Very cute.'

Ruby groaned. 'Why did I wear them today of all days? And my little legs let me down, couldn't even reach the rim of the dinghy.' Her legs were to be despised, just like her dreadful hair.

Lucy noticed her glum mood. 'Hey, come on, stop focusing on the negatives. We're nearly at the finishing post. What's a little flashing when we're so close to getting our wings?' She grinned. 'The "Boom Bottom"—' she did air quotes with her fingers — 'is but a moment in time.'

'I guess,' Ruby agreed doubtfully. 'We'll always have the Boom Bottom and Tampon Tragedy to cement our friendship.' She brightened at the thought.

'Why did you have to remind me?' Lucy's hands flew to her cheeks.

Ruby put her arm around Lucy. 'I have to deflect my embarrassment on to you, you understand, so that I don't feel too bad about my humiliation today. That's the way it works.'

Lucy giggled as they chinked glasses and she took a hefty swig of her wine. 'In the grand scheme of things such trivial moments don't matter.'

Ruby sighed. 'You're right, and that's what friends are for. We can take the piss out of each other without either of us being offended.'

'Exactly that, yes.' Lucy laughed. 'We should enrol Abbey into our team. She could be . . . I know, the *Distressed Drowning*, or the *Splendid Saving*.'

Ruby smiled briefly before frowning. She bit her lip. 'I hope she isn't sent home after this, that would be too cruel. We could offer to teach her to swim and she could try again. Maybe I'll mention it to Fiona?'

'Yes, you should, but right now, let's raise a toast to us. I think the final hurdle has been surmounted and as long as we both pass our exams we'll be red-shoe wearing, bone fide members of Celestial Air.'

Ruby hugged herself with delight. 'We can always pretend we work for Virgin as long as we have those shoes, but right now, Celestial Air is where I want to be.'

Soon she would be flying in a real aeroplane, wearing the coveted Celestial uniform. She had been rained on, covered in hot ash, almost eaten by monsters in a blackened cabin, flashed the Boom Bottom to all and sundry and been insulted by a handsome fireman, but what the hell, she had gained so much more than she had lost.

And she bloody well deserved those shoes.

CHAPTER ELEVEN

Finally the day arrived for Ruby and her colleagues to be presented with their wings. Lucy ushered Ruby into the ladies' cloakroom and dragged a stool in. 'Sit. I'm going to show you how to enhance that already beautiful face of yours.'

'I didn't know my face needed enhancing. I give it as much love as it needs to make me look presentable.'

'Hmm. I can show the world the beautiful woman you are, though. Watch and learn.'

Ruby shrugged. 'Okay, but I don't want to look like a drag queen.'

She sat down and allowed Lucy free rein on her face.

Lucy proceeded to brush a taupe eyeshadow over Ruby's eyes, added another two layers of mascara, swirled a large brush into a compact and swept blusher over Ruby's cheekbones.

Ruby peered at herself in the mirror. 'Wow. Is that really me?' She was transfixed, couldn't believe the difference. 'Thank you.' She smiled at her reflection. 'I do look . . . well, what can I say?'

'You look lovely,' Lucy said.

'Thank you!' Ruby made to stand up but Lucy pushed her right back down.

'I haven't finished yet.'

'No more. I still want to look like me.' Ruby laughed.

'Okay, but you need some lip gloss and then we're done.' She dabbed some pink stuff over Ruby's full lips. 'There you go.' She popped all the make up into a little bag, zipped it up and presented it to Ruby. 'A little present to remember this special day.'

'That's so kind — thank you!'

'Richie will be so proud when he sees you being presented with your wings. He'll realise how lucky he is to have such a talented and beautiful girlfriend. I knew a bit more make-up would work wonders for you.'

'Oh, Richie says he can't spare the time off work, but Mum's coming. She'll be proud as punch with her camera at the ready.'

Ruby knew that a professional photographer and hopefully Jerry from the *Devon Chronicle* would turn up to take group and individual photos too, so was doubly pleased with her new look. To Ruby, this day was as momentous as graduating from uni, which unfortunately she never managed to do. She had been lined up to go to Sheffield University to read history, but then she met Richie, who convinced her that no one needed a degree to get on in this day and age. She still almost believed that, but even so felt that she'd missed out on something that could not be replaced. So today was to be celebrated, no ifs or buts. It was her day along with her colleagues, who had worked so hard to reach this special moment.

The photographer duly arrived and Ruby swelled with pride as, with a shake of the hand from the CEO, she was handed her badge. It might only be a metal airline logo with her name engraved on it, but to Ruby it was the most precious thing she had ever earned. She badly wanted to salute the CEO, but fought down the urge and stood tall, shoulders back, unable to stop the wide grin that split her face.

The first thing she was going to do when she got home was polish her new red-leather shoes within an inch of their lives, prance around the sitting room wearing them and then . . . and then. She frowned trying to think what delight would come after that. For some reason Richie wasn't included in this daydream and it made her sad, although she wasn't going to analyse why. Instead she grinned at Lucy, who was also beaming, and with a pang she wished Milo was there to see such an auspicious moment, knowing that he would be grinning as widely as she was, celebrating her moment with her.

When the furore died down everyone decamped to the pub, but she declined the offer, deciding to get back to Richie and celebrate, hoping to recover the warmth they used to share. She headed for her moped, wondering how on earth she would ensure that her airline hat with its cute little tassel on top would make the round trip every day without ending up looking like a squashed blue rat.

She rounded the corner to the car park to see Jerry pushing himself out of his car. 'Hi, Jerry, you've missed all the action, I'm afraid.'

'I know, and I'm so sorry. We had a last-minute scoop, although when I say a *scoop* I mean the tiniest cow on the train track, cat stuck up a tree kind of scoop. That's what it's like living in the fast lane down Devon way.' He popped the boot of his car and picked out a camera. 'Just in time to catch you, though, so all good.'

'But it's all over, you missed it.' She indicated her weatherproof jacket. It swamped her but was big enough to wear over her uniform. She was ready to go home, not take part in a photo shoot.

'Nonsense. Won't take you a minute to put on those posh shoes and your hat. I want you pouting, mind, like a saucy air hostess leaning across your moped.' Jerry gave her a disarming smile and she could imagine him in his youth winning a charm offensive.

'I hope you're joking,' she said, and saw his eyes twinkling but nevertheless he levelled his camera at her.

Ruby sighed and unzipped her jacket, knowing a losing battle when she saw one. 'Yep. That's the angle of the story, but I also want you to look like a babe showing off your beautiful hair and wide smile. Sorry, can't help it.'

'This is for the *Chronicle*, right? Only, it sounds like you're selling me on OnlyFans,' Ruby teased.

'Darn it, rumbled again.' He grinned that disarming grin that made her think they could have been friends if the age gap wasn't so wide.

Ruby laughed and pushed out her boobs, pouting just as Jerry snapped an image.

'Hey, steady on,' she said, 'I don't want to get sacked before I've even started. Delete that one immediately, I was messing.'

'At least give me a Victory salute standing in front of an aircraft like those ladies in World War Two. I can get the lads on Photoshop to alter the background.'

Ruby obliged, stifling giggles as she mock-saluted and flicked her hair over her shoulders, allowing it to stream out behind her when the wind blew. She pouted slightly as she posed, laughing out loud as she became more outrageous, surprisingly enjoying herself.

'I'll try and coincide these photos with the launch of the new routes, now you're all raring to go,' Jerry said as the photo shoot wound down and he packed his camera away.

Ruby was eager to get home to Richie, so she said her goodbyes as she zipped up her waterproof and was back to being the girl next door. She gave Jerry a cheery toot and a wave and she was off; there was no stopping her now.

She wanted to celebrate with Richie, she really did, and prayed it would be a turning point in their relationship once he could see that she intended to make a go of Celestial as a proper career. When she brought in a decent wage and things settled down they would be fine, she was sure, although Richie barely asked her anything about her job and she had to endure his blank, uninterested eyes whenever she mentioned it.

She wished she was celebrating with her crew, though. If only Richie was the sort of boyfriend she could take with her, as some of the others did, but she knew he would be surly around her friends and criticise them once they were home. She had decided that she needed to focus on him for a while, and make him understand that her job was important to her, that it didn't stop her from loving him. She would win him around and they would be back to the way they used to be, laughing and teasing each other, and not caring if the world saw how in love they were.

Richie now spent hours in the farm shed where the car was waiting to be turned from a pumpkin into a souped-up dream machine, and it was good to see him come home in overalls, a splodge of oil on his cheek and his hair all tousled. The classic car club he joined were generous in their time and Richie's conversations were full of talk of spark plugs and manifolds. She couldn't help but laugh at the look on his face, though, when he discovered that the Porsche was only a rare colour because it had been resprayed and was not the early model he'd been led to believe. The inside was painted an undercoat grey as if the previous owner hadn't quite got around to spraying it before Richie foolishly bought it, but really, that was Richie all over — trying to bag a bargain and getting shafted instead. Every time.

So Richie had his happy place now and she hoped it would be a turning point for both of them. She'd achieved her own dream and there was nowhere else to go but up, she thought, with a wry smile, up into the sky where she had always wanted to be. And tonight she was going to celebrate that finally happening — with Richie, her boyfriend, the man she loved.

She parked the moped, pulled off her crash helmet and put a smile on her face as she burst through the door, determined to inject some of her enthusiasm into Richie. 'I passed with flying colours! Fiona showed me my test paper — ninety-eight per cent!' She threw her bag on the chair. 'Abbey didn't make the grade because she couldn't actually swim, but I've offered to teach her and she can just do the rescue bit next time, without taking the rest of the course, which is absolutely brilliant, although as Lucy said, it's all pretty pointless as the chances of swimming away from an aeroplane crash in the sea are nil to eff all, really. The other one who failed took a sickie and was spotted on Facebook at a friend's wedding. That was enough to give her the chop.' She stopped with an intake of air, finally running out of steam. 'It was really sad, actually. She came in to hand back her ID as we were all getting our wings. She looked gutted.' Ruby rallied. 'But yay, I did it!'

She couldn't stop grinning and rushed to the fridge to retrieve the bottle of Cava she'd hidden in the salad drawer. 'Not quite champagne, but . . .' She waved the bottle in the air. 'Ta da. It's Waitrose, so I know it'll be good.' The cork came out with a satisfying pop and she giggled as she poured it into two glasses. It was then she clocked that Richie, sprawled out on the sofa, had hardly moved and was glued to his phone, no doubt scrolling through mindless videos on TikTok.

'You okay? Has something happened?' She placed both glasses on to the coffee table.

He looked up. 'Happened? Nope, not really. You've got yourself the job you always wanted.' He raised a hand half-heartedly. 'Yay.'

'Yay,' she echoed. The lacklustre tone of his voice put her on her guard, but nevertheless she raised her glass again and took a large gulp, still eyeing him, deflating as she clocked his jutting lower lip, a sure sign he was in a mood. She took another gulp and put her glass down on the table, enthusiasm draining faster than the wine.

She'd been looking forward to recounting the funnier parts of the course as she hadn't had a chance to properly talk to him for weeks, being so immersed in the course and learning drills. Fire extinguishers, oxygen bottles and life jackets were all she dreamed about and she was drained from it all.

He didn't even know about the day at the pool and the rescue missions they'd enacted, which had turned into a real one for her. She was still amazed that she'd actually saved

Abbey from drowning and Richie knew nothing about it. To her mind it showed how far apart they had drifted, that Ruby, who normally didn't stop talking, hadn't bothered to share something so momentous.

Framing a sentence in her mind to put a funny spin on flashing her 'Boom' knickers as she climbed back into the dinghy, she saw clearly that she hadn't related any of it to Richie because he was so plainly uninterested in her new job. In a moment of clarity she knew that he probably would never want to listen to any anecdotes from Celestial. It gave her a moment's pause. Her job was going to be a huge part of her life and if Richie didn't want to hear about it, then how much of a life together did they have left?

'Why are you still mad at me? I thought you were okay with it now.' She blurted it out, although it probably wasn't the right question to ask.

'Well,' he said ponderously, 'for one, I haven't quite come to terms with you effectively imprisoning us both to living here.'

She flinched at his tone, having no idea what he was talking about, but she could tell a bad mood when she saw one. 'What are you on about? We're saving up for a place of our own, aren't we?'

'I don't mean this.' He waved his hand around. 'I mean *here*.'

She was still confused. 'But we've always lived here.'

'Doesn't mean I always want to. You're not the only one who might like to travel, you know.'

'But, but . . .' She was so genuinely confused she couldn't finish her sentence. 'Where do you want to go, then?' she croaked, a cold dread rendering her vocal cords useless. She couldn't move away now, not when she'd just landed the best job ever.

'That's not the point, but it'll be further than bloody Heathrow, which is about as far as you'll go, for all your plans of exotic trips.' He barked out a laugh, stood up languidly and yawned as he stretched his arms above his head.

He looked at the wine poured out for him and picked up the glass, knocking back her celebration fizz in one long gulp and toasting her snarkily. 'So here's to you and *your* dreams.' He slammed the glass down, picked up his denim jacket and slung it over his shoulder.

'Are we going out?' She scrambled to her feet. Maybe she'd got him wrong and he was going to surprise her by taking her somewhere lovely.

'*I'm* going out.' He slammed his feet into trainers barely looking at her.

She shook her head, blinking in disbelief. 'But it's my special day.'

He sighed loudly. 'It's not always about you, Ruby. You still don't seem to get that, do you?'

'But it *is* my . . .' She trailed off, realising that she was probably the only one who thought it was an achievement worth celebrating, and she *was* being incredibly self-centred. She sipped at her sparkling wine, which had turned into vinegar on her tongue, not even bothering to ask where he was going, for once not giving him the satisfaction of relishing the hurt in her eyes. The evening was already ruined. 'Richie?' she queried, hoping for an inkling of why he was behaving the way he was. It was futile really, as she was, in fact, already talking to his back as he stomped to the front door, grabbing his keys as he went.

'Ruby, I'm done with this. Get used to the idea, okay?' He didn't even turn around.

She waited until he'd slammed the door, blinking in shock at the void left behind. She stared hard at the front door, convinced he would swing back through the door shouting, 'Fooled you!' as he shrugged off his coat and threw his arms around her. But of course that didn't happen.

She slumped on to the sofa, glancing dully around at the sitting room she had furnished with such care: the fluffy grey pillows, toned down so as not to be too *girly* when she'd really wanted seashell pink; the quirky rabbit lamp with the ears poking up above the shade; the Persian Kilim rug that she couldn't afford but bought anyway, knowing it would be perfect nestled in front of the hearth. Richie had bought nothing as far as she could see, apart from the big ugly gaming chair that brooded in the corner next to his giant computer.

So, was that it? What did Richie mean? Had he simply gone out — or gone for ever? She wasn't quite sure, and had half a mind to lock the door so he couldn't get in — just to see if such an action would give her some backbone to deal with the situation.

As she now saw it, she had a few choices. She could wallow like a slob in her joggers, switch on the television and guzzle her sparkling wine until she *really* didn't care anymore; she could cry herself to sleep, which Richie probably expected her to do; or she could put him out of her mind and celebrate her achievement with people who actually seemed to like her company and were happy to be part of her world.

In days gone by, she would worry herself to distraction if she'd upset her precious boyfriend and be desperate to make amends, but he'd steadily eroded that urge, and the strongest emotion she conjured up now was resentment. What did it say about him, if he couldn't even be kind to someone he professed to love? Love was setting you free, was it, according to Sting and Richie *bloody* Shipman? Was disliking a person cause enough to set them free, too? She thought maybe it was, and it was high time she used that choice on Richie. She could be making new memories while he went off to stay at his mother's, no doubt to play pool and drink beer to his heart's content at his old local pub, not giving Ruby a second thought.

She necked another glass of wine while she deliberated, and decided, dammit, it *was* her special day and he wasn't going to ruin it. She went into the bedroom, changed into her favourite wide-legged black trousers that she could wear with high wedges and topped it with a black floaty shirt with gold threads running through it, even as she acknowledged that she wore far too much black. But with her ginger hair and white face, what colours could she wear?

Next, she picked up her phone and scrolled to Tom's Taxis. Decanting the essentials from her everyday handbag into a tiny one, she was just ready in time as Tom pulled up outside. She slammed the front door — just a fraction of a moment before she realised she'd left her door keys in her other handbag. 'Bugger,' she said, staring at the door. It was a bit of a shock to know that she was on her own right then, no Richie with his spare set of keys to let her in. She certainly wouldn't phone him, he would think it was a ruse to find out where he was, but she couldn't be arsed to think about him or how he felt. All she needed was a friend to talk to and alcohol in her veins to free her thoughts. And luckily that was exactly the direction she was heading.

Her resentment of Richie carried her forward into the pub as she marched in determinedly, although she faltered slightly on seeing everyone celebrating, her natural reticence holding her back. Everyone seemed far more drunk than she was, but she could soon remedy that.

'Ruby, you made it!' Lucy shouted, grabbing hold of her arm. 'Look everyone, it's Ruby.'

Ruby shushed her. 'Why do you always do this to me?'

'Because I love you — everyone loves you — and look, Milo loves you too, don't you, Milo?'

Ruby was surprised to see Milo, as he wasn't a new recruit — and he lived miles away, lording it over his minions in his castle or suchlike, didn't he?

'Here's Ruby, Milo.' Lucy was clearly so drunk that she wasn't thinking straight as she shoved Ruby in front of a puzzled-looking Milo.

He smiled in a distracted kind of way. 'Hello, Ruby, congratulations.'

She stilled her beating heart as she smiled up at him. Was it her imagination or was he looking over the top of her head? 'Thank you,' she said and stood there, unable to think of a single thing to add to her mind-blowingly fascinating conversation. Milo, scanning the room, was *so* looking for someone else.

'Yeah, well done.' He smiled faintly and turned back to his friends.

Lucy, watching this exchange and realising it hadn't gone as expected, said, 'Drink, I think?'

'A rather large one. My shout,' Ruby agreed, taking Lucy's glass. She was more than deflated at Milo's response to seeing her, but she had built their friendship up into something it clearly wasn't and it served her right.

After fighting her way to the bar and downing the best part of a large white wine, she calmed down and enjoyed the buzz, but after a while the conversation became too shouty and *matey*, with lots of back-slapping and hugging and she found herself retreating into herself. Richie was somewhere else — without her. *He* had done this, not her. Or was she to blame for chasing her dreams? Was this a new beginning or a sad ending? Maybe she should be the one to decide, rather than waiting for life to happen to her. A life without Richie telling her what to do and making her feel bad about herself? He hated her job, her laugh, her stature, even hated her Viking hair, which used to be her crowning glory until Richie came along. But he was her boyfriend, and they were supposed to be forging a life together, weren't they? She didn't know what to think anymore. Suddenly the fun had gone out of the evening. Her dream job had come with an unpalatable proviso of life-changing enormity and she didn't like it.

'Hey.' Milo sat down next to her.

'Said the horse to the bartender,' Ruby replied glumly.

'What?'

'It's a silly joke: horse walks into a bar, asks what's on the lunch menu, kind of thing.' Ruby's sad mood lifted slightly as the kind eyes of Milo did something flippy to her insides. So, he hadn't snubbed her?

Milo smiled. 'You are funny.'

'As in *weird*.' She sighed. 'I know. I am descended from the Vikings, who were not known for their hilarity.' She pointed to her head. 'I have a Viking helmet to prove it.'

He laughed. 'What are you on about? Where?'

'Oh, I don't have it with me. It's on the hall table; we throw our loose change into it. And the sad thing is, the only attribute the Vikings passed down to me was the ginger hair — oh, and the stocky legs. The Danish side of the Vikings were not willowy and beautiful, they left that to the Swedes.' She waggled her legs a bit to prove her dumpiness, swayed precariously and almost fell off her chair. She righted herself with great effort, wincing as she acknowledged that she was more drunk than she'd realised. Bum. She hadn't eaten since lunch and had started on the fizz a bit early at home. 'Did you know there's no proof that they even wore horned helmets?'

'The Vikings?' Milo asked, his lips twitching.

'Oh, yes.' Ruby nodded sagely. 'Not one raging horn between them.' She giggled, aware that she had said something vaguely smutty, even if she was unsure what it was. She looked down into her glass, sadly. 'I guess I need to do less thinking and more drinking, but I do sincerely believe it was important that I divulged to you the secrets of the Vikings and their helmets.' She giggled again, putting her hand up to her mouth. 'It's often my party piece when I'm drunk.'

Milo's forehead crinkled in concern. 'Absolutely. Definitely needed to share that with me.'

She gazed at him earnestly. 'I think so.'

Milo looked back at her steadily as if he didn't know what to do with her. 'Sure, I may have a wee drop o' Viking blood in my own bones. They settled in Scotland for over three hundred years, you know. Bit of rape and pillage must have cemented some DNA in our race.'

'Oh, sorry about that.' Ruby looked contrite.

Milo laughed. 'I'm not blaming you, and to be honest, you probably descended from them by the same route.'

'Oh, I never thought of that,' Ruby said wide-eyed. 'I assumed I was descended from a warrior — one of the ones doing the pillaging.' She sighed. 'That's a bit of a let-down actually.'

Milo laughed even as he pinched the bridge of his nose, his forehead crinkling with concern. 'You know, I don't think the two together — thinking and drinking — are doing you any favours. You look kind of glum, considering you should be celebrating.'

'Hey, I've just been told I'm not a direct descendant of Ragnar, how would you feel?' She huffed out a breath. 'Anyway, I'm not glum.' She was drunk and maudlin, bordering on miserable, and wished she was at home in her dressing gown, watching telly. Richie being there too was completely optional.

Milo took in their surroundings. 'It's a bit of a madhouse here, isn't it? Do you want to disappear?'

'Disappear?'

'Get out of here, yes.'

'With you?'

'If it's not too awful an idea? I'm hungry, are you?'

A distant part of her mind recalled that she shouldn't be around Milo, she should be in the bar with her co-workers, but she was bloody starving and not enjoying her new, shiny, happy friends as she should. She nodded and eased herself off the stool — very carefully. 'Okay, lead the way.'

She weaved out of the bar, smiling innocently as she passed Lucy, who pursed her lips and narrowed her eyes, miming *phone me* with her hand.

CHAPTER TWELVE

Milo took her hand — to steady her, she supposed — and they walked along the pavement together. His hand in hers was decidedly weird and she kept thinking he would let go, but he didn't and she quickly got used to the sensation of holding a hand that wasn't Richie's.

They were shown to a table in a quaint Italian restaurant and she vaguely wondered how she had wound up with Milo in an upmarket Italian when she should be doing the Conga around the tables in a downmarket pub with her airline mates. She knew which she preferred, though, traitorous as the thought was.

Milo suggested soft drinks for both of them, and after a chicken tagliatelle and two glasses of soda and lime she felt more normal, regretting her celebratory wine binge, but not regretting ending up opposite Milo. She didn't know what to think about this turn of events, but she was enjoying herself, even as a wash of guilt dulled her contentment, imagining Richie's face if he knew she was having dinner with a pilot — his worst nightmare confirmed. She wouldn't think of that now. If it *was* over between them she needed time to come to terms with it, dissect it and talk it through with friends before deciding whether she should be heartbroken or doing a happy dance of relief.

'So, you live in a castle, right?' she said conversationally. 'Like you do.'

Milo almost snorted into his drink. 'I can see the gossip-mongers have been out in force. No, I don't live in a castle. My father lives in a very large house in Scotland that just happens to have a turret, but I live on a farm down the road with my brother and his wife; it's a working farm, mostly.'

'Oh.' A working farm, not a mansion? That certainly put a different slant on things. 'That must be lovely,' she added wistfully as images of lambs frolicking on a carpet of daisies and buttercups filled her mind.

Milo quickly put her right. 'Peacocks screaming a dawn chorus competing with the crowing cockerels when I've just put my head down after a twelve-hour shift. Cows bellowing to be milked, donkeys braying at all hours. Donkeys, I might add, that should not even be living on the farm, eating our hay and batting their beautifully long eyelashes at the visitors. They don't even earn their keep, apart from the occasional handout from the sanctuary down the road for all the food they scoff. You wouldn't believe how much hard-earned money people donate — on a creature that does nothing.' He shook his head. 'One of the richest charities there is.' He laughed grimly. 'Yep, a herd of donkeys earn more money than their neighbouring farmers. Who's the *real* donkey, eh? Money down the bloody drain.'

Ruby was shocked at the tone of his words. Wasn't it an unwritten law of the world that donkeys were universally loved? Even Shrek ended up loving his annoying Donkey.

But Milo's face creased into a smile. 'And I wouldn't have it any other way, bloody noisy creatures. Tonto is my favourite, followed by Carrot, who has her own straw sunhat — that she's only partially eaten. She's really cute.'

Ruby heaved out a sigh of relief that he did actually like the donkeys; she didn't want her Milo-shaped bubble to burst quite yet. 'You live on your own at the farm — with your brother, I mean?' She could have bitten off her tongue, knowing that her question sounded like she was fishing to see if he lived with Loretta.

'Yes, I live there with my brother, his wife, Merry, and various members of staff. I have my own little home but we share all the duties, unless I'm flying.'

Ruby couldn't quite process this brand-new image of Farmer Milo with the smooth charm of his pilot persona. How come no one else at work had discussed this side of him?

Milo peered at her unblinking. He wagged his finger. 'I know what you're thinking. You're wondering how you can adopt one of the donkeys. Come on, fess up.'

She was actually wondering where Loretta fitted into this interesting lifestyle but she would rather die than admit it. Instead she laughed. 'Got me in one.'

'Well, I just happen to have some adoption forms that I carry around for such opportunistic occasions. Hang on.' He rummaged in his jeans pocket but his hand came up empty and his eyes crinkled at the edges in mirth. 'I'm joking.'

Ruby's now very sober mind couldn't help but notice how his smile softened his face and made him so much more approachable than the confident Milo at work. Here was the approachable *farmer* Milo and it appeared that she liked him just as much as *pilot* Milo. She took stock of her thoughts, accepting that she *liked* him, whatever his persona. It was perturbing, though, as she believed her head overruled the heart; it was the way things should be, to keep her world turning on an even keel. Liking Milo *was* permissible but she wasn't about to go falling in love with him now, was she?

'And you? Your life before this never-ending cycle of early morning flights and constant tiredness?' Milo asked, bringing her up sharp. She didn't want him to know that up until a month ago the pinnacle of her dreams was to live in a terraced house with her boyfriend. Luckily she did have her blog and Instagram posts, which she was happy to talk about, especially if it diverted attention from her personal life. 'Oh, I blog about Devon, the countryside, the seaside, the weather, anything really; I like taking photos. Since I've had my iPhone I've become lazy, though, and tend to just take snaps and put them on Instagram.'

'I've never got to grips with Instagram. I don't suppose I need to, but it would be good to advertise the goods we make and sell at the farm and the Fraser Estate. I guess the internet is the place for all of that stuff.'

The Fraser Estate, thought Ruby. 'It's easy, I'll walk you through it sometime.'

Milo nodded. 'You should come and take some photos of the donkeys. The sanctuary could amass trillions from people desperate to throw money at the little critters.'

She smiled even as she blushed and ignored the little leap of anticipation at seeing Milo in his home setting. 'I'd love that. I can already visualise Carrot with her straw sunhat on, ears poking out — I'll bring some props, turn it into a proper photo shoot.'

'Great idea. I'll bring the apples and you bring the sunshine.'

His smile was genuine but Ruby didn't know what to make of the sunshine comment. She nodded, even though Richie's jealousy would make it almost impossible to visit a farm to take photos of donkeys, when they didn't even know anyone who owned a farm, let alone one full of donkeys. Never mind, she would find a way around it. She remembered with a jolt that she and Richie might already have split up, but she could think about that tomorrow.

Milo's smile suddenly wavered and she wondered if Loretta was on his mind at the same time that she'd thought of Richie.

As if confirming her thoughts, suddenly businesslike, he said, 'We ought to get going, this fine establishment looks as if they are waiting to sweep the floors the minute we leave.'

'Gosh, yes, let me just text home.' Again a pang of guilt that she didn't actually mention Richie's name.

Milo insisted on paying and settled the bill as she tried to call Richie, but he didn't pick up. She wasn't worried, he was probably sulking.

Milo said he would take her home and she didn't really have a good reason to refuse. What could she say, that she would catch a bus when his car was yards away? She climbed in, grateful to be out of the cold wind, but her nerves kicked in as they pulled up outside her home, which was completely, ominously, in darkness. Surely Richie wouldn't still be at the pub? Did he seriously intend not to come home?

'Thank you so much for this evening, it was lovely,' she repeated, climbing out of his car. 'Night,' she added, hoping he would take the hint and drive away.

'I'll wait until you're inside,' Milo said.

She smiled thinly. 'Thanks.' The perfect gentleman, dammit.

She walked to the door, expecting trouble as she rang the bell, listening at the door for a commotion. But Richie's phone didn't ring and all was dark and quiet inside. She rapped on the door again. 'Richie,' she hissed through the letterbox. Surely he would be back by now? But if he was — and she suspected that he was — it was clear that he wasn't answering the door. She chewed her lip. What was she to do? Her mum would welcome her, although it was ridiculously late, but she was also forty minutes away on the other side of the bridge at Saltash. She couldn't ask Milo to take her there and a cab would cost a fortune. She turned back towards Milo's car to catch his eye as he peered out of the window, clearly realising something was wrong. Instead of rolling the window down to talk to her, he jumped out of the car. 'Problem?' he asked, peering at the door as if the fact that it was locked could be easily surmountable.

'I forgot my key, so I can't get in.' Once again no mention of Richie.

'Oh.' He gazed down the road and stared at her front door. 'No worries, I'll book you into the hotel where I'm staying.'

'Oh God, no, I'm fine,' Ruby said, panicked. A hotel would cost her the best part of her food money for the week, and it would look bad if she was seen going into a hotel at midnight with a pilot who apparently had a reputation for charming the ladies.

'Don't worry, I have a business account, it won't cost.'

'I can't.'

'Why not, and what else can you do? Do you have a friend you can call?'

She glanced at her watch and shook her head. It was far too late to ask anyone if she could crash on their sofa — apart from having to explain that her boyfriend had locked her out.

Reluctantly she nodded. 'Okay.' It didn't sit well with her and belatedly she remembered to thank him. 'It's very kind of you.'

The receptionist didn't blink when Milo checked her in; she had probably seen it all before, and Ruby curbed the urge to explain that it was all above board. And it *was* all above board, she reminded herself when Milo stopped outside her room and gave her a courteous nod of the head. 'Goodnight. I can take you home in the morning. I have to be at work for nine, so it's no trouble.'

'Thank you. I hate to put you to all this bother.'

'As I've said, it's no trouble. Sleep well. Oh, hang on, let me get you a tee shirt to wear or else you'll be sleeping in your clothes.'

'No, it's fine . . .'

But he was already striding down the corridor. 'Won't be a sec.'

Ruby had no choice but to wait. She hovered indecisively, uncomfortably aware that when he returned she could invite him into her room for a coffee or — was there a bar, a fridge? She could do with a swift drink right then, even though it would be a really bad idea. Would it be appropriate to invite him in?

She shot the idea down. Of course it wouldn't be appropriate. Glancing anxiously down the corridor, she noted, of all things, the pattern on the carpet and a large dirty mark that looked as if someone had dropped a bottle of red wine on it, long ago. A slamming door — and Milo appeared from one of the innocuous rooms along the corridor, smiling as he walked towards her, holding out what she presumed to be a tee shirt.

'Here you go,' he said.

She looked down at the pristine white top. It seemed too intimate a thing to take, as if he'd just removed it from his back and would smell of him. As soon as the thought crossed her mind she wanted to sweep it up and press it against her cheek, breathing in his scent.

As if spotting her hesitancy, he added, 'It is clean — just taken it out of my case.'

'Oh, okay.' As if *that* was the issue. 'Thanks very much.' She noted the raised eyebrow and quirky smile but smiled anyway. Was he teasing her, or worse, could he guess her thoughts?

'It's my Paul Smith one, my favourite, so don't lose it.'

He stood far too close for comfort and seemed reluctant to leave, but they couldn't stand in the corridor making small talk all night. 'Lose it? How could I lose it?' Too late, she saw the grin.

He shook his head. 'I know. Especially if you're wearing it in bed.' There was a flicker of a wink. Either that or he'd suddenly developed a tick.

Immediately, unbidden thoughts of being divested of her tee shirt by Milo reddened her cheeks. She blinked the images away but couldn't help wondering what her own lingering body scent was like and whether Milo would have the same urge to inhale it when she gave it back to him.

And still he stood outside her door, nonplussed. Did he expect her to invite him in? It was like playing a game where she didn't understand the rules. Richie was her first proper boyfriend and she certainly hadn't learned the art of flirting. Decisively she said, 'Goodnight, then, and thanks for everything.'

'The pleasure was mine. And for the record, your hair is better than my favourite *heilan' coo*'s hair.'

'A *heilan'* what?'

He smiled gently. 'A *heilan' coo* — highland cow,' he enunciated, 'for the uninitiated. It has soulful eyes like yours and her hair is exactly the same colour—'

'Great, you're likening me to a cow?'

'Yes, I am. My favourite cow. And she has horns, the same as you — still growing.'

Ruby burst out laughing. 'Oh, God, I told you about the Viking helmet, didn't I? Earlier, when I was pickled?' She put her hand to her forehead, giggling uncontrollably. 'I'm such a lightweight,' she said through her laughter.

'Yep.' He took out his phone, and Ruby for one heart-stopping moment thought he had the photos to prove it, but he simply scrolled through his phone and showed her a picture of a russet-coloured cow with a sweet face and curly horns. 'Best there is, you'd better believe it.'

'She's beautiful,' she said, aware that her voice had taken on a dreamy tone. She leaned against the wall by her door and Milo joined her, his shoulder against the wall as he angled his body towards hers.

Slowly he reached out to her hair, ran his hand down it briefly and twirled a strand of it around his fingers and let it drop back on to her shoulders, where it stayed in a perfect curl. Instinctively she reached up and found his hand and they entwined fingers awkwardly for just a few seconds.

'You trying to find my horns?' She meant it to sound sarcastic but her voice came out girly and breathy.

'You got me,' he said, a gentle smile on his face. He hesitated for one more beat. 'Night, then.'

'Night,' she said, letting her hand drop away.

Neither of them moved.

As if in slow motion, he leaned over and kissed her lightly on the cheek. 'Goodnight, Ruby Hansen with the Viking horns.'

'Goodnight, Milo with the Arms, and thank you.'

They grinned stupidly at each other, and the slight opportunity where they might have thrown caution to the wind and caved in to make a night of it passed. Entirely.

And so, Ruby undressed, slipped his top over her head and climbed into a cold bed having to be satisfied with inhaling the scent of Milo as her heartbeat slowed. It didn't really smell of Milo, just of fabric conditioner, but it was enough to know it was his, and no matter how much she told herself she didn't care, she did. She snuggled down, though, warming up as the duvet embraced her and, exhausted by the day and against all odds, managed to still her traitorous heart enough to fall soundly asleep.

CHAPTER THIRTEEN

Ruby surfaced to the sound of a godawful noise — something banging with ear-splitting monotony outside. She sat up, groggily gazing around the room, taking a moment to work out where she was. A soft light glowed under the door and there was a window that shouldn't be where it was. A fridge was under a desk. A freakin' fridge? She collapsed back on the pillow — and remembered.

She sighed, running her hand down Milo's tee shirt, the magic of last night returning guiltily to her consciousness. A slow smile spread across her face, but her pleasant thoughts were short-lived as the rapping noise became more insistent. Someone was knocking at her door and they seemed determined to break it down if she didn't answer it.

Unsteadily she lurched out of bed and yanked it open as Richie hurled himself inside, his face livid, lips twisted in an angry snarl. 'Where is the fucker?' Hands raised, he aimed a blow at her. The red mist had descended; he hadn't a clue what was going on.

She whirled around as he caught her on the shoulder, staggering backwards, hitting the bed and landing on it with an ungainly thump. 'Richie?' she breathed out, winded and so shocked she couldn't think of anything else to say.

'Where is he?' Richie's fists were clenched and his eyes were murderous.

Ruby, shaken, stuttered, 'Where is who? What's happened?'

Ignoring her, he scanned the room and kicked the bed hard, as if flushing out the culprit. His chin thrust out, ready and waiting for a fight, he dived into the bathroom, ripping aside the shower curtain. He grunted gutturally on seeing there was no naked body to beat up. Undeterred, he whirled around, ran towards the window and peered out as if he expected to see someone shimmying down the drainpipe.

Ruby, initially panicked that something bad had happened, started to laugh at his antics, belatedly realising that he thought she had a man in her room. 'You've been watching too many B movies, my love,' she said, stifling her annoyance, or was it the urge to laugh, she couldn't tell.

He rushed up to her, his face inches away from hers. 'You'll be laughing on the other side of your face when I find out what you've been up to.'

Ruby's smile dropped. Enough. She squared her shoulders even as fear ran down her spine. 'Are you threatening me?'

'That's nothing to what I'll do to you — and him — when I find out where he is.'

She stood her ground. 'Get out.'

'What?'

'Get out of my room.'

'Your room . . . what?' he blustered, clearly surprised at her retaliation. 'Who are you hiding?'

'No one. I forgot my key as you probably well know. Oh, wait, you've come to rescue me, have you? Silly me.' Her smile twisted as she fought down anger, knowing that rescuing her was the last thing on his mind.

'Not my fault you forgot your key, you dopey bint.'

She was used to this. He resorted to insults when he was wrong-footed, trying to make her feel that she was in the wrong.

He shrugged as she stared coldly at him, the first sign of unease crossing his features. 'Not my fault,' he mumbled again, but his anger had dissipated and he looked slightly embarrassed. 'Sorry I hit your shoulder — didn't mean to, wasn't thinking straight. I came to save you.'

Ruby scoffed. She couldn't even answer him, couldn't be bothered. It wasn't altruism that had brought him to the hotel, no matter how he tried to spin it.

She needed to calm him down and get him out of the hotel. He had made enough racket to wake the whole floor and it wouldn't be long before someone — maybe even Milo — came to see what the ruckus was about. She pulled on her trousers and made a grab for her top, but settled for wearing Milo's top for the time being, desperate to get out of the room and the hotel.

She stopped her frenzied exit for a moment as a thought crossed her mind. She was still as a statue. 'Hang on, how did you get here?' They didn't have a workable car between them and it was too far to walk.

'Cab's waiting outside,' a more rational but decidedly uncomfortable Richie said.

Only then did she wonder how he knew where to find her. How could he know where she was — unless he'd followed her all night? She sat down on the bed, trying to clear her mind as she slipped her feet into her shoes, overcoming the urge to throw them at her shitty boyfriend.

Richie, cold and unemotional as if trying to work out her misdemeanours, let his gaze play over her face and body, waiting to seize the moment when he could pinpoint where she had failed him.

Spent of energy and sick of trying to second-guess his motives, she motioned for him to follow her as she left the room. The soft click as she closed the door made her sigh with relief but it was short-lived. Milo, door slamming, hurtled down the corridor, jaw clenched and fists raised, looking for all the world like a tousle-haired, charging knight ready to protect his lady's honour.

Skidding to a standstill in front of Ruby, he demanded, 'Is this man bothering you?' He glanced from Ruby to Richie and back again before lowering his fists and rubbing the back of his neck awkwardly, as if realising he'd overreacted. 'Ruby?' He faltered, clearly puzzled. 'You're leaving?'

'Yes, early start and all that.' Why did she so often want the ground to swallow her up since she'd become an adult?

'Oh. Are you okay?' His brow furrowed as he took in Richie — baggy joggers, stained tee shirt, hair flattened to his scalp on one side and sticking up on the other like a broken pigeon wing.

'Yes, my taxi is here, that's all,' Ruby said.

'And I'm her boyfriend, so you'd better watch out.' Richie was suddenly *street boy*: chin jutting, legs akimbo, arms raised, ready for a fight.

Ruby grimaced involuntarily as Milo arched a brow, as if he couldn't quite believe what he was seeing, lip twitching in amusement: the full knight in shining armour realising he was fighting a grubby varlet.

Was he surprised because Richie, the dishevelled wretch in joggers, was her boyfriend, or because she had a boyfriend and hadn't mentioned it? She didn't know which scenario was worse.

'You have a boyfriend? *He* is your boyfriend?'

Cringingly, humiliatingly busted.

She spluttered out a vague answer as the ground swallowing her whole seemed to be taking its time. 'Well, *you* have a girlfriend,' she spat out accusingly.

Richie and Milo both gave her a perplexed look. She didn't even know herself what she meant by that statement. Tampon Tragedy and the Boom Bottom had nothing on this Corridor of Cringe.

'Which is nothing to do with anything, of course. I'm simply asking if you know this fellow, so I know you're not being . . .' He floundered. 'I don't know — coerced.' A mocking smile and slightly furrowed brow from Milo.

Ruby lifted her hand to her forehead knowing she had just made another tragic mistake by voicing her thoughts. She couldn't process so much, so early in the morning. Her brain hadn't come awake yet. Breaking up with Richie was too new, and now it sounded as if Richie had changed his mind and she didn't know whether to be happy or sad, pissed off or relieved.

Milo stared at Richie, who hopped from foot to foot as if he was warming up for round one in a boxing ring. The difference in their attire, stance and looks was vast, Ruby thought, glancing from Richie to Milo, done up in his pilot uniform, radiating good health and, she would bet her last pound, smelling of fresh pine shower gel.

There was a brief stand-off as everyone took stock in silence. Given Richie's earlier bluster, he no longer seemed inclined to ask Milo to *put 'em up*. He was staring at him in awe — as if he wanted to be his friend.

Could it get any worse? If there was a word that meant ten times worse than appalling, Ruby would own it right then.

'If you're sure everything is fine, I'll bid you good morning,' Milo said, looking directly at Ruby and sounding more like a Victorian accountant than a friend.

Ruby nodded in relief. It was *so* time to get out of there. She gave not a thought to the tee shirt that had recently occupied so much of her mind and hurried after Richie down the corridor.

'*I'll bid you good morning,*' Richie mimicked as soon as they climbed into the cab. 'Who the fuck speaks like that? Does he think he's on a film set?' But he sat brooding and Ruby knew he was thinking about Milo, his good looks, great job and good fortune in life. *Who wouldn't*, she thought with a pang. She too sat in the silence that shrouded them, trying to fight the urge to get as far away as possible from Richie, wondering at what point she'd started to loathe him. She had no intention of explaining herself anymore, or defending her right to be in a hotel, where a handsome pilot just happened to be down the corridor.

But something else wasn't sitting right about all of it. She glanced across at Richie, who wouldn't meet her eye. 'So, how *did* you know where I was?'

'Well, you weren't at home, were you, that's for sure.'

'I know that.' She stared at him, waiting. 'Did you go back to the flat last night?'

'Yes.' His voice was small and he didn't elaborate, which was unlike him.

She didn't want to ask why, when he'd been so adamant that it was all over between them, he didn't answer the door, knowing that it was childish pettiness that had stopped him from letting her in. She really didn't want to get into another discussion about their relationship. But this was a different matter. She wanted to know how he had pinpointed where she was. She asked him again.

'I always know where you are.' He didn't sound cocky or angry anymore, more resigned.

'Always. How come?' she asked calmly, although her heart was pounding.

'Put a tracker on your phone, didn't I?'

He didn't even have the grace to sound embarrassed. He sounded pleased, in fact — as if he owned her, as if she was his possession and he was right to keep her in his sights.

'You put a tracker on my mobile?' She had to stop from gaping, she was so shocked. 'You spied on me?' The urge to distance herself from him grew. She pressed her body into the door furthest away from him; it was the best she could do right now. 'How long have you been tracking me?'

'Since you started with *that* airline.' He fairly spat out the words. 'I was keeping you safe.'

She scoffed. 'So safe that you waited until morning to come and find me.'

'I was asleep.' He had the nerve to look affronted — as if that was the problem, not the fact that he'd put a tracker on her phone. He looked out of the window unconcerned, but she knew he was seething at being caught out — and saving his righteous anger for when they were indoors. His anger was his weapon and arguments were what he did best, twisting every fact until she ended up apologising. This time, however, he had gone too far and she was saving up a bit of her own wrath for when he started on her.

They were soon back outside the tiny apartment she had once loved so much and Richie paid the cab driver, who gave them a cheery goodbye, making a valiant effort at pretending he hadn't heard every word of their conversation.

They went inside silently.

Miserably, she gazed around at the place that, in her mind, Richie had now tainted. Summoning up her resolve, she faced him and took a deep breath. There was no pretending anymore.

But before she had a chance to say her piece, Richie, chin thrust out and fists balled again, demanded, 'So what were you up to with that pilot?'

He didn't know it but he'd already lost the game, having manufactured the same argument too many times, determined to wrong-foot her by convincing her she was at fault. He was probably sorry he hadn't caught her in a compromising position so his anger could be given free rein and make her suffering endless.

But not this time. 'You put a freakin' tracker on my phone, that's the problem. Not some man who was clearly in a room down the corridor. How bloody dare you try to make out I'm the bad guy here?' In the past she wouldn't have been quite so outspoken, but those days were gone.

'Just tell me.' His face was inches away from hers.

'There is nothing to tell.'

'Tell me.' His teeth were clenched and his eyes wild.

'Richie, I can't do this anymore.'

He held up a hand silencing her. '*You* can't? Is that right? Well, I can't stand to see your lying face anymore. I'm going to Mum's for a while.'

Ruby breathed out a quiet sigh of relief. If that was his idea of winning the argument, then who was she to change his mind?

He took a step backwards, his face scrunched up a bit, slightly puzzled and affronted as his words didn't have her falling to the ground sobbing.

Ruby stood her ground, almost smiling. He really had expected her to crumple into a heap on the floor.

'Give you time to think on what a relationship is. You know, being together, telling each other everything — being honest,' he reiterated.

He was really ramming it home, she thought, but he did have a point. Maybe the rot had set in when she purposely didn't tell him that she was applying to the airline because she knew he would talk her right out of it. She sighed. 'You're right, of course,' she acknowledged, but it was a bit rich coming from a man who sold their car and bought her a moped without giving her the slightest hint of his plans.

'You don't even support me — my hobbies and stuff,' he added, sensing victory.

Ruby sighed. He was scraping the barrel now. 'Like being supportive over a new job, you mean?'

'Exactly,' he agreed, realising a split second too late that she was being sarcastic. He quickly rallied. 'Most people would be pleased their boyfriend bought them a Porsche.' He sounded unsure of his ground, though; he knew he was reaching.

Ruby was not going down this unlikely rabbit hole with him and wanted to press home his promise to stay with his mum before he had a chance to change his mind. She marched into the bedroom and started emptying his clothes into a holdall.

'If you think it's best that you move out for a while,' she reminded him as they had strayed a bit off topic.

'Sorry, babe, but this one's on you and it will take more than an apology.'

She marvelled at his twisted logic once again. What was she even to apologise for? Him locking her out and trying to start a fight with her colleague in an upmarket hotel?

'No way can I stay with you right now,' he added for good measure as he watched Ruby scrunch clothes into a bag, his smile fading.

'I *so* agree that you should stand by your principles.' She hadn't got a clue what his principles were, but she needed to keep up the momentum.

She passed him the zipped-up holdall and he took it rather reluctantly as if it had only just hit him that he really was going to have to hightail it to his mother's house.

'If you just apologised . . .' He gazed at her with the brown eyes that she had loved, pleading.

She wavered for a second, but no, he wasn't getting away that easily. In fact, he wasn't getting away with his dreadful behaviour at all. Ruby fixed her face into a suitably sad and wistful pose and opened the front door. He put one foot on the pavement, flinching as if emphasising the sacrifice he was making. 'I thought I might have some breakfast—'

'Your mum will do you a fry-up,' she interrupted. She was not letting him back down their hallway for love nor money — not that they had much of either anymore.

He looked from left to right as if he didn't know where he was going. He probably didn't. He didn't even like his mum — and what was more, he didn't even have a bloody car to drive off in either.

She wanted to laugh.

'Just for a week or two, babe, while we sort out our emotions. I need to be able to trust you — you do see that, don't you?' He sounded like he might cry.

Ruby nodded sadly, waiting for him to put his other foot down on the pavement and wondering if a little shove to speed him on his way would be in order. 'Wait!' She put her hand up.

He turned, eyes shining, a smile restored to those full lips — the lips that actually seemed a bit effeminate to her now.

'Take the tracker off my phone before you go.'

'Oh.' He shuffled back through the door and she held out her phone.

Putting his bag down he took her phone silently, concentrating, pushing buttons, pulling out his own phone, frowning and then shoving it back at her. He looked bleakly at her. 'All done,' he said. 'Sorry.'

She nodded, staring at her phone. She had no idea if he had or hadn't taken off the tracker and she made a mental note to take it to a repair shop to have it checked over.

He straightened, gave her another long, sorrowful look, and when she didn't say a word, he picked up the holdall, took a deep breath and left.

Ruby watched his retreating back until he eventually turned a corner and was gone from sight. She nodded slowly and released the breath she hadn't known she was holding. Closing the door silently, she slid down it and rested on her haunches, weak with relief and spent adrenaline. 'What a perfect twat you turned out to be,' she said out loud. Then surprised herself by bursting into tears.

CHAPTER FOURTEEN

The weeks flew by and Ruby took to flying like she'd been born to it. The unsociable hours were a bit of a shock and she was actually glad that Richie wasn't home as she knew her erratic shift pattern would have caused yet more arguments. She loved the camaraderie of the flights, quickly working out who the best crew members were — the ones who were happy in their work and of a sunny disposition. It was a small airline and word soon got around if there was an upset, who was grumpy, who was mean on a night stopover and who ate Pot Noodle in their room to save money rather than eating in the restaurant with the crew. Some people were just not made for serving their fellow man or accepting life's little inconveniences, and they were the ones she steered away from.

She soon found her footing with the passengers too. Apart from inevitable delays, which caused a terrible knock-on effect for some of them, mostly they just wanted to be treated like the paying customers they were: to be fed and watered with a guarantee of reaching their destination with all their limbs intact.

If she kept a running supply of tea and snacks to the flight deck they would give her a shout when there was something interesting to see out of the window, and her Instagram account quickly filled up. Images of deep-orange sunsets, moon-tinged clouds, egg-yolk sunrises, deep-blue sea and the unfathomable blackness of night silvered by stars soon became regular images.

But she felt deeply guilty about the way Richie had left and knew that the trouble between them started because of her career change. Richie had been texting and calling her, and he was back to being the kind and funny Richie of old. He said it was his insecurity that made him behave the way he did and if she could only try a bit harder, they could meet halfway.

She couldn't say she missed him terribly but she was lonely and the evenings on her own seemed to go on for ever. She needed to make a decision one way or the other, so she texted Lucy to see if she was at the airport hotel. Quite a few of the regular crew normally hung out there after their shift, and it could be a laugh. Mostly, though, she needed to talk through the positives and the negatives of going back with Richie.

'Come on down. I'm here with Harry and Emily, and a few of the others are milling around. Get a cab, don't come on your moped,' Lucy said.

Ruby was relieved she wouldn't have to spend another night on her own and called up Tom the cab driver once more. She was inside the hotel shortly afterwards, greeting her colleagues, all of whom were in their civvies, having learned that valuable lesson on their training course: drinking in uniform was another sackable offence, so they all bought spare clothes with them on the off chance they would go out after work.

She bought drinks for herself and Lucy, exclaiming as always at how ridiculously expensive the wine was at the hotel, as she sat down next to her friend.

'So, what's with the glum face?' Lucy asked.

'I was going nuts at home, the same thread going around and around in my head.' She took a swig of her wine and grimaced. 'I need to make my mind up about Richie. Everything between us went wrong when I started this job, as you know, and I feel so bad about it, knowing I pushed him away.'

Lucy narrowed her eyes. She had never said anything derogatory about Richie, but Ruby had the feeling she didn't like him; the narrowed eyes and downturned mouth were a bit of a giveaway too.

'The job you love?' Lucy pressed.

'Yes, but if I love Richie enough I would give it up, surely.'

'Do you want to leave your job?'

'No, I *love* my job.' Ruby was horrified at the thought. It was what made everything worthwhile in her life — even riding the bloody moped home at eleven o'clock at night when errant muntjacs threatened to topple her off it and flying *creatures* batted around her face, scaring the life out of her.

Lucy gave her a measured stare that went on for too long.

Finally, Ruby sighed loudly. 'Are you saying I've answered my own question?'

'I haven't said a word.' Lucy picked up her glass and twirled it around in her hand. 'Wait there, I'm getting us another one each. Down that one while I'm gone.'

Ruby gulped her wine, which brought about a fit of coughing as Lucy returned and rubbed her back, after placing two more large glasses of wine on the table.

'So, give up the job you've dreamed of having ever since you were a teenager and had a girl crush on that beautiful hostie on the flight to Malaga? Is that your plan?'

Ruby had forgotten she'd told Lucy that story. She smiled at the memory. 'Yes, but—'

'Drink,' Lucy commanded. 'So, this last month or so you've acted as if a cloud has lifted — smiling, laughing, and giving big eyes to one of the firemen, if I'm not mistaken.'

You are mistaken about that, Ruby thought, but said nothing, just bit her lip.

Lucy stared at her, waiting for her to speak, but when she didn't she continued. 'Let me get this right. You didn't even dare tell Richie that you applied for the job because you knew he would veto it? I'm just wondering what kind of a boyfriend would do that?'

Still no reply.

Lucy eyed her steadily over the rim of her glass as she took a sip of her wine. 'Okay, here's another truth for you. Richie won't change. He might *appear* to be a different man if you get back together, but if you stay with him you will be toeing his line for ever. And what job are you going to *do* if you leave? He'd have you in a basement scrubbing bricks if it was up to him. He *likes* demeaning you.'

Ruby knocked back her wine. She knew Lucy was right. What had become of the happy girl she used to be, always up for a laugh and an adventure? Richie had drained the spirit out of her. What made her even sadder is that she was relieved to be told what she already knew — that the love she'd had for Richie had faded and it was time to get out of a toxic relationship. For good.

It wouldn't take much adjusting but she would have to find a lodger. She nodded. She could do it. Never fretting about arriving home late off shift, or tiptoeing around Richie's moods if she woke him up accidentally or her roster was changed at the last minute, messing up their plans once again.

She smiled to herself: it truly was as if a heavy load had been lifted from her shoulders. She'd already had a taste of freedom since Richie had been at his mother's and she knew deep down that she would be taking him back because she felt obliged, or heaven forbid because she felt she had no choice but to obey him. What was worse was that Richie would spin it as if he had graciously taken her back and try to make her grateful — for ever.

Harry, one of the crew, plopped himself down next to Lucy, who obligingly changed tack and launched into a story about a Japanese passenger who put clotted cream in his tea, not realising it was for his scone, and then complained that his tea was off.

Harry bested her with a story that Ruby had already heard ten times in different versions.

The punchline came quickly. 'It was an electric tooth-brush going off in a cabin bag!'

Ruby had to stop herself from rolling her eyes. It was a classic tale that everyone in the airline world attributed to their friend, or a passenger on their flight.

'They thought it was a vibrator, can you believe that?' He practically gave a drum roll as he laughed hysterically, thwacking the table with his palm.

Ruby and Lucy both laughed obligingly.

Ruby's eyes swivelled as the door swung open and a half-dozen pilots strode in radiating confidence, walking in synch, hands in pockets, looking like a posh Rat Pack. With a lurch, Ruby spotted Milo in the mix, laughing with his colleagues, absolutely the best of the bunch. Finally admitting to herself that she had hoped to see him there, she nevertheless feigned nonchalance as the men strutted through the foyer as if they owned the place. Wearing a pilot's uniform had that effect, she'd noticed. People looked at them. They walked taller, their smiles were broader and their strides longer.

An ostentation of peacocks, she mused as they passed by. She hadn't realised that she'd been staring until Milo slowed his stride, catching Ruby's eye. He winked. 'Hello, ladies.'

Her cheeks heated up as his eyes fixed on hers, and she prayed he'd walk on by. 'Hi, Milo,' she said, barely able to look him in the eye. She was still not over the disastrous morning at the hotel when Richie had humiliated her so badly, or was the humiliation all of her own making? Whatever. Having washed and ironed Milo's tee shirt, she'd left it in his pigeonhole with a thank you card, and then changed her mind and taken the card back; it seemed a bit over the top. She squirmed with indefin-able embarrassment, though, whenever she remembered the morning of the Cringing Corridor.

She smiled her best smile, expecting him to say nothing more than hello, but still she felt let down when that was entirely all he did, and did indeed walk on by. Inexplicably crestfallen, she watched as he retreated, finally accepting that she liked him more than she should. How ridiculous of her.

She would have more chance with the fireman who thought she was a cleaner on their firefighting day — and that was no chance at all. Would she have noticed Milo if she was happy with Richie, or wasn't life that straightforward? There was no denying he made her heart skip and flip, so didn't that in itself constitute a form of unfaithfulness? *Oh Richie, I'm so sorry*, she thought, reeling from this new reality.

Lucy was side-eyeing Ruby. 'I get it.' Her eyes were positively brimming with mischief. 'Milo's a pretty good reason to break up with Richie.'

'No, *Richie* is a good reason to break up with Richie.' As she said the words, she bizarrely felt like crying. 'I just wish I could rewind my life back to last year. I've made such a mess of things.' She sighed heavily and bent down to pick up her bag. 'Nothing has happened with Milo, Lucy. Can you imagine him fancying me?' She eyed the lift doors wistfully; Milo was so close and yet so far.

'Come on, finish your drink and come back to mine, before you ask for his room key at reception or something equally cringeworthy.' Lucy clearly thought the idea hilarious.

'Oh my God, don't even go there.' The horror of doing such a thing would follow her to her grave. Ruby looked mournfully down at her drink and her head snapped back up as Lucy elbowed her.

The lift doors pinged and Milo strode out, his uniform gone, hair damp around his neck and wearing a fresh blue shirt and jeans.

Her eyes fixed on him like a limpet to a rock as he weaved his way past chairs and around tables, issuing an apology when he bumped into someone. She was still riveted when he drew near and smiled cheekily.

Sitting down next to Ruby, without hesitation, he said, 'Sorry, just needed to shake off the chaps I was with. They wanted to go to a rather salubrious bar and — well, I'm not in the market for that.'

'Because you have a girlfriend?' Lucy asked pointedly, leaning forward, her words slurring a little.

Milo sighed and rolled his eyes as he turned to Lucy. 'My girlfriend, or girlfriends plural, as it now appears to be, seem to cause an inordinate amount of interest in Celestial Air. I swear Loretta has more fans at Celestial than she does on Instagram.' Milo fixed Lucy with a laser stare, a muscle jumping in his jaw. 'We used to have a captain here whose nickname was Captain Duff Gen — it's an RAF term for giving out bad information. He spouted the most outrageous gossip and so we began to feed him duff gen, just to see how long it would take before the lies showed up on the circuit, so to speak.' He smiled and said no more, letting the words speak for themselves.

Lucy drained her drink. 'Well, that's told me,' she said, but she was grinning. 'Not my fault you're worth gossiping about, but I swear I'll only spread the truth, the whole truth and nothing but the truth from now on.' She glanced at Ruby and back at Milo before enunciating theatrically, 'My, is that the time?' She checked a non-existent watch on her wrist. 'Must be off.' She picked up her phone and winked at Ruby.

Ruby was worried that she herself had been the one to start the rumour about him having more than one girlfriend, as she had asked a few crew members if they knew a woman called Daisy, but Milo didn't look at her accusingly. In fact, he gave her a slow smile, as once again they were alone together.

'So, your Instagram is becoming quite famous, I see,' Milo said after a beat of silence.

'All thanks to Celestial.' It was true. Ruby's Instagram had taken off alarmingly since she'd started putting up reels of pilots flying the aircraft and hosties working in the cabin. She had even enacted a few emergency drills with some of her colleagues to explain that being a flight attendant wasn't all about serving tea and biscuits or looking glamorous. The hashtag #CelestialAir had picked up thousands of followers since Fiona had given her the go-ahead to start using it.

Milo angled his head. 'I think you've done most of it on your own, along with a huge amount of free advertising for Celestial Air. Shares have tripled in the last month. We're now known as an international airline serving the South West, instead of just a two-bit airline escorting farmers to and from the markets.'

Ruby nodded. It was true. 'And Bananarama seems to be quite the hit too. I've had messages from the manufacturer asking if I'd like to do some promo work.'

'Have you? That's marvellous.'

'They seem to like the plastic flowers on the front mud-guard and the flower-power stickers all over it.' She gave him big eyes to show she was being sarcastic. 'Classy, hey?'

'One hundred per cent,' Milo agreed.

'I've even had a company offering to buy me a new crash helmet.' Ruby nodded. 'Maybe I'll get a colour that doesn't clash with the moped. They've said the gold stars I painted on it might degrade the fibreglass, making it unsafe if I had an accident.' She shrugged. 'Who knew?'

'You have some really great photos on there.'

Ruby nodded, her mind miles away from the stilted conversation they were currently having. She was in no way drunk but she'd had just enough wine to be slightly reckless, and in light of her deciding that she and Richie were over, took a deep breath and said, 'Can I ask you something?' She had a rethink the second the words were out of her mouth, but Milo stopped talking and looked at her with interest. 'Of course. What is it?'

'Oh God, I know I'm going to regret this already but, am I wrong in thinking that you and I have some kind of connection? Not in a creepy *ET phone home* kind of way, but . . . I dunno.' She rubbed at her face, appalled with herself. 'Oh God, sorry, I'm being too presumptuous. It's just that . . . you know, the hand-holding and bearhugs. Is that just *you* being *you* or is it an *us* thing?'

Milo looked confused and right then she would have welcomed a tsunami sending her to a watery hell.

'It's okay. I realise now that none of that adds up to much — the occasional hug and suchlike.' She pointed at Milo and then back at herself, waving her hand around in between both of them for good measure. 'You know me, overactive imagination and all that.' She shrugged. 'It's fine, I shouldn't have said anything.'

'Some kind of connection?' He scratched the back of his neck and looked uncomfortable. 'What makes you say that?'

'Nothing really, I'm so sorry, I've embarrassed us both.' She held up her almost empty glass and shook her head. 'This is where two glasses of wine gets you, one step away from being a psycho stalker.'

Milo's eyes grew round and his Adams apple bobbed as he swallowed.

'Not that I am, I'm really not.' She almost groaned out loud with embarrassment. Whoever thought she could be let out into the civilised world should be banished along with herself.

'So, ignoring the psycho-stalker comment, which I'm hoping I can safely do,' Milo now said, 'you're basically telling me that you like me.'

She screwed up her eyes as if it would help to eradicate Milo's words. She was *so* regretting necking the wine. What was she thinking asking him such a question?

He leaned towards her, hand raised, and she thought he might be about to swat her away like an insect, but instead he cupped her ear. 'Can I let you into a secret, but you mustn't tell anyone?' He took his hand away but his cheek was so close it could skim hers.

She nodded, his warm breath setting her ear on fire.

'I liked you the minute I saw you drag yourself through the doors at work and almost get your arm ripped off. Or was it when I spotted you through the window holding your *mobile* above your head, as if it would keep the rain off your beautiful hair?'

Elation bubbled up inside Ruby, relieved that the imaginary tsunami hadn't swallowed her whole after all. Milo liking her *weirdness* didn't automatically mean he wanted to be with her, although it was nice to hear — but he said he liked her hair, that was always a bonus. She found herself smiling inanely, until she remembered the sophisticated Loretta. What *had* she been thinking?

'So, *do* you like me?' His mouth was twisted slightly into a sardonic smile and Ruby hoped there wasn't a bit of sarcasm going on there.

But she wasn't going to give anything else away. It was time to weasel her way out of a situation she'd caused by speaking out of turn. Loretta was everything a man could want and she was *nothing* a man would want. Loretta was the fairy on top of the tree, the icing on the cake, the yin to Milo's yang, whereas she was the leftover, dried-up crumbs on the plate, the melted chocolate tree decoration that fell on the floor and tasted cheap anyway. She caught herself. She'd be in tears if she carried on. Giving a bright smile she said. 'Of course I like you, I like all my friends.'

Milo's expression tightened. 'Likewise.'

'Great. All good, then?'

'Yep. Though I'm not sure we've gained anything by this conversation, as I'm pretty sure we liked each other without feeling the need to reiterate it.'

'We did?'

Milo nodded slowly. 'I thought that was a given.'

'Okay.' Ruby nodded and waited for what was to come next — which turned out to be not a lot.

Milo's fixed smile wilted as they both ran out of words — and actions. 'Right, then. I'd better get off, I suppose.'

Ruby was so bewildered she didn't know whether to shake her head or nod in agreement.

He looked at her sternly as if picking up on her confusion. 'Ruby, do you or do you not have a boyfriend?'

The question took her by surprise, but it really shouldn't have. Milo had almost had a fist fight with her delightful boyfriend in a hotel corridor, when Richie wasn't all about protecting her honour so much as being an arrogant . . . well, *dick* really. Her brain whirled but her words when they came out were slow. 'Is that . . . is it the only reason, you know . . . *stopping* us?' She was about to tell him that Richie had left her, but in a moment of clarity she remembered a girl called Daisy who, it seems, had never quite recovered from Milo's charms, and there was still Lovely Loretta to think about. 'Would I be waiting in line after Loretta and, err, others? Daisy, off the top of my head, for one.'

Surprisingly he stifled a laugh, but he recovered quickly. 'Ah, Daisy, bless her.' He smiled again.

Why did he keep smiling? This was serious stuff — and he wasn't even denying that he had more than one woman in his life. 'Anyway, two wrongs don't make a right — right, Ruby?'

She shook her head automatically. It seemed to be expected of her. 'No. No, they don't.' She thought for a moment and lowered her voice. 'What do you actually mean by that?'

'Well, if you have a boyfriend and I have a girlfriend, we would both be in the wrong if we . . .' He waved his arm in a circular motion between them both.

'Ah, I see,' she said, not understanding much at all, apart from his admitting that he had a girlfriend. Her head was muddled with all the swerves in the conversation, not to mention the wine that had gone to her head and was now souring in her stomach. But it was clear that he did understand her question, which was probably worse than him being as confused as she was.

'So?' She looked at him, waited for a definitive *yes* or *no*, even for one foolish moment considering that she would happily be a welcome addition to his harem. He looked lovely in the darkness of the pub with the table light highlighting one side of his features, half mysterious shadow, half long lashes, and his soft smile with a little hollow in his cheek, just above his jaw. It made her sit on her hands as the desire to stroke his face became ridiculously overwhelming.

'So . . . ?' she ventured.

'So, nothing.'

That floored her and it was time she left. Instinctively she stood up, leaned over and kissed him on the mouth, lingering long enough to inhale the smell of his aftershave, or it might have been shampoo, lemony and spicy. His lips, if she thought she could tell by the touch of lips on lips, were a tad surprised but then yielding — just a little. He barely kissed her back, that much was a definite, and she pulled away in seconds.

But still, he smiled and said, 'Thank you,' as he brushed her cheek with the back of his hand and . . . that was it.

Ruby smiled half-heartedly. 'I think the saying "Least said soonest mended" might be appropriate at this time, although I'm pretty sure that boat has already sailed,' she said ruefully.

'Ah, we do seem to have had quite an enlightening conversation.' But he smiled with his eyes, all crinkly at the corners and mellow and blue — so, so blue.

She sighed, already regretting running her mouth off — and kissing him — but it was done and couldn't be undone. 'Bye, then,' she threw at him, hoping, even as she knew it was futile, that he would grab her arm and beg her to stay. She gave him a self-deprecating smile, put her head down and hurried away, her bad choices already close, like a shadow, waiting to taunt her later.

CHAPTER FIFTEEN

Ruby opened the front door and almost fell over the ever-growing pile of detritus that was necessary for her journey to work every day. Crash helmet, insulated gloves that made her hands look reptilian, airline bag, airline hat — safely ensconced in a different bag — and biker boots.

She kicked at the boots, which always seemed to have a mind of their own — maybe they went walkabout when she wasn't looking. Never in her wildest dreams had she thought she would be a biker girl. Maybe that was one favour Richie had done for her, given her a bit of personality. She had booked a couple of lessons with a view to passing her motorbike test, thinking that if she was going to be a biker girl she might as well have a proper motorbike. Yep, maybe one good thing had come out of Richie selling their car and buying a knackered Porsche, even though it still sent her blood pressure soaring when she thought about how he'd hoodwinked her and she'd let him get away with it.

Sighing with relief once she'd disentangled herself, she appreciated the tranquillity of her own space: no TV in the background or stupid computer games beeping and roaring. She was going to head straight for the bathroom and have a long and leisurely bath to mull over her conversation with

Milo and remind herself that she was not a *hot hostie*. She giggled; it sounded like something a fast-food place would serve up.

In retrospect, she should have been thankful that the conversation with Milo had ended when it had. Although, she wondered wistfully, what might have happened if she had taken it further?

She slung her bag on the sofa and headed for the kitchen, wondering if it was too early to pour a glass of wine. Was that a familiar black rucksack next to the sofa? She spun around, her eyes swivelling: a set of car keys she didn't recognise sat on the hall table, and a pair of trainers that certainly weren't hers were haphazardly positioned by the door. The Stupid Porsche keys? Richie's trainers? Pushing the kitchen door open, she came face to face with Richie, who had clearly been sprawled out on the sofa just minutes before, judging by the dent in the cushions, the empty mug and the foil cartons on the coffee table, leftover Chinese takeaway congealing in the bottom.

Richie was back. Of course he was. Why did she think for one minute that she was free of him and she could live the life she wanted?

'What are you doing here?' Her sharp tone surprised herself and it clearly surprised Richie.

He thrust his chin out, already aggressive. Pushing his hair out of his eyes he said, 'What am I doing here, in my own home? Watching television. Where have you been?'

'I thought you were going to your mother's?' She sighed wearily.

'I did — and now I've come home.'

Determined not to let him get the upper hand she said, 'I think we need to discuss this, Richie. You seemed quite determined when you left.'

'Nothing to discuss, babe. We had time apart for us both to reflect on our relationship, and now we're back together, stronger and wiser.'

That was debatable, she thought, but held her tongue.

Richie's tone was reasonable, quiet, measured, but she knew that underneath he was gloating. Nothing had changed with Richie; he certainly wouldn't be wiser. In sixty seconds, from walking into her own house and being free, she was now Richie's woman again. She wanted to tell him to leave, but she knew he wouldn't. He was waiting for an argument. He wanted nothing more than to goad her, prod her and back her into a corner.

She rubbed a hand across her forehead. If Milo had given her one crumb of hopefulness that there could be more between them, it would have been enough, but right then, she was bone-tired, weary of the world in general, men in particular, and just wanted to put her head under a pillow and howl. And she didn't even have the luxury of doing that on her own.

Richie grinned as if sensing her defeat. 'You jump in the bath and put that nice silk negligée on, the one with the slit up the side, yeah?'

'No, Richie. I'm going to bed,' was all she said. He could think what he wanted, but when he came upstairs she would not be wearing the nightdress with the ridiculous slit up the side. All she was going to do was put a good night's sleep in front of her and see what the morning brought. She walked into the bedroom and slammed the door, hating herself almost as much as Richie right then.

CHAPTER SIXTEEN

So she and Richie were sharing a home once more. It was almost as if Milo predicted the future when she had more or less propositioned him; he knew she wasn't a free woman. But all was not lost. She was still at Celestial and loving it and if she could forget about Richie while at work her life was fine. She didn't actually see very much of him anyway, as many weekends were taken up with flying, while Richie was often out tinkering with his new toy, the Porsche.

She settled nicely into the job and learned more every day as a cool spring turned into a stifling summer and the mysterious workings of the aircraft became clearer. Of Milo she saw nothing, and was both relieved and saddened. She knew it was for the best if she intended to make a go of it with Richie, but sometimes she found herself reminiscing and wondering: what if?

But no one spoke of Milo and by some miracle she never bumped into him, briefly toying with the idea that, as he was friendly with Fiona, he might know her rota and know when to keep away. It saddened her greatly but she made it through most weeks with only the occasional wistful thought, which she quickly brought to a halt when it became too fanciful.

She was pottering around the flat one rainy day in September on stand-by, and as sure as eggs were eggs she was called out for duty, to crew a flight with disgruntled, stranded passengers up to Inverness. The flight should have taken off at seven o'clock that morning, and the worst of it was the aircraft was up in Bristol with the stranded passengers. The crew were travelling to Bristol by minibus, as the current crew were out of hours and legally unable to fly, having been on duty since early that morning.

She didn't mind as she had time on her hands and was eager to get out of the stifling atmosphere in the flat. Richie, working from home, needed quiet when he was on one of his frequent Zoom meetings, and she ended up sitting in the tiny bedroom messing around on her phone rather than doing anything constructive.

So, once again she folded her uniform into the top box — shoes in first, hat in last — and with difficulty she pulled her jeans over her tights and heaved on her waterproof coat. Finally she tugged on her sturdy, wet-weather boots and pushed on her helmet, fastening it tight under her chin. She set off feeling a lightness of spirit the closer she got to the airport, and was practically fizzing by the time she was back in her uniform, painting on a smile along with her make-up in the ladies' loos.

They all piled into the minibus and prepared for a long journey. The trip was uneventful and Ruby gave up gazing out of the window at the unrelenting dreariness of black, bony-fingered trees against a washed-out grey sky and tried to doze. She could vaguely hear the chatter of the other crew, mostly women. At one point she pricked up her ears on hearing that someone had been murdered and dumped in a wheelie bin, only to realise it was a storyline from *Eastenders*.

Vanessa, attractive with big blue eyes and a mass of curly blonde hair, tried to engage Jack, the elderly captain, in conversation, but he was having none of it and hid behind his copy of the *Financial Times*. He harrumphed loudly and shook his newspaper a few times, and Ruby could tell that his patience was being sorely tested as Vanessa twittered away about her career to date. Why she imagined Jack would be interested was anyone's guess. Maybe she thought he had the power to promote her.

This is not going to be a good trip, Ruby thought, deciding that most of the crew were not her sort, especially when she overheard them bitching about some poor unfortunate who had upset them simply by her chest being slightly bigger than her uniform jacket and having to squeeze her boobs together to fasten the beautiful gold buttons up.

She prayed that she'd remembered to pack her Kindle.

On arrival they lugged their flight bags out of the boot and trudged up to the crew room and then straight out to the aircraft, which they boarded in a flurry of rain, thoroughly bedraggled and fed up by the time they were ready to greet the passengers.

The passengers were also being rained on as there wasn't an airbridge available and they ran up to the steps, shaking out their jackets and coats in the galley. The aeroplane soon smelled like wet dog, the windows steamed up and everyone was grumbling as they took their seats.

'God, what a miserable lot,' Vanessa hissed to Ruby as the last passenger trundled up the stairs.

Ruby could hardly blame them. They had been delayed for hours and told to remain onboard a broken aircraft before decamping to the one Celestial Air were now operating.

'Hang on a minute, I'll do a PA,' Ruby said as she grabbed the handset. 'Good afternoon, ladies and gentlemen. We would like to apologise for the unavoidable delay today and hope that our complimentary newspapers and drinks service will show our appreciation of your understanding and patience.' She put the microphone back in its cradle. 'That should do it.' She was confident that Celestial Air would be more than happy to soothe their disgruntled customers with a free drink and newspaper.

The flight was uneventful, if bumpy, and they landed in a crosswind, the aeroplane dipping down three times before it settled on the runway. Everyone seemed relieved to disembark, and thanked the crew quickly as they escaped down the steps to stability.

Jack relayed to the rest of the crew that the operations department said they were to stay overnight at a hotel in Inverness and await further orders, as the original aircraft still hadn't been fixed. This suited Ruby fine, and she sat herself down next to him on the crew bus, also being disinclined to chat.

But surprisingly Jack seemed to have perked up and enthused about wildlife and birds as they trundled along in the slow, noisy bus, the driver grating the gears and appearing to aim the bus directly at the potholes. 'Do you know that Inverness and the surrounding area has golden eagles and the most beautiful red deer? I make sure we stay in the hotel near the River Ness when we come up here. It's a beautiful walk.'

'Well, it will be if the rain stops,' Ruby agreed conversationally as rain splattered against the window.

'I shall go for a long walk along the river when we get to the hotel. Shame I didn't bring my rods.' Jack laughed as he mimicked casting a line. 'Mind you, last time I came up here I spotted a couple of those nasty signal crayfish. Hateful, invasive creatures, so wouldn't fancy getting my fishing line tangled up with one of those.'

'Ooh, I know the ones you mean,' Ruby said, grimacing obligingly, a vague memory of reading about the ugly beasts clogging up the rivers.

Ruby liked the idea of going for a rain-drenched walk and she had a thin coat with her that would do, but just as she was going to suggest she joined him they were interrupted by Tom, the young first officer, who had stood up in the aisle of the bus and was trying to convince all the crew to go drinking with him.

'Coming to the McTavish Inn with us? I know they have Happy Hour cocktails from five until six, I've been there before.' He bounced from foot to foot in agitation, possibly desperate to get his fill of pina colada or tequila sunrise before they ran out.

Ruby wasn't sure if the invite was aimed at herself or Jack but she knew all about happy hours with adults who turned into boisterous teenagers, necking two-for-one drinks at the speed of light as soon as they were let loose. After her last drunken ramble, when she practically tried to drag the perplexed Milo off to bed with her — that's how it played out in her mind anyway — she decided she was never going to lose control of her sensibilities again. She declined politely. She would rather read and have a glass of wine in her room. Jack had already shaken his head vehemently and Tom should have known better than to try to persuade him. She peered over at Jack, squinting at his *Birds of Scotland* book that he'd just dug out of his bag, and much to her own surprise, said, 'I'll come with you, if you'd like the company.'

If he was unimpressed by her offer he was too much of a gentleman to show it. 'That would be lovely. I don't suppose either of us have walking boots, so we can stroll along the easy route.'

Ruby agreed happily and the walk was settled once they'd checked into the tartan-decked hotel. Random moose heads and stuffed fish in glass boxes dotted its walls and walking sticks and umbrellas, free to borrow, were in a stand by the door, their use irrefutable.

By the time they found the river the rain had stopped and an aura of calm descended. The sky was already turning a dull pink and darkening on the horizon. Ruby had changed into her jeans and fluffy mohair jumper, which was a few years old but still a firm favourite, and they tramped along the side of the river in companionable silence. Every now and then Jack would exclaim when he saw an interesting bird. 'You don't see the throated divers around so much at this time of year, it must be because the ground is churned up. They'll be after their dinner,' he continued as they watched a bird with a long beak dragging hapless worms from the comfort of their damp, earthy homes.

The walk was surprisingly restful and she half wondered about getting Richie a book on birds so that he could add it to one of the hobbies that he'd allegedly been dying to start. She'd thoroughly relished the pleasure Jack got from spotting the nesting site for a Scottish crossbill, slightly in awe that a bird could be the source of so much pleasure for a man.

The ethereal light that often occurred in northern parts of Scotland had been guiding their way, but as the evening drew in, the path, full of deadly hillocks, slippery leaves and shoe-size rabbit holes designed for spraining ankles, became their enemy. Reluctantly they turned back, but Jack seemed to have enjoyed the walk — and her company. She also had a good clutch of photos for Instagram: a heron swooping into the river and a gleaming silver fish leaping out of it, among others. All in all it was a good haul, she decided, looking forward to editing and posting them — and as usual hoping Richie didn't see them, to give him more ammo about her easy life.

Stamping their feet in the foyer to dislodge the wet leaves and mud from their shoes, Ruby said, 'Let me buy you a drink to warm us up and to thank you for such an entertaining walk. I'll never look at a river bird again without wanting to look up its species.' She headed for the bar. Reaching for her purse, she turned around to ask Jack what he wanted to drink . . . and stopped dead. Jack was warmly hailing the person she had spent months erasing from her mind.

'Milo! There you are, my boy. Good to see you, good to see you.'

The colour drained from Ruby's face as she simultaneously caught sight of herself in the mirror behind the bar: nose as red as Rudolph's and unruly hair corkscrewing out at every conceivable angle — and actually, didn't her ears look more hobbit-like than they used to? She turned away from the face that had disappointed her for so long, the pale and wan countenance, plain grey eyes set too far apart and the ridiculous orange freckles, all topped by cartoon character hair. She tamped her hair down, knowing it was a thankless task, as she acknowledged the irony that the only make-up on her face was leftovers from the rain, black mascara adding to the dark circles under her eyes. Where was that magic invisibility ring when she needed it?

'Ruby, what are you doing here?' Milo took a step towards her and then stopped, looking slightly stricken. His fists clenched and unclenched, much to Ruby's consternation, but Ruby didn't know what it signified. Did he want to turn his back on her or throw his arms around her? She would never know, but she had no choice but to face him as she stood awkwardly in front of him, at a loss for words.

She drew a finger under her eyes to wipe away the mascara, a leap of trepidation making her heart jump. She'd managed to put him out of her mind mostly, but the ill-timed kiss was forever at the forefront of her mind, the taste of his lips and the scent of him always there, lingering.

'You two know each other?' Jack asked as he brought Milo out of his trance with an affectionate man-hug. 'Good, that makes it easier for us chaps to talk shop without having to entertain you.' He turned to Ruby, smiling. 'Know his father well, known him for years.' He ushered Ruby to a comfortable seat. 'Leave the drinks to me. Wine, was it?'

Ruby shook her head. 'I'm okay thanks.' She needed to freshen up before anything else. She turned to Milo, fighting down nerves. 'What a coincidence. I came up in the aircraft that replaced Yankee Charlie, but how come you're here?' She aimed for light and breezy, and although she wasn't fooling herself, Milo seemed to take her words at face value. Inside, she was a turmoil of squirming worms and fluttering butterflies at seeing him in this unlikely place. She needed to remember that he'd turned her down and had reminded her, pointedly, that she had a boyfriend. He hadn't laughed when she'd kissed him, though. Oh God, did she need to keep bashing herself with that particular stick?

She tuned back in: Milo was speaking to her.

'It's not a coincidence at all, Jack is one of the old flying school gang and swung the job for me at Celestial. He knew I needed a challenge that wasn't all cowpats and brandishing hay, and I had my pilot's licence, although it was admittedly in crop spraying.' He smiled ruefully. 'So, I owe him one and we always catch up when he's up this way.'

Realisation hit. 'Ah, your parents' turreted ancestral home is up here.' She grinned, remembering.

'Absolutely. Spent the last three months up here helping out. Might end up here for good, who knows?'

So that's why she hadn't bumped into him at work? At least he wasn't avoiding her. Ruby was about to reply when his gaze shifted to over her shoulder and his eyes narrowed. 'Hello, there. Oh, you've changed *again*.' There was an edge to his voice and Ruby turned her head, intrigued.

Vanessa, undoubtedly the leader of the pack, hovered behind Ruby, all long legs and jutting hips, as the rest of the crew, done up in sequins and Lycra, strutted around the bar hotel as if it were a catwalk. Ruby thought she looked as if she was on a mission to win a bondage award: a cross between an early cavegirl and space-age babe. She wore a plastic-looking crop top that was as thin as a piece of toilet roll around her boobs, along with a sparkly bandage that masqueraded as a miniskirt.

They had obviously already had a few drinks, and Ruby wished with all her heart that she'd gone straight to her room after her lovely walk. She wanted her memories of Scotland to be a burnt-orange sunset shading to a navy sky studded with diamonds, but if she went out with the crew, her overriding memories would be lurid orange drinks with plastic straws and someone vomiting in the toilets and having to be put to bed.

Vanessa sidled over to Milo in a way that set alarm bells ringing, and Ruby wanted to sandwich herself between them. *Oh dear*, she thought, *I still have a crush on him.* She sighed. It would be so much better for her if she never saw him again, but it was *so* lovely to see him and her heart hurt at the thought of losing him again, so quickly, to Vanessa.

'Where did you go, Milo? We haven't seen you around for ages.' Vanessa neatly sidestepped Ruby and twined her arm through Milo's in a very proprietorial way.

'Been sorting stuff out up here,' was his gruff reply, and it gladdened Ruby's heart. 'Just waiting for Jack,' he added, nodding over to where Jack had ensconced himself in an easy chair and was studying a menu, indifferent to the shenanigans of his crew.

'I thought you were coming with us.' Vanessa snuggled up to him and gave him big cow eyes with fluttering eyelashes that looked as if they would take wing at any moment.

'No, thanks.' Milo laughed. 'I've been down this route before and I always end up with a thin wallet and a fat head.' Ruby really, really wanted Vanessa's pleather crop top to ride up and strangle her, and watched with deep happiness as Milo disentangled his arm, extracting her grip on him, one varnished red fingertip at a time.

Ruby wanted to purr with satisfaction. She waited with bated breath as Vanessa tried her hardest to include Milo in the fun that was Happy Hour, until she finally gave up. Even so, when it was clear that she'd lost the battle, she said, 'Play your cards right and I'll let you buy me dinner tomorrow.'

Tomorrow? How long were they staying, then? Ruby thought they were in Inverness for one night, but had to concede that she was normally the last person to know what was going on unless she was told officially. Stories on the grapevine were not for her ears, although she didn't know why she'd never managed to infiltrate the cool gang, the way Lucy had. She was, however, gratified to notice that Milo, having loosened his arm from Vanessa, was slowly but firmly distancing the rest of his body from her too, taking almost invisible steps backwards.

Vanessa's pink-glossed, dewy lips pouted as she stared from Milo to Jack, dismissing Ruby as of no consequence; clearly she could never be in the running for Milo's affections. She gave Jack one more icy stare before reluctantly accepting the lie of the land. Her face contorted as if she'd swallowed a toad, and she finally turned her gaze to Ruby, giving her the once-over and finding her lacking, barely worth the effort of talking to. Still, she did muster an easy insult. 'You look a bit bedraggled, love. Been out in the rain, have you?'

Ruby's cheeks heated up as Milo looked at her, as if noticing for the first time that her hair was wild, her chin and cheeks no doubt pink from the cold, and her lips thin and white, as they often became when she was nervous. She put her hands up to her hair, trying to smooth it down — a pointless task, she knew, hating that Vanessa had drawn attention to her particularly fetching 'drowned rat' look.

'Yes, actually, I went for a walk along the river.'

Vanessa's eyes widened in shock. 'Why would you do that?'

'Erm, the weather was perfect for a river walk — to blow away the cobwebs.' Could she get any more lame?

Vanessa gave her a look that told everyone what she thought about blowing the cobwebs away.

Yep, the lamest of the lame. 'Maybe I blew away too many. I'd better freshen up,' Ruby said, gazing wildly around for the lift or a door to disappear through.

'Yeah, for sure.' She gave Ruby another disdainful once-over. With a sigh, she said, 'We're all going out for pizza.'

Good, thought Ruby.

But then Vanessa half-heartedly asked, 'Coming?' as if it killed her to be polite.

'Yes, okay.' Ruby needed an excuse to get away from Milo, who looked far too delectable for her heart rate, wearing an open-neck, pale-blue shirt and jeans that fitted in all the right places. 'See you in a little while,' she said to Vanessa, who had already lost interest, clearly considering her no threat whatsoever in her quest to land Milo, or whatever it was she intended to do with him.

Ruby, wrung out by this cringeworthy exchange, sighed with relief as she threw a goodbye smile to Jack and Milo before hurrying to the safety of her room. She let out a deep breath as she opened her door and headed straight for the bathroom, leaning against the sink, weak-legged and grimacing at the face that stared back at her. Splashing warm water on her cheeks, she screwed up her eyes and took deep breaths. *This is silly*, she thought, *I'm a grown woman, I can handle this.*

But she was alarmed at her shaking hands as she reapplied mascara and lipstick, unsure what had rattled her the most: Vanessa's bitchiness and determination to be with Milo, or Milo appearing out of the blue like he had, looking casually gorgeous.

She unfastened her overnight bag and pulled out some clothes, settling on her soft green angora sweater, which she slipped on over her knee-length grey jersey skirt and zipped up her suede boots. Very early she had learned to cram her overnight bag with as many alternatives to wear as she could, catering for every unexpected occasion, but there was nothing in there remotely similar to Vanessa's bandages, so she would just have to be herself.

She carefully applied her make-up as Lucy had taught her, the pink lip gloss being her favourite addition, making her finally appreciate her wide smile. Surveying herself critically in the mirror, she decided she looked a little like a 1960s supermodel — or maybe Velma from Scooby Doo — but she had to admit it was a look that suited her. She looked . . . hmm . . . interestingly wan, at a push? She snorted. Yeah right. Of course she did.

There was nothing she could do about her attire, though. She didn't have a pleather bralette to her name, and would never dream of showing her midriff outside the bathroom. She fastened the amber pendant around her neck that her mum had bought her for her twenty-first birthday and blew herself a kiss in the mirror, half wishing that she'd treated herself to a drink from the minibar for Dutch courage. Why hadn't she stood firm and declined Vanessa's offer? Probably because she wanted to get away from Milo. So wouldn't it just be her luck that Milo had, after all, been persuaded to join Vanessa and was already in her poisonous embrace. Loretta would be history by midnight, for sure.

Nervously she descended in the lift, only to be greeted by a deserted lounge and deafening silence, empty glasses piled high by the bartender on the counter. Her remaining confidence drained straight into her suede boots as she stood confused, hot embarrassment racing around her veins and heating up her recently calmed cheeks. They hadn't waited for her. She wanted the floor to open up and swallow her.

Jack sat by the fire nursing a drink and she turned away quickly so he wouldn't see the humiliation etched on her face, but he spotted her and hailed her over.

'C'mon over, I've kept your wine on hold. I'll get Samuel to bring it over. That noisy lot have gone out — told 'em you'd rather join me for dinner. That's right, isn't it?' He winked as he smiled benignly.

She stared at the empty bar again and glanced over at the comforting fire. The lack of noise and the warmth and calm were infinitely better than going out for pizza. She nodded as she sat down, grateful but flustered. 'When did the others go?' she asked weakly.

'Oh, a few minutes ago.'

And Milo went too, she thought. *With Vanessa.*

'The food's very good here.' Jack was oblivious to Ruby's discomfort and she smiled wanly, determined not to be ungrateful. Jack was the perfect gentleman and great company. She appreciated his being there, but her sense of self-worth had plummeted and she just wanted to go to her room, take off her stupid Velma outfit and put on her pyjamas.

Jack signalled to the bartender. 'There'll be three of us for dinner now, Samuel, if that can be arranged, and get this young lady a glass of the Mouton Rouge '86, please. You know the one.' He turned to Ruby. 'I'm a regular here; it helps if you know the locals. Now, indulge me; even if you're not a red wine drinker this is one of the best.'

A wan smile, fast becoming a trademark of hers, said that she would indulge him. A glass of red wine appeared in minutes with the assurance that the table was now set for three.

She stuck her nose into the glass and inhaled as she had seen connoisseurs do, and was amazed at the aromas coming off from the depths of the glass. She took a sip and her eyes widened in surprise. It was fruity, yet smoky and earthy. 'Who would have thought a sip of wine could send all my troubles to hell?' She smiled into the glass as the drink warmed her soul and wrapped her heart in a glow of contentment. Her bad vibes evaporated as quickly as a puddle in sunshine. 'This is delicious.'

'Take it slowly; it's quite a strong one,' Jack warned gently as her sips turned into rather large gulps.

She nodded, determined not to drink too much and start blabbing — once bitten twice shy, although she was nicely mellow now. Stretching out her legs, she fought the urge to close her eyes for a moment or two. The third guest could be Hannibal Lecter and she would be pleased to see him, as long as she didn't have to make too much effort to chat.

As the thought entered her head, Jack boomed, 'Ah, here he is. He doesn't know it yet, but he's paying.'

His words ended on a chuckle and Ruby blinked as Milo appeared like a miracle sent from heaven, or a temptation sent from hell, easing his body into an armchair next to Ruby, a waft of citrus and wood surrounding him.

Rolling his eyes, Milo said, 'Ha, my turn again, is it? I guess I can swing it as a business meal for the salmon farm. I haven't used that one for a while.' Safe to say they were joking, then.

Ruby tried to ignore the thrumming in her veins and the sweaty palms as once again she was more aware of Milo sitting next to her than she was of her own feet attached to her legs. Sadly, she would still choose Hannibal Lecter over Milo as he was a lot less of a threat. Why did it have to be Milo, who, she had to remind herself, over and over, she had forcibly kissed? Who did that, uninvited, to a person they barely knew? And what had he done in return? Thanked her and said goodbye. Women were supposedly queuing up in front of him, so he was probably used to being attacked like that. But she would not join the end of the queue. She would not.

'The Aberdeen Angus steak is the best I've ever had, and their cranachan is out of this world,' Jack enthused.

'Who needs a maitre d' when you've got Jack around?' Milo laughed as he studied the menu, glancing at Ruby as if they were comrades in awe of Jack. 'It's true, though, the food here is the best there is.'

Ruby studied the menu: lobster thermidor, hand-dived scallops, tomahawk steak and something called white pudding haggis, which was one of the cheaper dishes, but she absolutely couldn't go there. She tried not to gasp at the prices and hoped her credit card would take the hit as Milo ordered a sixty-pound bottle of wine. Her heart fluttered with panic; this one meal could clean out her finances for the rest of the month, but she could live on porridge and pasta if need be, although Richie wouldn't be impressed. At least fuel was cheap for her moped. *Jesus, what have I let myself get dragged into?* Perspiration gathered under her arms and her face grew hot. She would have to suck it up, what else could she do?

In the end they decided on a sharing banquet and Ruby, accepting her fate as a pauper for the foreseeable future, embraced it, trying out everything including the haggis, which was . . . interesting. It was all so delicious she wanted to text all of her friends with photos and surprised herself by wondering what Richie would think of it.

For once she couldn't help showing her Instagram followers the feast she'd eaten, settling on a few 'look at my dinner' photos even though she considered most food photos a huge yawnfest. Even the Scottish trifle went on there. To her mind it was practically identical to English trifle — maybe a *wee drop o' whisky* in it instead of sherry, but whatever, it was all delicious.

Finally the food was all gone and the conversation at a lull.

She thought she should be the first one to leave as Jack and Milo might have private business to discuss, but wasn't sure how to ask for her part of the bill — dreading it, in fact. 'Thank you, I had a really . . . calm time,' she said to the two men, as Jack poured the last of the wine into her glass.

'It was delightful, I agree,' Jack said, 'but I'm ready for my bed now.' With a wink he picked up the bill and tucked it underneath his credit card on the silver tray. 'Leave this one to me. I couldn't in all honesty make Milo pay. He has lambs, cows and donkeys to feed.' He stood up, wincing as he straightened his legs. 'Bloody arthritis,' he said, rubbing at one knee. 'Now, we don't need an early wake-up call, Ruby, as the return flight isn't until late evening — if it's not cancelled again for another day — so you two go and have a nightcap and I'll see you in the morning.' He pulled out his room key as he headed off, giving a vague salute to the waiter.

Hugely relieved and stammering grateful thanks, she said goodnight to Jack and sank back into her chair, feeling that a weight was lifted. She couldn't begin to imagine how much the bill for three meals and wine would be in such a wonderful restaurant.

'If you have an early start tomorrow, don't let me keep you. You've already gone above and beyond the call of duty,' Ruby said as she stretched out her legs, not meaning a word of it. She would happily sit with Milo until the world stopped turning. The fireplace in the corner spread its cheer and the wine was still giving her mellow vibes.

Like the true gentleman Milo was, he simply smiled a gentle half-smile and said, 'Not at all, the present company is far too good to call it a day.' He frowned. 'I'm not in a hurry, are you? We *could* settle down by the fire and order more wine, but don't feel obliged — even though Jack suggested it,' he said with a smile.

She nodded. 'I'd like that. Yes, please.'

Milo called over the waiter and placed his credit card on the round tray as he ordered two more glasses of wine. Ruby liked the understated way he did it. Richie would have made a big show of it, being the big *I Am*. Besides, Richie's credit card was welded to his wallet and was mostly for show.

Milo held her arm and guided her to the fireplace, where they sank into comfy armchairs, cosy and secluded. 'First rule of aviation, the captain is always right.' He laughed and it was melodious and charming and she wanted it to stop as it made parts of her melt, but instead she leaned towards him as if drawn by an invisible thread.

The logs gently sank into the fire, giving off sparks of white light and pockets of heat as a sudden stillness surrounded them. The world disappeared, leaving them in their own bubble of time.

Milo looked thoughtful. 'Thank you for this evening. It's been too long since we had a catch-up.'

Ruby thought this was her cue. 'I'm so sorry I kissed you the last time we met.' She said it so quietly that she wondered if she'd only thought it.

'Are you? Oh dear.' He made a sad clown face, pulling his lips down and blinking. 'That makes me sad.'

'Oh, I didn't mean it like that, it's just . . .' She tailed off. 'I don't even know what I meant.' But she did know. She was sorry that Milo hadn't fallen for her charms — lacking as her charms clearly were — and had not returned the kiss.

Milo laughed. 'I didn't mean it to come across that way. It's just that my father taught me to be wary of situations that could get one into trouble. I guess having a well-known family, up around these parts anyway, taught me to be on my guard. Ask any one of the many girlfriends I'm supposed to have.' He smiled and Ruby giggled, hoping that he was joking.

He continued. 'I have thought about you, and I wanted to tell you the last time I saw you that I wasn't heading down south again for three months, but I didn't know how to, being as we're not, you know, an *item*.'

His words were like manna from heaven, although strangely it made her want to cry. She was wasting her life without him, that much was clear to her now. She *needed* him in her life and wanted to tell him so, but of course she couldn't. She had no right to utter any words of tenderness, not while she was with Richie. She stared at the man she truly believed she was falling in love with and realised with great clarity that what she wanted the most was for Richie not to be her boyfriend anymore — ever again.

Milo watched her with gentle eyes as if waiting for more, but there was nothing that she could say that could be acted on or clarified; her mind was a muddle of emotions and thoughts.

She tried out a few sentences in her head, aware that the beats of silence were lengthening. She wanted to ask Milo if he thought about her the way she dreamed about him. But again, of course she couldn't. The urge to return home as soon as possible and pack her bags, to be rid of Richie, became all-consuming, so what she needed to do was call a halt on this wonderful day and stop her emotions and dreams from running away with her. 'I guess it must be time to go.'

Milo glanced at the clock over the fireplace. 'Yeah, before Vanessa and her gang return and try to make me the life and soul of an impromptu room party.'

Ruby grimaced. 'I can't imagine them trying to get me to join in, but then I'm not an eligible man with impeccable manners, a trillion sheep and a dozen guffawing donkeys — whose dad lives in a castle.'

'Pretty sure it's only half a trillion sheep,' he shot back, grinning. 'But God, yes, we need to get away.' Suddenly all brisk, he glanced at his mobile and with an air of finality drained his wine.

The waiter came scurrying over as if he'd been listening in to the conversation and could tell the night was finally over — or maybe he was just desperate for his bed. Milo signed the chitty not even checking the amount. 'Right, I've got a way to go, so I'll say goodnight.'

'Are you not staying in the hotel?' She was shocked at the thought that he had to go out into the dark and cold. Besides, he'd been drinking; surely he wasn't foolish enough to drive?

'No.' He tapped his mobile as it pinged. 'My dad's house is about fifteen miles away.' Looking at his mobile again, he added, 'My driver's outside.'

'Oh, I feel bad for keeping you now.' She was relieved that he wasn't driving, but still surprised that he'd spent his evening with her, when he could have cosied up with his family.

'Nonsense. Anyway, I came to see Jack.'

That's told me, she thought, until Milo added, 'You were an added bonus. Come on, I'll walk you home.' He grinned as he angled his head towards the lift.

Ruby's heart started thumping again as she obediently picked up her bag and they walked out of the restaurant, even though they both knew she could perfectly well make her own way. The tension between them was palpable as they waited for the lift to arrive. Was there the remotest chance that he was thinking along the same lines as herself and would kiss her goodnight? She remembered *that kiss* again.

The lift bell chimed and Milo seemed suddenly riveted by the shiny metal doors as they opened. She couldn't look at him for fear of what he would see in her eyes: longing and probably a fair bit of lust. She most definitely kept her lips zipped shut. She had tried that gambit before and it hadn't ended well. Milo smiled gently down at her and put his hands on her shoulders.

'Well, I've learned a thing or two about photography tonight — aerial and otherwise.'

That was the trick, she thought wryly, keep away from anything personal. Still, she rose to the occasion, thinking that she had gone on at length about her love of photography. 'Have I bored you? Sorry, but I love taking photos, especially the ever-changing skies, although you will know more than me about cloud formation.' She could do innocuous as well as the next man.

He smiled. 'I think I probably know more about milking cows, but I like your faith.' He paused. 'You should come up with me sometime — up in my aeroplane.'

'Come again?' Ruby was confused. 'Wait, you have your own aeroplane — not the ones that Celestial own?'

'It's tiny, tiny.' He held up his thumb and forefinger, leaving a small gap to indicate how small it was.

Aware that she sounded slightly breathless and maybe a bit too excited at the suggestion, she shrugged nonchalantly. 'If it's that small, no thanks. I only fly in huge aeroplanes.'

'Oh, it was just a thought.'

'I'm joking, of course. I'd love it. The aurora borealis. Now, that's a dream. Imagine photographing that from the sky.'

She took a step towards the lift. 'Goodnight, and thank you for dinner.'

He put his hand out and touched her hair. 'Thank you for keeping me company. Your lovely smile was much appreciated over the steak.'

Another silence. He took in a breath as if he was about to speak but instead smiled tightly, brushed her cheek briefly with the back of his hand and turned around to leave. 'Soon, yeah?'

He disappeared back through reception and swung out through the double doors into the cold night, out of Ruby's sight.

Soon, what? *Come back*, she wanted to shout after him. *What does* soon *mean?* She huffed out a breath. For God's sake, would that man ever talk plainly to her? After staring into the empty space of the reception area for a full minute, with no other options, and anxious not to bump into Vanessa and the others, she took the lift up and away from Milo and hurried to her room.

Undressing in a stupor, dazed by her own rekindled emotions, she ran through as much of the evening as she could remember. Milo hadn't said one inappropriate word but he'd *looked* at her, really looked, as if he was trying to reach into her soul. What that actually meant she didn't know, but it gave her a warm glow like being shrouded in soft cashmere. And he had missed her. Surely that meant something, didn't it? And an invite to go up in his aeroplane? Did he mean it? And he hadn't said a word about the gorgeous Loretta, not one word.

Her mind went around and around replaying the same reel over and over as she tried to sleep. Finally giving up, she found a hot chocolate sachet on her welcome tray, boiled the kettle and filled up a mug. Taking it on to the tiny balcony, she sat in a peaceful if rather cold silence, looking down at the pine forest just beyond the hotel walls. Her troubled thoughts calmed and she finally headed back to bed, reflecting that at least she had breathed in some good Scottish air — her mother would be pleased. And she was drinking a nourishing drink, even if it was from a sachet.

CHAPTER SEVENTEEN

'Hurry up with your breakfast, we're keeping Milo's man waiting.' Jack pounced on Ruby as she sat down, her breakfast bowl of pineapple and apricots slowly sinking into thick Greek yoghurt from the self-serve buffet. She'd also guiltily piled pancakes on to a plate and ladled warm maple syrup over the top and couldn't wait to dive in.

'Sorry?' Spoon poised, she wished she could eat her breakfast in peace but was too polite to start as he hovered over her.

'We need to get to the farm before lunch so we can take the aeroplane up.'

'We? What?'

'I've just spoken to Milo and he said I was to make sure you came too.'

'He did?' His words slowly sank into her consciousness.

'You like taking photos of the sky, apparently.' He smiled dryly, having been witness to her taking a million photos along the river the day before. 'Along with everything else on this wonderful earth of ours,' he added for good measure.

'I do indeed.' The stack of pancakes cooled by her elbow, the syrup she'd happily ladled on them dripping over her plate and on to the table. She sighed. After last night's farewell, she'd decided in the early hours of sleeplessness that she didn't want to go up in an aeroplane with Milo; she really didn't need to be near Milo any more than necessary. In fact, she was scared that in her slightly drunken state, she had lifted her bright, shiny, expectant face up to his shadowy confused one, expecting to be kissed again. She all but groaned into her yoghurt.

Taking a moment out, she ran through the night before — again. Specifically when she said goodnight to Milo by the lift. Had she given him a little wave or blown him a kiss? She didn't think so, but couldn't be sure.

Sighing, she tried out nonchalance in the hope that she could worm her way out of leaving the hotel. 'I was going to read my book, and anyway I don't imagine that he meant it.' She shrugged to prove the point.

'He wouldn't have suggested it if he didn't mean it,' Jack said rather tersely. 'What will you do all day stuck in this hotel otherwise?'

It was a fair point. There was no sign of the rest of the crew and she wasn't that keen to spend time with them anyway, although she did have a book to read and photos to edit.

'Come on, I'll enjoy showing you around,' Jack continued. 'A lot of my misspent youth was whiled away on the Fraser Estate, mostly trying not to fall into rivers, getting charged by deer and shot at by the gamekeepers thinking we were vermin. It was great! Of course, it's changed a lot now. It's much more commercial — has to be, to keep going.' He had a waterproof jacket over his arm and was definitely pacing.

Ruby sighed, aware that she had lost the battle before she'd even taken a mouthful of yoghurt, probably before she'd even woken up with the slight surreal daze that sleeping in a strange bed gave her. 'Okay, give me a minute.' Jack was good company and Milo would be flying the plane, so not a lot of conversation would be going on there. She picked up her spoon and started to eat, feeling more uncomfortable by the second as Jack sat opposite her watching every mouthful go in.

'Stop watching me. I swear you'd spoon-feed me, given half a chance.' She laughed, glad that she was comfortable with him.

'Time is of the essence,' he said, glancing pointedly at his watch. She sighed, put down her spoon and abandoned her breakfast. 'I'll get my bag. Give me five minutes.'

'Atta girl,' Jack said, slapping the table for extra effect. 'I'll be out the front. I wasn't joking when I said Milo's man is waiting for us.'

After a half-hour journey in a clattering Land Rover, Ruby and Jack arrived at the Fraser Estate.

Climbing down, she was greeted by a tall man who looked like a slightly faded version of Milo: the same dark wavy hair but peppered with grey, the same angle of the jaw and twinkling eyes. Milo's father.

'Hello, Jack, welcome to my humble, err, castle!' His deep voice rumbled with laughter at the long-standing joke that it clearly was. Jack wheezed with laughter and Ruby smiled politely.

'Come in, it's been too long, come.' Milo's father walked out of the cold and into the not much warmer vastness of his family home.

Ruby gazed around in awe at the huge hallway, at the giant-sized full-length pictures of ladies done up in posh regalia, cradling tiny lambs or posing as their faces hovered over ancient-looking books. Whatever the symbolism was, it completely missed Ruby. A couple of deer heads were more self-explanatory: some bastard had shot these beautiful animals just to put their antlers and heads on a wall. A full suit of armour stood to attention by the door and she peered closely, waiting for signs of movement, half expecting it to take her coat, like a valet.

'It's like something out of the movies,' she said, taking in the moose head fixed over the sweeping staircase, great antlers reaching up to the vast ceiling. She was actually almost sure that you didn't get moose in Scotland, and if you could, anyone who tried to shoot them should be thrown in jail for ever.

She peered at the staircase, waiting for it to tilt and rotate like something from Hogwarts. Sadly, it stayed exactly where it was, which was probably for the best, Ruby reflected with disappointment.

She was dimly aware of her hand being pumped up and down in welcome, as she continued to gaze at this incredible entrance hall that was bigger than the hotel foyer where she was currently staying. She blinked and people came back into focus as she finally took a moment to greet the man who owned the spectacular dwelling. 'Oh my God, this is amazing.' She was gushing, but she couldn't help it. 'This should be on the telly.'

'Well, actually we're working on a programme right at this moment.'

Ruby's eyes were on stalks. 'Really?' She pirouetted, taking it all in once again. 'Amazing,' she breathed, until she finally noticed that everyone was looking at her. Waiting for her? Possibly so they could all move out of the hallway. 'Sorry,' she murmured, eyes still swivelling.

Milo stood behind his father, smiling as his gaze fixed on Ruby's face.

She risked a look at him and their eyes met for a moment, which seemed to spur him into action.

'Morning, I hope you slept well?'

Bit too polite for Ruby's liking, but she nodded, hoping they hadn't reverted to politely distanced conversation again. 'Hi, yes. I was just saying, this is so incredible.'

'Yes, you did mention it once or twice.'

Ruby all but snorted. 'Yeah, all right!' But she grinned. 'It is, though, isn't it?'

Milo grinned as he too gazed around the entrance hall. 'Something special, all right. Listen, Jack and Douglas have a lot of catching up to do, and I'd hoped that I could take you up for a spin in Doris, my little aeroplane, but the cloud base is awful.' He looked slightly abashed. 'Dad also needs me, as we have an unexpected appointment about the sale of some machinery and something to do with a televised documentary, so . . .'

'Oh.' Doris was clearly the name of the aeroplane, and an awful cloud base, she assumed, meant they couldn't take it up, so there was no reason for her to be there — at all. She rallied quickly. 'Don't mind me, I'll just wander around, if that's okay with you?' She prayed she could find a quiet corner and pretend to be busy. She wondered if it would be rude to ask to be taken back to the hotel.

'Nonsense. Ah, Loretta.' His voice changed tone. Happy? Irritated? Ruby couldn't tell. 'I hoped you'd get out of bed before teatime.'

Ruby's heart sank to the floor as she took in the willowy blonde with a haughty bearing, the same one who had skidded into the pub car park in a sporty Jaguar so long ago. And she was here, at Milo's home, with Milo. Oh God, she'd got it so wrong — again.

Loretta yawned and stretched her arms, her bed hair looking suspiciously like it had been artfully scrunched. Her make-up was subtle and pretty, which was a shame, as Ruby would have loved her to be made-up like a drag queen. She sighed. You can't win 'em all.

Douglas interrupted. 'Ruby here needs someone to show her around. You can saddle up Horatio for her, can't you?' He turned to Ruby. 'You do ride?' He looked at Ruby expectantly, it being a statement not a question, as if riding a horse was equivalent to breathing.

Ruby looked back blankly before she understood. Loretta was not wearing 'just got out of bed' sweats, she had on jodhpurs and a heavy-duty sweatshirt. She picked up a riding hat and crop from a nearby low table and began to swish it back and forth.

'A horse?' Ruby's voice suddenly sounded very small. She was expected to ride a horse, wearing a long flowery dress and two-inch heels? Her mouth dropped open as she tried and failed to voice an objection.

'Yes, splendid,' Douglas answered for her.

Clearly a gaping mouth and floral dress meant *yes* in Douglas's language.

She almost shook her head but, on seeing Loretta gearing up for an expected sneer, agreed. 'Absolutely, I love horse riding.'

Loretta snorted loudly, looking Ruby up and down and quite blatantly grimacing. 'Horatio would crucify her, Douglas. It's a shame you don't have one of your little donkeys braying around the place, Milo. That would do her perfectly.'

It took Ruby a moment to realise the enormity of the insult but Loretta hadn't quite finished.

'I didn't know you were bringing one of your little *hosties* with you, Jack.'

'Ruby. Her name is Ruby,' Jack growled out.

Ruby was glad to see she had an ally in Jack as Milo was staying decidedly on both sides of the fence. *I hate horses almost as much as I hate Loretta*, she thought. Out loud she said, 'I'm fine to just wander around, really I am.'

But Loretta talked over the top of her. 'Try these on, you can't ride in *those*,' she commanded, plucking a pair of boots from a wicker basket piled high with wellingtons and other footwear. She glanced at Ruby's shoes with disdain, as if she'd worn them just to be difficult.

Ruby tugged off her shoes and pulled on the giant-sized boots, which flapped as she tried to walk.

'No, they won't do.' Loretta stared fixedly as Ruby pulled them off and put them back in the wicker basket. 'Your feet are so *small*.'

Loretta was the only person Ruby had met who managed to make her small feet sound like a disfigurement. *She'd get on well with Richie*, she thought bleakly.

Loretta rummaged around in a box inside an old oak settle and produced a pair of red wellingtons.

'You can wear these.' She thrust them at her and Ruby took them doubtfully. They were shiny and very red and looked suspiciously like they belonged to a child, but she had no other choice really, so she took off her boots and put the dreadful wellies on. They pinched her toes and on closer inspection it looked as if they were two left feet. Ruby started to protest but Milo, Jack and Douglas were already drifting away, deep in conversation.

'You'll ruin your coat if you wear that.' She pointed at Ruby's coat. 'Here, take this.' Loretta shoved an ancient Barbour jacket at her next and the unmistakable odour of fish wafted up from its depths, making Ruby's nose crinkle.

'Follow me,' Loretta said, waving a hand as if Ruby was a servant.

Ruby couldn't bear it. 'I really don't want to go horse riding. I'm happy to stay here.'

'God, me too, you'd better believe it.' She threw a look over to where Milo, busy on his mobile, was gesticulating to reiterate the point he was making. 'And I'd be happy to let you, but Douglas has spoken.'

This intrigued Ruby, who wondered why Loretta would bow to Douglas's requests. It was all very confusing. What was worse, though, was that the bright, shiny day that had started off so promising was turning into a nightmare.

'Come on, then,' Loretta shouted, already heading outside, waving her riding crop imperiously above her head.

Ruby followed reluctantly, thinking about where she'd like to shove Loretta's riding crop, as a stablehand introduced her to a brown horse with a white star on its forehead. She barely had a second to say, 'Hi, Nutmeg,' when she was lifted ungainly up on to it. She landed bottom up with her face buried in its mane. Sputtering horse hair out of her mouth, she righted herself with difficulty, trying to make light of her predicament. Loretta watched the undignified hoisting silently and shot off on her own huge black horse the second Ruby was upright. Ruby had expected more of a flourish of showmanship, surprised Loretta wasn't riding bareback or pirouetting on top of the horse as if in a circus.

The stablehand patted her horse's rump and it trotted off in the same direction.

Ruby did have some experience of horse riding but it was years ago and she'd never enjoyed it. She would rather have done ballet like her friends but her mother had looked at her sadly and shook her head. *I don't think you'll ever be a ballerina, love, do you?* And that was that. Clearly Vikings didn't make good ballerinas. Ruby hoped they would be better on horses.

But hoping didn't make it happen and she now found herself out of sync with the horse, her bottom whacking down on it, jarring her spine all the way up to her teeth at every slow trot and canter. The combined effect made her feel sick and saddle-sore and she would happily have fallen off and crawled back to the house just to be back on terra firma. She stood it for as long as she could, up a windy little path and down another one, tree branches narrowly missing her eyes and the wind chill making her nose run. She was so cold she was sure her bottom had frozen to the saddle.

They crossed a stream that seemed to be taking them further away from Douglas's castle. 'Loretta,' she croaked, 'I think my hands might snap off if I don't warm up soon.'

Loretta had the grace to slow down. She glanced at Ruby and Ruby noticed her leather-gloved hands, and the cape covering most of her body looked as if it had a fleece lining.

'Well, you're hardly dressed for horse riding,' Loretta said.

Ruby didn't know how to answer that without being rude. She hadn't wanted to go horse riding and Loretta had offered no more than the silly little wellingtons to wear and a smelly Barbour. She supposed the fact that she'd gone along with it was her own fault. She needed her steely core again.

Just when she thought she might welcome death, her horse slowed down and then stopped, raising its head and snorting. Like a miracle, it slowly turned around and began to walk back the way they'd come; it knew the way home. It trotted obligingly down to a canter and then a gentle walk as they headed back to the stables. Loretta hardly said anything, clearly considering Ruby's ears unworthy of her precious words.

CHAPTER EIGHTEEN

Milo stood, hands on hips, stifling a laugh when he saw Ruby sitting on a horse wearing a coat that was too big and boots that were too small. 'I see Loretta's been looking after you. What on earth are you wearing?' He peered closer. 'Good Lord, I thought we'd binned that old coat years ago. Didn't we use it to carry fish home after a day by the loch?' He looked up at Loretta, who arched her eyebrows, baby-blue eyes the picture of innocence. 'And what have you got on your feet? You only need two little frog eyes on top of those and I'd swear you were wearing children's bootees.'

'They were Rupert's,' Loretta said.

Milo's chuckle confirmed that they were indeed children's wellingtons.

'She has elf feet,' Loretta said deadpan.

It would have been better if Loretta said her feet were petite, maybe even fairy-sized, but elf feet was only one step away from saying she was deformed. It was true, high arches and a size three was not standard and had caused hilarity and faux wonder over the years, and to Ruby, it was just another thing to add to her list of defects. It was a wonder that they'd found a pair of airline shoes to fit her, but she supposed they were made in a factory somewhere that catered for all needs — elves included.

Loretta slipped off her horse with the grace of a ballet dancer, almost pirouetting as she landed with what Ruby would swear was a plié.

Ruby stayed resolutely on her horse, looking at the ground, which was squelchy with mud and an awful long way down. She was numb all over and had no idea how she would ever have the courage to reach the yawning distance between her saddle and the ground. She hoped a footman, or whatever they were called in posh castles, would come to her aid — they were always on hand in the movies. But no one appeared with a foot stool or a hunched back ready for her to stand on. She wiggled her legs; maybe the horse would kneel at a command — a command that she of course didn't know. Probably expecting too much, she mused, ready to just fling herself off sideways and take the inevitable broken shoulder and hip.

Milo, seeing her discomfort, reached up to her. 'Swing your leg over and I'll catch you.'

She mulled over the simplicity of the sentence for a moment; swings were made for swinging, numb legs were not, but she would try her hardest. She did a bum shuffle and a forward lunge and launched into thin air. 'Uh-oh!' she cried out as her arms flew upwards and her legs flailed under her.

Luckily Milo opened his arms and broke her fall as she landed, reassuringly safe. She definitely heard a bit of an 'oof' from his lips, but he held on tight until she was steady as he righted her. Slight stubble on his jaw rasped against her cheek and he smelled wonderfully of the great outdoors, fresh grass and hewn wood. It was all she could do to stop herself from inhaling deeply into his neck.

His hands on her waist were firm and he held her as if she was no more than a doll. That was impressive enough — but as an added bonus he ran his hands over her arms and smiled down into her eyes. 'You're cold?'

'That must weigh a ton,' Loretta said, glancing at Ruby as if she were a sack of coal.

That? thought Ruby with indignation. Were there no depths to her spite?

Milo laughed, which didn't go down well with Ruby, especially when he added, 'I've carried a pregnant sheep over the moors before now.'

'And your point is?' Ruby was piqued but she laughed. She was so relieved to be on firm ground again that she could see the funny side of anything, and she instantly forgave him. What else could she do? If she hadn't spent so many years absorbing Richie's insults she might have been mortally offended. Richie was an expert at insults, and Milo and Loretta would have to go some to beat him. 'I'm sure you didn't just compare me to a pregnant sheep!'

God, she wished someone could take a photo of this perfect moment, with her standing bravely in the circle of radiance that was Milo, the sun in the sky and the bloom of fresh air on her cheeks. She would crop the bloody kids' wellies out, of course, but her Instagram followers would love it.

A smirk from Loretta took the smile off her face even as Milo smiled back. Loretta's eyes smouldered with resentment, her normally full lips a thin line, her eyes mean.

'Well, you're not *quite* as fluffy.' Milo set her away from him, ran his hands up and down her arms and looked her over as if checking for broken bones.

'But probably just as hefty.' Loretta was now grinning brazenly as she took off her riding hat and ran her fingers through her silky hair.

Ruby watched jealously. Oh, to be able to run her fingers through her own hair without it ending up looking like a clown wig.

'Loretta, for goodness' sake,' Milo chided, and Loretta pulled a face. He tugged her horse by the reins and the other horse plodded behind; they knew the drill.

'What?' Loretta looked all big eyes and sweet smile.

Milo shook his head in despair. 'Just 'cos you're part of the furniture here doesn't mean you can get away with being rude.'

'So sack me, I dare you. I think your father would have something to say about it, having been friends with my dad for over fifty years.'

'It's okay, it was funny,' Ruby said.

'Blew the cobwebs away, did it, your ride?' Milo, attentive once more, seemed to take it for granted that she'd enjoyed herself.

They were heading for the stables and Ruby sped up in anticipation of a hot drink.

'I don't have much of a riding seat, I'm afraid.'

'It's just *seat*, you don't need to add the *riding*. That's implied,' Loretta said, kicking up stones, her arms crossed and looking like the wicked stepsister Ruby never wanted.

'Oh, okay, thank you.' Although why she thanked her for highlighting her ignorance was anyone's guess.

She didn't think she would sit down for a week and was desperate to rub some life into her frozen bottom but settled for clenching her bum cheeks a few times in the hope that her circulation might perk up a bit.

'I suppose someone will have to rub down the horses, but it isn't going to be me,' Loretta cut across their conversation, the scowl back in place. She flounced past the stables, down the path and kept walking until she reached the house, where she slammed the door so loudly that it rattled and shook alarmingly.

To Ruby's surprise, Milo looked more amused than upset at Loretta's display, his countenance unruffled to the point of indifference. 'If she knew how rotten that timber was she wouldn't go slamming the door as hard as that.' He shook his head. 'It looks as if I'll be sorting out the horses. Coming?' Ruby couldn't imagine what the alternative would be, so she followed Milo and the horses into the stable on stiff legs and frozen feet, blowing warmth on to her hands to regain some movement.

She was pleasantly surprised when the pungent aroma of fresh hay greeted her, mixed with the smell of old leather, having braced herself to endure the smell of horse dung and stale urine.

'Would you like me to help?' she asked hesitantly, having no idea what one did with a horse after a ride. Rub it with a teacloth to dry it off?

'No, just take a seat and keep me company,' Milo said, pointing to a hay bale. She sat down gingerly, shifting her weight from her left buttock to her right, hoping the bale wouldn't collapse on her. 'Put that blanket around your shoulders and you'll soon warm up. It's clean.'

She did as she was told and soaked up the stable's smells and sense of calm, the only noise coming from the horses munching on hay and invisible birds chirping in the distance. In fact, it was eerily quiet outside and it made her realise how little quiet she had where she lived. If it wasn't the tourists making a racket, it was the bloody seagulls lining up to terrorise the tourists — and making a racket.

Sitting in the quiet with Milo, free to study him as he rubbed down the horses and filled up the water trough, his face a picture of concentration, she was close to her idea of heaven. Silently she extracted her phone and snapped an image of the chestnut horse with Milo's hands brushing down its hind legs.

Watching Milo tend to the horses was as endearing as watching a man with his children, bringing out his soft side as he soothed and petted the animals that he obviously loved. The rhythmic effect was soporific and her thoughts drifted as she studied Milo in an abstract way: the well-defined muscles in his arms that were all-year-round weathered and the control he had in his legs as he stooped down to tend to the horses. The look didn't really go with being a pilot, as they were often a bit pasty with soft white hands, but then, he was a bit of an outlier. She decided to risk a question. 'Do you fly because you need the job or is it the flying *thing* that grips you pilots?'

He stood up from his prone position and stretched, hands on the small of his back. 'Bit of both really. As I've probably said before, I'm scared that the farming life will suck me into it so completely that I'll suddenly find I'm a middle-aged, weather-beaten old leatherface, wearing a bobbly winter cardie and a flat cap talking about the price of raw wool. I guess I'm fighting against my destiny, but let's be honest, if the farm in Devon doesn't suck me in, this place will.' He glanced around and smiled slightly. 'It probably is my destiny and has pretty much everything I need in my life.' His eyes took on a wistful look. 'Almost, anyway.'

Ruby wondered about such a cryptic comment and hoped it wasn't Loretta that would complete his dreams.

He shrugged. 'You won't believe it, but this house is called *The Destination*. It's quite a landmark around here and collectively it employs an awful lot of the locals, one way or another, even if it's only getting someone to pick the roses for the garden centre or labelling the honey the bees produce. We rely on loyalty, and luckily there's plenty of goodwill as we're a tight-knit community.' He sighed. 'Father will need me or Gabriel — and anyone else prepared to do their bit — before too long as he's not getting any younger.'

'You have bees here?'

'Yes, although we don't even have anyone experienced enough to tend to them properly, it's all a bit "winging it".' He smiled. 'Excuse the pun.'

Ruby's heart turned over as Milo spoke. He was such a different person from the one portrayed in Celestial Air. She loved that he loved the Destination and she wanted to stay for ever — with him, of course. The urge to shoot her hand up and say, 'Pick me, pick me' was overpowering. She could imagine herself wearing an antique muslin veil chasing honey bees around with a big net. In fact, if anything was ever her destiny, beekeeping was it. Okay, she had only decided on such a career change one minute ago, and Milo's presence clinched it, but right then, it was all she wanted to do.

'Loretta, as you can imagine, is great at promotions, planning new ideas for the summer and winter balls that take place here at the castle, forcing the gentry and the *new money* to cough up for all sorts of fêtes and causes.'

Suddenly Ruby's fantasy evaporated in a haze of Loretta's expensive perfume. Although, if she was reading it right,

Douglas was her boss, which was an interesting development. She had noticed that Milo didn't touch her and wondered what kind of relationship it could be. One where they — Loretta and Milo — didn't touch each other was certainly her preference, but seemed unlikely to be Loretta's fantasy. Loretta kept giving her evils and throwing *moony eyes* at Milo, who seemed impervious to it, or maybe he chose to ignore it. Whatever was going on between them was not a full-blown love affair. Most intriguing.

'The upkeep of this place is phenomenal, so having a *proper* job to fall back on makes sense and it gives me back my life a few days a week. And of course, as long as I work for Celestial, I can be freelance.'

Ruby nodded. She could understand the urge to escape from reality; she did it quite often in her head, but to live on a working farm or castle or whatever it was seemed like the best job opportunity ever.

'What about you?' he asked.

Ruby laughed. 'I find my castle tends to look after itself.'

Milo chuckled. 'I mean, are you planning on broadening your horizons? Is Celestial just the beginning of your dream, or are you looking for a rich pilot to take you away from the woes of the world?'

Are you offering? Ruby thought, but she said, 'That's rather insulting to say in this day and age, Milo. Women can look after themselves. They don't need to "capture" a man.' She did air quotes as she spoke. 'But yes, my ideal is to wear the red uniform of a certain famous airline, even though I know my hair will clash badly with the colour.'

'Sorry, didn't mean to sound sexist, but I do circulate in a society where a certain type of woman thinks a rich man is a meal ticket for life. They hear that I live in a castle and assume I'm some kind of lord and rolling in it.' He sighed as he ran his fingers through his hair. 'They need to spend a weekend up here to see what routing out wayward sheep and mending a mile of wooden fence can do to the beauty sleep regime.'

'You do have an aeroplane, though, right?' If ever she sounded like one of his gold-diggers that would clinch it.

'Yep, but there are aeroplanes and there are *aeroplanes*. Ours is a two-seater and we use it mostly for rounding up the animals, or more often than not rescuing dumb hill walkers who go out in rain and snow equipped with a woolly jumper slung around their shoulders and a packed lunch in a string bag.' He glanced at Ruby. 'How are your hands and feet, by the way — warmed up yet?'

She caught on quickly. 'You are *so* including me in those daft hill walkers.'

'*Nooo*, never.'

She laughed. 'Hey, come on, I wasn't dressed for horse riding because I wasn't expecting it, but, for sure, I would be one of those *dead-in-a-ditch* statistics cuddling my rucksack for warmth.'

'What with all that airline training?' His eyes crinkled as he smiled and Ruby's heart contracted with silent longing.

'They don't teach you how to do a bushtucker trial, you know, although I could totally save myself from all those unexploded devices we learned about, if they were littered around the Highlands.'

'Aye, although I did hear you weren't so good at climbing into dinghies, so steer clear of the lochs.' He leaned against a wooden stall and folded his arms, his eyes dancing with mischief.

Ruby groaned. 'No!' She put her hand up to her face in embarrassment. 'I knew that would get out, but Lucy said I was being paranoid.' She prayed the Boom Bottom wasn't being discussed along with her inability to climb into a dinghy with her lily-white legs and fuzzy ginger bikini line.

'Don't worry, I'm teasing. I'm on your side. One of the pilots mentioned it, as he knew I . . .' Milo faltered, coughing into his hand. 'Nothing.' He picked at a splinter coming away from a wooden strut, turning his face away.

'As he knew what . . . ?' He was talking about one of the most embarrassing moments of her adult life here, and it was *nothing*? She waited.

He looked uncomfortable. 'It was just a conversation.'

'Right. I hope they were kind.' She waited some more, but clearly nothing else was forthcoming.

In fact, he changed the conversation completely. 'I'm sorry that today was a bit of a washout. We had an important business connection turn up out of the blue, plus the weather was crap for flying in a small aircraft.' He shrugged. 'Out of my hands, unfortunately.'

She'd give him the change of conversation. 'It's fine. It's lovely to be here — Paddington Bear boots and frostbite on my hands notwithstanding. At least Loretta ensured I made it back. She could have lured me into a forest and stuffed me down a handy well.'

Milo looked puzzled. 'Why would she do that?'

'Oh, err, just—' she shrugged — 'you know.'

But Milo clearly didn't know, and she felt mean for her uncharitable thoughts even as she wanted to hex Loretta to kingdom come.

'I'd love to see your Viking cows — if you have time.' It was her turn to change the subject, but they did sound cute and some shots for her Instagram account wouldn't hurt. She'd gathered so many new followers recently she felt she needed to diversify; surely they were sick of seeing pictures of her moped and images of the sea from 15,000 feet?

'My Viking cows?' He laughed. 'Brilliant name. They really do look like shaggy-haired Vikings. Love it.'

'Do you think they'll recognise a sister-in-arms?'

'Hmm.' Lightly he ran a hand over her hair. 'No horns yet?'

'Viking horns grow very, *very* slowly,' she declared.

His hand on her hair had unnerved her; if she was really unlucky, he would have felt the shiver running through her body.

She wanted to ask where Loretta stood in his complicated life as she was beginning to feel she had the wrong end of the stick where she and Milo were concerned, but as she was framing the words in the most polite way she could think of, the stable door flew open and then slammed shut and there stood Loretta, as if conjured up by a demon.

'What are you bloody doing, Milo? You've been ages — your father's waiting for you. You need to come now.' She acted as if Ruby wasn't even there, or if she was, she was no more than the milkmaid or the wench who swept the stable floor. Whichever it was, she barely glanced at her and turned her attention back to Milo.

'Stop panicking. I've told you, you don't need to worry about me and Dad, it's not your job,' Milo said calmly.

'No, but I'll get the blame from Promo Live if you don't get the deal.'

Ruby was all ears; she couldn't help it. Nosey was in her genes.

'Promo Live won't give up the chance to film our house and grounds, you know that.' Milo patted the horse he'd returned to rubbing down. 'I'll be a minute or two, don't fret. And don't forget that he's *my* father. He knows I would *never* let him down.'

Loretta huffed and stormed back out again.

Standing tall and turning to Ruby, he said, 'I think I'd better get you back to the hotel, as who knows how long this might all go on.' He ran his fingers through his hair, agitated. 'It really was lovely spending some time with you up here.' He ran a hand around the back of his neck.

Ruby had never seen him look so uncomfortable.

'Look, I feel we need a lucky break but it's all so manic here and . . .' He sighed and looked into the distance. 'I don't know what I'm trying to say, to be honest, but . . . we always seem to be a bit "eat and run", you know?'

'Well, we do work for an airline, it's not a job that's conducive to excess amounts of chill time. Talking of which, did you get your tee shirt back? I never did ask you. I washed and ironed it.' Immediately, she wished she hadn't drawn attention to the hotel fiasco and had just kept her mouth shut. Milo was possibly in the middle of saying something really important, and she'd already sent him off in a different direction.

Milo nodded distractedly. 'I did, thank you, and I was most upset that it didn't smell of you — your perfume, I mean,' he added quickly.

'Really?'

Milo leaned against the stable door and folded his arms, smiling gently. 'Really.'

'Well, that's splendid, indeed,' Ruby said, wondering when she'd started talking like an extra in a Richard Curtis film.

Milo grinned but looked bashful. 'Anyway, we'd better get on,' he said, and his hand ran through his hair once more.

'Splendid,' Ruby repeated, knowing she was letting a golden opportunity disappear.

'Tally-ho and all that,' Milo said, smiling.

'Erm, can you run that by me again . . .' she started, but Milo interrupted her.

'I'll get Bruce, our driver, to drop you off.'

'Lovely.' *Not lovely, not lovely at all.* She didn't want to leave this newfound revelation hanging in the air, not knowing what they meant to each other, or where they were heading — if they were heading anywhere. She didn't want to leave him to the dubious charms of Loretta. She didn't want . . . just didn't want to leave.

But of course she did leave, following Milo meekly out on to the vast driveway, where an open truck covered in dust and piled high with hay bales stood to return her to the hotel.

'Sorry to dump you in the truck, but we need the Land Rover to show the production company round,' he said as if that explained everything.

'No, it's fine,' she said, climbing into the truck with a heavy heart.

'We should make a date for you to photograph the donkeys at the Devon farm, yeah?' Milo said.

Ruby couldn't keep the delight from her face. 'That would be perfect. I'll put up more pictures on my Instagram account, and I can ask Jerry if he'll put it in the newspaper, like we discussed.' She was breathless with relief. 'Do you want to swap phone numbers?' She could barely believe she'd summoned up the nerve to ask him, but she needed something more tangible to hang on to.

'Yeah, of course.' Milo pulled out his mobile and Ruby relayed her number as he punched it into his address book. He beamed at her and nodded. 'Okay.'

She beamed too. 'Okay.' It was a pact, and once more the good part of the world righted itself and she could deal with the rest when it happened.

And so it was time to return to the flatness of flying home, each mile taking her closer to Richie, second by dispiriting second. Vanessa huffed around, quizzing Ruby about whether she'd spent time with Milo, but the passengers were pliant and made for an easy working day.

They landed to clear skies and watery sunshine, which was a pleasant change and it cheered Ruby up. At least she would have a dry journey home. *Home.* Her heart sank. Home meant Richie and petty arguments and annoying niggles, or did it mean one big showdown which would lead to her packing her bags? She sighed. The choice was hers and she knew what she should do. She was cheating on Richie in her mind, and if she and Milo never became an item, she was still cheating and no one deserved that — not even Richie. The truth was clear; she no longer loved Richie — hell, she didn't even *like* him. Unfortunately, Richie seemed to think they were back on track and everything was hunky-dory. Was she about to destroy his happiness?

She left the crew room reluctant to call it a day but said her goodbyes to Jack and thanked him for such a lovely time. The rest of the crew all said a breezy goodbye until the next time, apart from Vanessa, who more or less ignored her, which was no loss at all.

CHAPTER NINETEEN

Ruby always felt drained after a long shift but this time it seemed worse than usual as a stultifying lethargy overcame her. It had been so delicious spending time with Milo in Inverness and she felt as if a new life was just within touching distance, if only she knew how to grab it. She always went to great lengths to hide her tiredness after work from Richie, not wanting to add more fuel to his determination to bitch about her job. He was right, of course; weekends were messed up and spontaneity had gone out the window, and she was always tired. Even so, she was reluctant to go straight home after they'd landed and thought she would see if Richie wanted to go for a drink — maybe see what came out in the wash.

Already, now she was away from Celestial Air — and Milo — her emotions vacillated. This was *her* Richie she was thinking about leaving, and for what? Was there enough left to try and salvage their relationship? One last stab at it, perhaps? If she pretended hard enough that Richie was still the love of her life, maybe it would happen.

But when he didn't answer the text, even though she knew he'd seen the message, she wondered how long she could continue with the charade she was acting out. So when

Lucy texted, *Just landed? Fancy a drink?* she knew that was exactly what she needed and agreed with alacrity. She could take home fish and chips as a peace offering to Richie after a quick catch-up with Lucy.

'Let's go to that pub we went to after the fire training day where that fireman said I should be a model,' Lucy suggested.

Ruby agreed and did the usual divesting of outer garments in the car park, stuffing everything in the top box of the moped. She breezed into the pub, relieved she could put off going home for a while longer.

They bought drinks and sat down on the table under the window, bringing back memories of the first time she met Milo at the firefighting course. She launched into her story about visiting the Destination, knowing that she was gushing and behaving like a starry-eyed teenager.

'There he is,' Lucy hissed, eyes widening and fluttering her eyelashes. She started laughing loudly and elbowed Ruby as if she'd said something hilarious.

Ruby's stomach lurched as for one mad moment, so caught up was she in her own little world, she thought Lucy meant Milo had turned up — even as she knew it was impossible. The way the butterflies danced in her stomach made her realise — as if she needed any more prompting — that she had to find a way to leave Richie.

'Oh, hi again, Billy,' Lucy called to the fireman, giving him a little wave. 'Look, his eyes lit up,' she hissed again to Ruby.

Billy picked up his bottle of beer from the countertop and sauntered over.

Ruby smiled too, not begrudging the interruption, but was soon feeling like a spare part and found herself checking the time more than once. One of Billy's friends looked over for a minute or two and, as if deciding she wasn't worth the bother, looked down into his pint almost sorrowfully and took a large slurp. While that was all for the good, of course, she couldn't help but feel a bit slighted. She didn't even have an engagement ring to put him off — just herself and the labradoodle hair which she'd recklessly taken out from its clips and slides and allowed to tumble freely. And she thought that someone with the attributes of Milo could fall in love with her? She was living in cloud cuckoo land.

After a few more mildly entertaining minutes of watching Lucy and Billy flirting with each other, she picked up her bag and excused herself.

'Have fun, you two.' She winked at Lucy, who smiled broadly and mouthed, 'I'll call you,' before giving Billy her undivided attention.

Piling on her layers again, she drove home via the fish and chip shop, the cold starting to seep into her bones as the day lengthened. That was the thing with England, she decided: as soon as the sun disappeared it turned freezing.

She pulled up resignedly outside the apartment and let herself in. 'I'm home,' she called out, throwing her keys on the hall table and peeling off her layers once more, before carrying the fish and chips through to the kitchen, preparing to play out the charade for a bit longer until she had made a proper decision.

She was greeted by a stony-faced Richie glaring at his phone. Her heart sank. She couldn't face another one of his silent treatment evenings, she really wasn't in the mood.

'Where have you been?' His tone was icy and almost threatening.

'At work, you know that.' She thrust her chin in the air, but despite her bravado an icicle of fear slithered down her spine.

'No, I mean where have you been since you finished work?' He finally dragged his eyes away from his mobile. His pupils were large in his eyes, giving him a menacing edge.

She didn't know why she didn't fess up to going to the pub with Lucy; maybe it was to stop another pointless argument. 'Nowhere. Why, what's happened?'

'What's happened is that I've cottoned on that you're lying to me.' Richie's face coloured a dull red from his neck upwards and his brows beetled together. 'See, you think you're smarter than me, when you're just the dumbest person I know.' He turned his phone around and thrust it in her face. 'I have all the times here. It doesn't take a genius to find it.'

Ruby, who had until then been holding on to her flight bag, took it off her shoulder and dumped it in the hall. She shrugged out of her coat, adopting a nonchalance she didn't feel. 'What are you talking about, where do you think I've been?'

Richie, still puce in the face, was mute as he stabbed at his phone screen.

She peered at his phone, displaying a website that was ticker-taping down in a permanent scroll like it was spewing out football results. She didn't know what she was looking at until she registered the pair of gold wings, Celestial's logo, at the top of the page. The website announced the arrival and departure times of Celestial flights to the world via Google. There weren't that many, so she could clearly see that her flight had landed two hours ago.

'I *know* when you landed.' He glanced at his phone. 'Approximately 118 minutes ago. So what have you been doing since then?'

Ruby took a deep breath, containing her anger. How dare he check up on her! 'Apart from the fact that our work doesn't stop when the last passengers disembark, you have no right to check up on me.'

Richie looked genuinely puzzled at her comment. 'I have every right — you're my girlfriend.'

She shook her head dumbfounded. She was starting to think she didn't know the man she lived with. He was clearly descended from the Neanderthals and should still be living in a cave. 'We have duties once we've landed.' The grain of guilt for not mentioning that she'd been to the pub decreased, as she counted off tasks to do before she left the airport. 'First off, we have to sign off the catering trollies and the bar, then we check the cabin for lost property, ensure everything in the galley is turned off and sometimes we have to clean the aircraft if there is a tight turnaround and the cleaners are on another aircraft—'

'Two-bit airline makes you clean it? I told you it was nothing more than a glorified waitress job,' he interrupted, sneering.

If that was the best he could come up with, insulting her job and her airline, then it wasn't worth arguing with him.

As if he hadn't spoken, she continued, 'Then it's everyone to the crew room, where we sort out the bar money and write a report about the flight, if anything untoward happened, which, as it happened, did. We had to call out one of the firemen to check an extinguisher that was accidently knocked out of its cage by an overzealous caterer manoeuvring one of our trollies. It was quite an event, squirting crazy foam everywhere. Anyway, that took a good twenty minutes.'

'Oh, we have firemen in this mix as well as pilots, do we?' He followed her into the kitchen and towered over her as she poured a glass of water.

It was too much for Ruby to take. She rounded on him. 'Yep, I'm shagging them all, one each night because they all find me *sooo* irresistible with my ginger hair and freckles and my dumbass personality and the Viking helmet with two horns that I like to bring out as a party piece.'

Richie actually laughed at that comment, but she wasn't laughing. 'They'd probably have loved my crossed-over front teeth too, if my diligent parents and the local orthodontist hadn't intervened. What a shame they did, eh? Then you could have found something else to criticise.' She ran her fingers through her hair, knowing it was a bad move as it would just make it frizzier than ever. She shook her head in despair. 'This is so pointless.'

The smell of the rapidly cooling fish and chips that had been so enticing now turned her stomach. Exasperated by another ridiculous argument that stemmed completely from his jealousy, she said, 'I can't keep dealing with this Jekyll and Hyde personality of yours. Face it, Richie, you don't even like me, you just want to own me.' She stared at the fish and chips lying in their paper wrapper, picked them up and dumped them in the bin. 'Your dinner's in there. I'm going to bed.'

She dashed tears away as she undressed, wondering why she'd let their relationship unravel so badly. She'd lied to him because of his jealousy and his need to control her. She'd put up with it, tried to be the perfect girlfriend, but she couldn't take it anymore.

The tears stopped as anger bubbled up again. She climbed into bed praying that Richie slept on the sofa, preferably his mum's sofa. He wouldn't be happy until she left the airline and he was in complete control of her, and she wasn't having it. She turned out the light then lay down, turned over and tried to settle, plumping up her pillow in an action more akin to punching it, if she was honest. It didn't help.

CHAPTER TWENTY

Ruby's head was a mess — full of disloyal thoughts alternating between Milo playing the lead role in her life and hot anger about the way she let Richie treat her. She had actually enjoyed being on her own when he'd gone to stay at his mum's and life was so much easier without him. She had even grown to love her labradoodle hair again and she certainly laughed more with her work friends than she ever did with Richie. She was free to go out on impulse, something that only angered Richie; spontaneity was only for him.

All she wanted was a peaceful life, but his latest stunt with the website was just another way of spying on her and she was so over it. She didn't know how to leave him, but she did know that she didn't care enough to try and stay.

He had sold her car, bought himself a Porsche and had joined a gym, which was a real slap in the face, as when she'd wanted to join — it had a lovely pool — he'd said they couldn't afford it. She was still merrily, or not so merrily, riding to work, and mostly in the rain as it was a very rainy summer. Although the early mornings were mild, she still arrived a cold, straggly mess most days, and had to leave so much earlier to change into her uniform, put her make-up on and wrestle her hair into a bun in the ladies.

She would have to fork out for a car before winter as it really wasn't feasible, even in Devon, or maybe she would buy a motorbike, if she passed her test — which would also no doubt offend Richie's manhood. She smiled grimly, knowing he would resent it to the point of madness, which would be one silver lining in a sky full of dark clouds anyway.

For once she wasn't in the mood for work. She was distracted and upset knowing that, although work was fabulous, her personal life was a mess.

This particular morning she was working at the rear of the aircraft with Cara, a new girl she knew only slightly. She went through the motions, checking the food trolleys were stacked with breakfasts and not cream teas, which had happened to someone else a month ago. They'd tried to make light of it to the passengers, asking them to consider it brunch, and they were mostly fine about it. It wasn't as if they were getting nothing, although she did wonder how the other crew reacted when they discovered their aircraft was loaded up with two trolleys of full English on an afternoon flight.

She checked the milk, tea and hot water urns, and signed it all off. She was still freezing as the heating hadn't been switched on and she hadn't thawed out from the journey. Rashly, she had worn her stiletto crew shoes on her moped instead of her bike boots in an attempt to save time, and now they were wet and adding to her misery. Sighing, she slid them off and pulled out her flight bag to put her low cabin shoes on. There was half an hour before take-off and she could dry out her stilettos for a bit in the oven ready to change into them to greet the passengers.

She turned the oven on to minimal heat and sighed with relief as her toes hit the dry warmth of her cabin shoes. Five minutes later she turned off the oven and was about to take her stilettos out, when Cara asked her if they had one more seat belt extension as the one at the front had already been used.

'Yes, sure, I'll get it for you,' she said, reaching up into the locker and handing the extension to Cara. 'You know how to use it, don't you?'

Cara assured her that she did and Ruby turned away as a passenger asked if she could have a glass of water.

They prepared to board the passengers and Ruby heaved bags into lockers and ensured able-bodied passengers were sitting in the emergency exits. Smiling unfailingly, she began to relax. She loved her job and couldn't understand the moaners who seemed to dislike the very people who paid their wages. The checks and demonstrations were completed and Ruby and Cara took their seats for take-off. As they tore along the runway, Ruby, thinking through the service in her head, was brought up short as a distant alarm began to clang. It was coming from the flight deck.

She sat up straight, adrenaline coursing through her body as she strained to see down the length of the cabin if anything was amiss, peering around the bulkhead and listening out for any kind of commotion. She could see nothing amiss. The aircraft steadied out and Ruby relaxed slightly; there were often strange beeps and dings coming from the flight deck and she'd learned to ignore them. But without warning, another alarm, a high-pitched wail, started up. Passengers who had acknowledged the alarm were alternately swivelling their heads to the front and the rear of the aircraft, some with fear in their eyes and others simply intrigued. Many eyes were fixed on the cabin crew to see how they were reacting.

The captain's voice came over the intercom. 'Cabin staff remain seated,' he said in a calm and measured voice. 'Ladies and gentlemen, we are returning to base as an alarm is signalling a slight problem. Please remain seated and keep your seat belts fastened. There is no need to worry, everything is under control.'

Wide eyed with fear, Cara turned to Ruby. 'What do we do?'

'We sit tight for now and we'll be on the ground before you know it. It's more than likely just a switch malfunctioning rather than an actual problem. One of the engineers talked me through it all once.'

'Okay.' Cara's hands reached down to her seat and she held on tight.

Ruby ran through her drills, not knowing what kind of emergency it could be, while simultaneously praying it was a false alarm. 'If we need to, you grab a fire extinguisher and I'll get the insulated gloves. Don't forget, if the oxygen masks drop down, grab an oxygen bottle and put your mask on — we'll need to be able to move around.'

Ruby swallowed back her own fear, seeing the terror in Cara's eyes. She had just discovered that the metaphor 'legs turning to jelly' was not an exaggeration; she wasn't entirely sure she could stand up unaided. She felt the contents of her stomach turn to water and determined to get a grip. She was not going to let Celestial Air down; it had been her promise to them when they gave her the job and she would make them proud of her, come hell or high water.

She placed her feet firmly on the floor and ran through the brace position to adopt when facing the rear of the aircraft. She felt Cara's hand creep into hers and she held on tight, giving her a reassuring nod. Looking out of the window, she could see land and her heart lifted. 'It will be fine, Cara, don't you worry. Just a false alarm.' As she spoke a loud beeping emanated from their end of the aircraft.

Ruby glanced up to see a dull red light flashing in the rear galley. 'It's the rear smoke detector. Is there a fire in the toilet?' She picked up the receiver to tell the purser at the front so she could relay the message to the captain. 'I think there might be a fire in the rear of the aircraft. It's not coming from the toilet. I don't know what it could be.' Her voice was shaky and she coughed to steady it.

'The captain is already on it. The fire service will meet us. Don't open the toilet door. See if you can collect a fire extinguisher without alerting the passengers. The one by the bulkhead door?'

'Will do.' She felt more in control now she had something to do. 'Stay here, Cara, I'm going to get the fire extinguisher.' The aircraft was holding steady and there was no sign of any external difficulty, but to make sure, Ruby peered out of the windows to view the engines. She heaved a sigh of relief. No sign of fire on the wings. Grabbing the fire extinguisher, she slid back to her seat, keeping low. 'We'll be on the ground in five minutes, I can see the tower,' she reassured the frightened young woman.

'Ruby . . . look.' Cara's voice was high pitched in her panic as she pointed, with a quivering finger, to the ovens.

Wisps of smoke were creeping out from around the seals in the lower oven door like a whisper of fear insinuating itself throughout the rear galley.

'Shit, shit, shit.' Ruby was glued to her seat, wasn't supposed to get up and all she could do was watch. Terror engulfed her as she prayed that there wasn't a fire raging inside the oven about to spill over into the galley. Even as she thought it, more faint tendrils of smoke snaked out of the door, as insipid as a mare's tails in the morning sky but as deadly as a nuclear mushroom. A fire on board an aircraft rarely had a good outcome, as Fiona had taught them.

Six chimes carried through the aircraft; an emergency had been called.

Ruby picked up the intercom and told Anthony that there was smoke coming out of the right-hand oven. Once again, he already knew. The captain must have been alerted by an alarm and was relaying everything to him.

As she spoke she happened to look down at her feet and grew cold with dread. She had turned off the oven before take-off, she knew she had, but had left her shoes in there in the confusion of boarding. What if it was her *shoes* smoking and burning up? She couldn't think of any other reason why the oven would be smoking. And what if it was more than smoking? What if it was a full-on fire? If she opened the door to check it could be devastating. She wouldn't, of course; she knew better than that. It could flare out and cause an inferno. Oh God, her stupid, precious shoes were going to cause everyone on board to die in a fireball.

175

She couldn't see the oven dial from where she was sitting. Calmly, she asked Cara, 'I don't suppose you put the bottom right oven on, did you?' Cara was rigid with fear and her lips were turning blue with shock. Bloody hell, that was all she needed — her colleague to keel over to add to her worries.

'Are you blaming me?'

'God, no, I just wondered . . .'

'Well, I did, because I was taught to put the ovens on before take-off so that they're hot when we put the breakfasts in.' Her lips were a thin line and her bottom lip wobbled as she spoke.

'Right. Okay. Perfect. No problem.' *Shit, shit and double shit.* She could see land now and knew she couldn't get up out of her seat to turn the ovens off — and anyway the damage was done.

If the rear of the aircraft didn't explode, after they landed the fire brigade would open the ovens and find her charred shoes and she wouldn't have a leg to stand on. For some reason the analogy made her want to giggle and she suppressed a snort.

'Are you okay?'

'If we get out of here alive I'm completely screwed, but apart from that . . .' She would be sacked, she knew it, and deservedly so, but right then she needed to focus on getting everyone out of the aircraft alive. Bizarre thoughts ran through her head. Who would tell her mother that she was dead? How long would her moped sit in the car park until someone moved it? She had the only set of keys with her. Wet shoes and cold feet were a ridiculous reason to die in a fire.

'One minute to touchdown. There is no reason to suspect that there will be a problem with the landing, but please refresh the brace position shown on the diagram in front of you and locate your nearest emergency exit. I repeat, there is no cause for immediate alarm.' At least the captain wasn't losing his cool.

Ruby could see the ground rushing up to meet them as she peered out of the window and relaxed slightly. But on the words 'Brace for impact,' she gripped her chair and prayed fervently to a God she wasn't sure she believed in.

CHAPTER TWENTY-ONE

Fire engines chased alongside the aircraft, sirens blaring as they touched down; the smoke in the rear of the galley was acrid and black albeit not thick and choking, but any fire necessitated an emergency evacuation.

'Deploy the forward slides. Passengers evacuate to the front of the aircraft and leave all belongings behind.' The command came from the captain and Ruby's training once again kicked in; she knew what to do. The captain obviously didn't want the passengers to head for the rear steps, so she directed them to the front of the aircraft, shouting forcefully with positive commands, as she had been trained to do. 'Go, go, move. Now!' She turned to Cara. 'Herd the passengers out to the front slides and then jump yourself. Got it?'

Cara nodded, seemingly incapable of speech. But she shepherded the passengers to the front and blocked the aisle off so no one could return if they were daft enough to try and retrieve a case or bag.

The rush to get to the front was reasonably organised, although, as she always suspected they would, the women grabbed their handbags and clutched them to their chests when they were clearly told to leave all belongings behind. But she wasn't going to be the one trying to separate someone from their handbag.

Ruby touched the oven door with the back of her hand. It was red hot. Definitely a fire brewing. She was ready with her fire extinguisher when the fear hit her. She was twelve years old again, startled by a fire that she had caused. She tried to calm herself by breathing deeply, even though she knew it wasn't a good idea with smoke filling the cabin. She could get an oxygen bottle. No. Not oxygen, that could exacerbate the situation. Or would it help? She was no longer sure; her mind was scrambled. One thing was for sure, she would not desert her post. Faint with terror, she planted her legs apart as she took up her position, determined to do the right thing.

A firefighter pushed his way against the flow of traffic towards the rear of the cabin and Ruby heaved out a sigh of relief as she recognised the bulk of John, her trainer. She wanted to weep with relief; someone was taking control.

'It's this oven,' she yelled shrilly, aware that she sounded slightly hysterical.

'Righto. I want you to leave the aircraft now,' he shouted to Ruby, who was aware that a roaring noise was drowning out their voices. But she couldn't move. It was as if her feet had grown into the floor. She wobbled and swayed, watching as if in a trance as John felt the oven doors with his hands. He opened the rear aircraft door gingerly, so as not to let in a rush of air. A crew of firefighters wearing full firefighting gear rushed in carrying all sorts of paraphernalia.

'What are you still doing here? Go!' one of the firemen barked. It seemed that rain had started to fall on the aircraft and what looked like soap suds dripped down the outside of the windows. Ruby recognised what it was by the smell. They weren't taking any chances: the whole aircraft was being doused in anti-inflammatory liquid.

She stood, transfixed, watching, heart in her mouth as John slowly opened the door to the oven, squirted a whole extinguisher inside it and slammed it shut. He turned round and spotted Ruby. 'All crew off the aircraft, for fuck's sake!' he yelled, waving an arm in her direction.

For the first time the surreal situation became fact and she jumped at his command, waking up from the trance that had shut down her body. 'I'm going,' Ruby shouted back over the din of extinguishers, the liquid thrumming on the aircraft roof and the hullabaloo at the front of the aircraft. Quickly, she grabbed her own handbag, a manoeuvre that was most definitely frowned upon, and legged it down the cabin and out to sweet, fresh air.

She huddled with the rest of the crew, shivering, although she wasn't sure if it was shock or cold that was causing it. Eyes fixed on the entrance to the aircraft, she waited for the captain to come down the steps.

Finally, someone who seemed to be thinking about the crew shouted, 'We're waiting on a paramedic, but if anyone needs a doctor give us a shout, otherwise we're taking you to the crew room.'

Ruby, once again, couldn't move. She needed to see the outcome of this terrible fiasco.

One of the engineers tried to steer her into a waiting crew bus as John appeared at the top of the stairs, his face a mixture of elation and horror. Sure enough, in his gloved hand dangled a pair of very charred, beyond repair crew shoes, heels black stumps and no sign of the beautiful red leather. He walked down the steps and headed for the huddle of crew, who were all peering, trying to see what the black clump of matter he waved around was. Ruby knew exactly what they were looking at.

'Have I taught you nothing?' John boomed, waving the shoes theatrically in the air, a look of satisfaction on his face. She didn't know whether to own up there and then or keep quiet until she could confess quietly to Fiona and the management, who would no doubt gather for a meeting after such a disaster. It would all come out anyway, in the end. If only her shoes had burned to a crisp. Would she have owned up then or kept quiet? That was a question she would never need to answer, unfortunately.

Slowly, all pairs of eyes swivelled around to look at Ruby and Cara. Completely ashen, her eyes wide and lips trembling, Cara asked, 'Why are you all staring at us?'

'It's okay,' Ruby said. 'It's all my fault.' Louder now. 'They were my shoes.'

Cara turned huge eyes to the aircraft and then slowly swivelled her head to the black clumps of burnt leather John held aloft, as if the cogs in her mind were falling into place. She put her hand to her mouth. 'Oh my God, I put the ovens on. Did I roast your shoes?' Cara clapped her hand to her mouth.

'Roasted is putting it mildly. Overcooked is more the result, I would say.' Ruby attempted a laugh that threatened to turn to full-on hysteria.

All eyes swivelled to Cara, whose eyes were like saucers, her lips still a fetching shade of ice blue. She looked as if she was about to faint, and indeed, she did stagger backwards and put her hand to her forehead in a great imitation of a swoon. Someone caught her before she went down and then didn't quite know what to do with her as he held the dead weight of a body against his chest. Someone phoned for help, as an ambulance, as if by magic, pulled alongside the crowd of angry and shaken crew members.

'I put my shoes in the oven to dry out.' Ruby attempted to justify her actions to anyone who would listen, herself wide-eyed in shock and disbelief that she could have been so irresponsible. No way was she going to let Cara feel guilty for doing her job properly. Her eyes filled with hot tears that she blinked away furiously, the enormity of her actions just starting to hit.

'Is she okay?' Ruby knelt on the floor where Cara was now deposited and grabbed her hand.

'Yes, she's fainted. It's better if she's out for the count, her breathing will steady. Don't worry, she'll be fine.'

Shock can sometimes kill. Ruby remembered that much from her training, and she eye-balled the rest of the crew for signs of imminent death, but they mostly looked relieved and grateful to be alive, glancing away if she caught their eye. How could she ever apologise enough?

'Girl, you are in so much shit,' one of the stewards muttered.

Anthony, white-faced with fists clenched, took a step towards her and pointed a long finger. '*You* have put us through this,' he said dramatically. Ruby couldn't help but want to giggle at his camp theatrics.

'Chill, we got to practise our drills. Think of the positives,' Emma said, but her voice was shaky and weak.

'C'mon, everyone. We're safe, aren't we? There'll be time to discuss the fallout of this later. In the meantime let's get to the crew room and we can write a report up. God knows they'll scrutinise this, so don't make anything up.'

'Fucking idiot nearly killed us all,' Sasha said in her lyrical Latvian accent that made even the insult sound rather pretty.

Suddenly the captain came thundering down the stairs. 'Whose were the shoes?' The normally mild-mannered, gentle man bore down on the small group, united in the aftermath of relief and shock.

If ever Ruby had heard a collective gasp before, it was nothing to the intake of synchronised breaths she now heard.

Nobody as much as batted an eyelid.

'They were mine, Captain, and I can't say enough how sorry I am.' Her legs were the texture and strength of boiled spaghetti as she faced him, like a schoolgirl being told off by the headmaster all over again.

'Blithering fool!' he said. 'What were you thinking?'

There was no point in explaining that she'd turned the oven off. She should never have put the shoes in there in the first place — it was all her fault. 'What can I say?' Her voice was small and wobbly as the captain, hands on hips, glowered at her, fury in his eyes.

'There will be consequences,' he said ominously, another long finger thrust in her direction, and she rather thought that he and Anthony would make a great double act as the baddies in a Christmas pantomime.

Ruby nodded mournfully, although a tiny part of her mind still held out hope that this whole thing would be played down and she would be forgiven.

There seemed little else to say and they all trooped into the minibus to take them to the crew room, although Ruby rather expected everyone to shuffle along the seat and say, 'Can't sit here,' when she boarded the coach, like a re-enactment of the scene from *Forrest Gump*.

Everyone sat in silence until someone's phone rang and the excited voice at the other end was put on loudspeaker as they said the emergency had already been reported on the news, although the details were sketchy.

Ruby bowed her head, tied up in her own thoughts, envisioning prison at the least, her face on everyone's Twitter feed, posters saying, *Have you seen this woman?* If she decided to make a run for it, where the hell was Acapulco or Cartagena and why didn't she know such things?

Customers would sue and the slides alone cost a fortune to replace. Did they have to pay for the fire engines? She didn't know and she certainly wasn't going to ask. The airline, the company she loved, the company who had given her the chance to shine, might go bust because of her stupidity.

She trooped in behind the crew to see Fiona sitting by the window biting her lip and staring at the runway where the aircraft sat, doused in foam with two slides blown and what seemed like a million people in high-vis jackets surrounding it: engineers, security, firemen, Celestial Air staff. Even the baggage handlers seemed to have found a bus to come and gawp, although to be fair they probably did have to collect people's bags at some point.

Ruby didn't think for one second about the consequences of hugging her boss and didn't know why she did it, but as Fiona stood up, she ran over to her, put her arms around her and said, 'I'll make it right, I promise. I'm so sorry.' Then she promptly released the flood of tears she'd been holding back.

Fiona unwound Ruby's arms from around her neck and stood back, rubbing at her arms as she looked into Ruby's eyes. Calmly she said, 'Ruby, everyone knows that you would never do anything to harm a single person in this world. We all know that and hopefully your colleagues will forgive you, but I don't think the shareholders will be quite so accommodating.'

'It's okay, I know. I'm just glad that no one was hurt.' She sniffed discreetly and wished she had a tissue to hand. 'Is it okay if I go home now? I can be reached on my mobile.' She wiped the heel of her hand across her eyes regardless of her make-up. 'I won't go to jail, will I?' she pleaded.

Fiona burst out laughing. 'Of course you won't. It was an accident and accidents happen. No one died.'

'I know but the airline might go bust.' She put the heel of her hands into her eyes to staunch the tears. 'What have I done? You can't afford this, you said on our training course that blowing a slide cost a fortune.' Ruby's voice hitched up a notch and she started breathing in raggedly, sobs wracking her body.

'Ruby, please calm down, we're insured. What's happened is not good, but we do have three other aircraft and we can get Tango Yankee up to muster pretty quickly.'

'You can?' Her relief was palpable, even though Fiona's brave face looked doubtful.

Taking deep breaths, Ruby gazed at her fellow workers. One came forward. 'Come on, Rubes, it's okay. We're all fine, look.' She held up her hands. 'Still have ten fingers.'

One by one the crew agreed, holding up their own hands. A few smiled like it killed them, forced smiles that were more like grimaces, but others were more forgiving.

Anthony, obviously relenting, gave her a hug. 'Hey, if nothing else, you've proved that we can all handle an emergency. That's a big deal, you know.'

'Yes, actually it is. I thought I was going to die with fright earlier on, but . . . I didn't. Instead I proved to myself that I have the courage to do my duty.' Ruby looked around, hoping that everyone would agree. Some did but some gave her evils, and she could imagine the grief they would give her when they got home. She was glad she wouldn't be able to hear it.

Fiona put a gentle hand on Ruby's shoulder. 'Go home, love, it's all over bar the shouting.'

And the sacking, Ruby thought as she glanced with longing at the pigeonhole with her name embossed on top of it. She walked towards it and pulled out a couple of memos. Stuffing them in her handbag, she said, 'I'll wait to hear from you.' She gave a little wave to her colleagues. 'Thanks, guys, it's been great working with you.'

Receiving a few sorry little waves in reply, she was gone.

She needed to get away — fast. Her whole body trembled as she walked out of the building on weak legs and she didn't know how to stop it. Instead of taking the lift she ran down the two flights of stairs and jogged, as fast as was ladylike in her uniform, to the car park, needing to expend the energy in her body. A literal smell was coming off her, sulphurous and cloying. Was it adrenaline? Could fear and shock give out a smell? She sniffed surreptitiously at her armpits, which were decidedly moist, as she pulled her biking outerwear over her uniform. Unlocking her moped and taking out her crash helmet from her top box, she couldn't focus on anything apart from getting home to her sanctuary. But her arms couldn't even grasp the handlebars and her legs didn't seem to want to help her climb on to her bike.

Tears began to course freely down her cheeks and she slumped on the grassy hill by the bus stop close to where she parked her moped. Gazing around at the airport she loved — the buzz of families going on holidays, polite businessmen tap-tapping on their laptops as they waited to board and the bustle of crew leaving and arriving — she envisioned instead reporters with wide-lens cameras pointing at the aeroplane now standing on the tarmac. She swiped at her eyes and stood up, knowing she'd be a sitting duck once reporters got wind of the situation. They might even now be heading her way. The thought boosted her into action and she once more climbed on to Bananarama, giving it a little pat to ensure it treated her well.

She set off, peering at the road through a veil of tears, trying not to think of the bleak future that lay ahead of her. But she couldn't help re-enacting her actions over and over, almost crashing into a bollard as her vision blurred. She was so humiliated. Milo would find out and he would tell Loretta, a sad smile on his face. And Jack, who was so kind to her. Everyone at the airline would relish the gossip and maybe cross themselves for their own lucky escape. There but for the grace of God and all that. She couldn't bear it.

CHAPTER TWENTY-TWO

It wasn't until she arrived outside her own door that she thought of Richie and wondered if he'd heard about the emergency. What would she say to him? What would he say to her? She would have to tell him. She couldn't keep it a secret. Would he be kind, making a good fist of pulling together as a couple, soothing her and reassuring her that they would be okay until she found another job? It was unlikely, she had to admit, and it brought a fresh bout of tears. Anyway, she didn't want another job, she wanted the one she had — if indeed she still had it.

Deep down she knew Richie would gloat, but if she heard one single 'I told you so' from him, she would . . . She would what? She didn't know jack shit about anything right then, apart from having the creeping and overwhelming urge to speak to Milo. He would know where she stood and what she should do. Pulling off her crash helmet and fishing around for her house keys, she took deep breaths, in and out, and readied herself for a showdown.

She saw that Richie wasn't home, the old fail-proof signs of a car parked outside no longer being valid since he'd bought the stupid Porsche. But it gave her time to organise. She would have to face him, yes, but if she had a contingency plan she would be saved the worst of his wrath. The less he knew for now the better, and maybe it would not end up as disastrous as she feared.

But almost as soon as she formed the thought a key scraped in the lock. Richie was back. Keys hit the hall table with a clang and he strode in.

Ruby looked up through her tearstained face but Richie didn't even notice she was upset, just gave her a throwaway glance and said hello.

'Listen, Richie, I have a big problem.'

Richie tensed. 'What do you mean, have you come off your bike?' He actually sounded concerned, and for a second she felt all warm and loved up, just for a second, and then she smiled at her gullibility; he'd be more worried that she'd hit someone's car or damaged the moped.

Ruby sighed. 'I need to tell you something. There was an incident, Rich. Just listen.'

She indicated the sofa and Richie sat down. 'I've only got a few minutes — just came back to get my overalls. I've said I'll go to the barn for an hour or two,' he explained, looking agitated.

She sat down opposite him and explained what had happened and watched the range of expressions flit across his mouth, from smirking to pursing his lips in annoyance and then, as the realisation hit that she might be sacked, pure thunder.

'You're a joke, you know that? You can't even work for a two-bit airline without messing up. Afford a lawyer, can you, when you're sued for negligence?' His eyes darted around the sitting room as if he was metaphorically packing and she wondered for a moment if he was actually considering leaving her. He stood up, shaking his head and huffing through his nose in annoyance.

'Are you still going to the barn? What, to tinker with your *Porsche*?' She wasn't surprised.

'I said I would.' He looked slightly abashed. 'Anyway, they might come and arrest you, and might start looking in my direction if I'm here.' He shuddered theatrically and reached for his keys.

Ruby stiffened at his words. 'What do you mean? And why would they arrest me?' Fiona had assured her that she would not be in any trouble with the police, but what if she was wrong? A shiver of fear ran down her spine but she squared her shoulders and, after a moment of thinking about it, relaxed. She hadn't committed a crime, had she?

'You're probably right. Google it, see if you can be arrested for burning down an aeroplane.' He smirked and then, unable to keep it in, let out a belly laugh. 'It *is* quite funny really,' he said, and Ruby knew she was on her own with this one.

'Well . . . don't wait up for me, I might be late.' He stopped suddenly, looked sorrowful and shook his head. 'I do think it's time you realised this job isn't for you, and to be frank, I don't really need all this crap. We'll discuss it when I get back, yeah?'

Ruby nodded, wanting him as far away as possible so she could try to think clearly. 'Goodbye, Richie.' She hoped he didn't come back, just to save having a showdown. It was all over as far as she was concerned.

Once he had gone, with a slamming of doors and a promise to call her later — by which, she assumed, he wanted to see if it was safe to come back — she sat dully over a cup of too-milky tea and a warming dry white wine. She hugged herself, one arm wrapped around the other, and tried to stop rocking. It was strangely comforting, though, and she didn't see a reason to stop. One leg twisted around the other, she rocked towards the electric fire that she'd cranked up for comfort as she alternatively swigged from her too-cold tea and her too-warm wine.

How long she sat there would forever remain a mystery, but she finally rallied when her phone rang and a leap of fear hit her in the chest. She glanced down, fully intending to ignore it, but there was no caller ID and she panicked that it might be the police. Or would that come up as 999? The thought set her smiling, if weakly, pretty sure that wasn't the case. Her stomach hollowed out and she felt instantaneously sick, but she did answer it, fearing the worst.

'I'm coming over. I need to see that you're okay. You might be in shock. How are your pupils? Are you shaking — shivering? What colour are your lips?' Milo's voice was like a gift from the gods and she could have cried with relief.

'Yes to the shaking, and I haven't looked in a mirror but I don't feel great. I'm surprised how long it's lasted.' Her voice did indeed sound shaky and her legs weren't yet back to being the sturdy pins they usually were.

'I'm on my way,' Milo said simply, and she knew that he was the only person in the world who could help her right then.

Lucy phoned then, having just heard the news, and although she was reassuring, she knew no more than Ruby did about whether she would be sacked. She promised to call later and Ruby ended the call to tidy herself up a bit as she waited for Milo.

A few minutes later, he rapped on the door and when she answered it he instantly took her in his arms and peered at her face. 'Your lips are too white but your pupils are okay.'

'Thank you, Dr Fraser.'

'I'm serious, I've seen shock before. I know what I'm talking about.'

Ruby wondered if there was anything he didn't know about as she relaxed into his arms. For a second she knew what it was like to feel safe and treasured, but he quickly let her go and led her into the kitchen. 'Have you had a hot drink with sugar?'

'I'm okay, Milo, really I am.'

He gazed at her intently again and seemed to come to a decision. 'You're here on your own?' It was a question and a statement and she was glad that she could truthfully say she was.

'Pack a bag, then, you're coming with me.'

'Where to?'

'The farm. A few days in the countryside will do you the world of good. You can finally meet the donkeys.'

With those words, Ruby perked up considerably and, just for a moment, all thoughts of being sacked flew from her mind. 'I'd love to,' she said. 'I can't wait to meet Carrot.' And although that was true, her heart was singing more at the thought of spending time with Milo. What was even better was that Milo clearly cared, or was he just being kind? Right then, it didn't matter. She was getting away from it all to exist in blissful oblivion for a few days, before it all came crashing down on her.

'Don't forget to bring your camera. We can have a play around with some photos while you're there,' Milo added as Ruby rushed to pack a bag.

For a split second, she thought guiltily of Richie, who wouldn't know where she was, and then the haste in which he legged it out of the door pulled her up short. He couldn't wait to get away from her in case her misdemeanours tainted him. It was a punch in the gut to realise he didn't give a toss about their relationship and she wondered what kind of madness had kept her shackled to him for so long.

She and Milo were both quiet on the journey to his farm and she was grateful that he didn't expect a blow-by-blow account of what had happened. He'd probably heard most of it anyway, and hopefully it wasn't too damaging to her, although she had to admit that whatever the spin, the story wouldn't cast her in a favourable light. Even if she told him that Cara had put on the ovens without her say-so, it wouldn't change a thing. She wouldn't, of course — it wasn't fair. No, it was all on her and her burnt red shoes, now Exhibit A in the case against her, and she had to accept that.

Surprisingly, she dozed on the journey down, probably all the spent adrenaline wearing her out. She awoke as the car slowed and Milo patted her thigh. She groaned as the blissful sleep ended and her imminent predicament kicked her in the head again.

'You'll be okay, honestly you will.' Milo's voice instantly soothed her as she remembered that she was with him and that made everything fine.

'What doesn't kill you makes you stronger?' she said, pushing herself upright.

'Something like that.'

Ruby put her own hand on top of Milo's without a hint of flirtatiousness. 'You have no idea how grateful I am for this. If I wasn't here with you I'd be sitting on my little sofa chewing my nails and waiting for the letter of doom — or even worse, a phone call.' She paused reflectively, gazing at the verdant fields full of picture-perfect black-and-white cows looking nonchalant. 'Do you think I might just get a telling-off?'

Milo took his hand away to steer the car around a corner, shaking his head the teeniest amount, as if thinking it over himself. A deep breath and then nothing. His silence said it all really.

'Of course not, what am I thinking?'

'I honestly don't think they'll want to sack you but I don't think they'll have a choice. The shareholders will be baying for blood. It costs a lot just to repack a slide, for starters, and if they were damaged . . .' He shrugged. He didn't need to finish the sentence.

Ruby's eyes widened. 'Don't even go there.' She shook her head vehemently. 'I'm sure they weren't damaged.' But she wasn't sure. She'd never been less sure about anything in her life. 'And the ovens will be a burned mess,' she added. 'The whole aircraft will have to be checked.'

'Anyway, we're here now.' Milo's voice was overbright and she felt like a kid being jollied along on a school trip.

Ruby didn't move. She was suddenly filled with the urge to go back and face the music. 'I need to go home, to know what's going to happen.'

'Ruby.' He turned off the engine, turning to face her. 'Listen, your career right now is no longer governed by anything that you choose to do. It is, in effect, out of your hands.'

The enormity of what she had done hit her again and she found herself breathing too deeply, panic hitting. She rubbed at her face and looked up briefly, trying to mask her fear.

Milo was out of the car in seconds and pulling open the passenger door. For a second she thought he was going to hug her, but he held out his hands, palms upwards and she took them gratefully. They held hands for a full minute just staring at each other, but to Ruby it seemed as if secret promises were passed between them, that he would be there for her, that he cared for her, that he would keep her safe. She clung on to him and felt warmth and courage pass from his hands to hers.

'Come on, Carrot is waiting. Have a therapeutic hug with a few of my animals and you'll be right as rain in no time.' He lifted out her overnight bag and swung it over his shoulder as he whistled a tune. A large, sandy-coloured dog came barrelling towards them, jumping around in excitement at the sight of Milo.

Milo reached out and ruffled the dog's fur, laughing as it barked and spun around in mad circles.

Slowly it calmed down and turned its head to look at Ruby, who took a step backwards. She was good with dogs but this one was a mighty big one, jowls flapping and hefty chest thrust forward.

'Hey, Loki, heel boy.' And just like that the dog sat docile and pretty, large paws together, head cocked on one side. Waiting.

Ruby nodded. 'I'm impressed.'

'Wait until you see me with the cows. You will *so* love me.'

I already do, Ruby thought pensively.

'I can make them lie down, really I can.' Milo went on striding ahead of her.

Ruby laughed, playing along. 'What an accolade,' she said. 'Cow tamer extraordinaire, Milo Fraser.'

'Just you wait and see.' Milo sounded like a little boy who couldn't wait to show off his talents and Ruby's heart, which was already well on the way to melting, liquefied completely.

'Come and have a quiet cuppa and then we'll have a catch-up,' he said, heading towards a large thatched cottage with pale-pink exterior walls.

Ruby didn't need telling twice; a cup of tea was just what she needed, although she wasn't so sure about the catch-up. She quite liked living in suspended animation, pretending all was well in the world.

She found herself being seated in a homely kitchen, a huge range cooker dominating most of it, along with a battered wooden table and chunky rattan chairs that looked as if they'd been chewed and clawed at by an assortment of animals for many, many years.

Milo deposited her bag in the narrow tiled hallway and pulled out a loaf of fresh granary bread from the larder, sliced and toasted it as he waited for the tea to brew in a brown, chipped teapot.

Ruby, barely paying attention, gazed out of the window at the blue sky and green grass, trees dotted around, mulchy leaves thick on the ground beneath. Cows roamed indiscriminately in the distance, an occasional bellow adding to the bucolic atmosphere. 'It's like a stage set here, it's all so perfect,' Ruby said.

'That's Daisy,' Milo said, pointing to a large black-and-white cow that was contentedly chewing away at the grass.

Ruby laughed. 'Daisy as in the *star* Daisy, who had a photo shoot with Jerry?'

'That's the one. Why, did you think it was a woman?' Milo was all eyes, as if surprised, but he clearly knew.

He chuckled as he piled buttered toast on to a large plate and plonked a jar of jam next to it.

'Yes, I did think Daisy was *another* girlfriend, as you well know.'

'I like the people at Celestial to think I'm spoken for.' Then he winked and added cryptically, 'A bit of healthy competition never goes amiss, either.'

Ruby wondered if he was referring to her, but said nothing, just dolloped strawberry jam on to her toast. She took a bite and immediately focused: it was the most delicious toast and jam she'd ever tasted. 'This is so good,' she said, and for a moment as she ate, all was well in the world.

Milo gave her a minute before saying, 'So, do you want to talk about what happened?'

'I think you probably know — it doesn't take long for the jungle drums to pass on bad news.'

'Okay, I won't pretend I haven't heard a version of the incident. You put your shoes in the oven and forgot about them? Right?'

Ruby sighed as she debated telling Milo that she had turned the oven off, and her fellow crew member had whacked it up to put the breakfasts in after take-off. It didn't redeem her, but maybe made the whole thing slightly less incriminating. She so badly wanted Milo to think well of her. 'Actually, I turned the oven off and another crew member turned it up. Doesn't excuse the fact that I put the shoes in there in the first place, I know that.'

Milo thought for a moment. 'But it does give it a better slant. Does Fiona know about this?'

'No, and I can't tell her 'cos it sounds like I'm trying to shift the blame, and at the end of it all, it's still my fault.'

'True.' Milo shrugged. 'So, what's your plan of action?'

She bit her lip as she thought. 'I'm thinking of stealing a new pair of shoes from the uniform stores and pretending that the ones in the oven didn't belong to me. What do you think? Would it work?'

Milo's smile was half-hearted to say the least. 'It'll all be okay,' he said unconvincingly.

'Well, it won't, will it? Sadly, my own stupidity has made me lose the only job I ever wanted. I'll never get a job at another airline either, when I tell them I was sacked for whatever crime cooking shoes in an aeroplane oven amounts to.' She laughed ruefully and Milo put his hand over hers again and squeezed. Clearly he didn't have a magic formula to make it all okay, but she appreciated the sentiment.

'What does your boyfriend say about it?'

This time her laugh wasn't so rueful. 'He legged it the minute I told him, didn't want the taint of trouble touching him.'

'That's a surprise. He seemed such a treasure when I met him,' Milo said deadpan.

Ruby burst out laughing. 'It's all over, bar the shouting. The annoying thing is, I've been wanting to end it for ages now. If only I'd known all I had to do was set fire to an aeroplane to find out what an unsupportive coward he was. Easy-peasy.' Her laugh was hollow. 'Thing is, he did leave and I was happier without him — but then he came back and I didn't know how to make him go away again. Sounds silly, but he was my life until I started flying and saw a better world out there. It's hard to let go of a dream. But my dream with Richie has well and truly turned into a nightmare. Time for it to end.'

Her laughter quickly turned to suppressed sniffles as it hit her all over again that she'd lost *everything*. She'd have to get a dead-end job immediately just to buy fuel for her moped, let alone find the rent for the apartment. She breathed in deeply as panic threatened to overwhelm her.

The door opened and a man who could have been Milo's double but with a more weathered face smiled at Milo and then glanced at Ruby, still smiling. 'You're back, then, with your precious cargo.'

Milo looked slightly abashed at his words. He ran a hand around his neck. 'Yeah, back safe and sound.'

Ruby's eyes widened. 'Don't tell me you were already here? You drove all the way to Plymouth to pick me up?'

'It's nothing. I'm used to driving hundreds of miles. Don't forget our parents live in Scotland.'

The man took a few steps forward. 'I'm Gabriel,' he said to Ruby, holding out a hand.

Ruby took his hand, still amazed that Milo had taken time out just to pick her up. 'Pleased to meet you, Gabriel.'

'And before you ask, he looked like an angel when he was born — no particular country of conception,' Milo said.

Gabriel smiled at that and nodded. 'You've had the Venus de Milo conversation, then.'

'Several times,' Ruby agreed, warming to this man.

'Hey, if you can put up with that, you're welcome here. What's ours is yours.' He waved an expansive hand and turned towards the dog. 'Come on, Loki, time for your walk.' On seeing the leather lead picked off a hook, the dog once again started spinning in circles and disappeared out of the door the second it was opened. 'See you later,' Gabriel said with a small salute.

'Bye, bro. We'll probably go out for dinner, so tell Maddie not to worry about food for us.'

'Will do,' Gabriel said as he shut the door behind him.

'That was my brother,' Milo said unnecessarily.

'I'd never have guessed,' Ruby said, amused.

There was a moment where they both seemed to flounder for conversation but Milo looked out of the window and said, 'Come on, get your camera and let's go on a photo shoot before it gets dark.'

Ruby leaped up. 'Can't wait to meet Carrot.' Taking a last bite of the delicious toast, which was crunchy on the outside and just the right amount of softness on the inside, she metaphorically dusted herself down. 'Okay, change of career coming up.' She put on a practised smile, the one she used when greeting passengers at five in the morning, when really she wanted to be in bed dreaming.

'Yes, let's do this *thang*,' Milo said in another one of his strange accents that she couldn't pin down. Clearly, she hadn't watched as many films as he had.

She nodded. 'This is the last thing I imagined I would be doing after setting an aeroplane on fire, but hey-ho.' She rooted out her camera from her backpack and they went out into the weak sunshine and the fading blue sky. She walked through the soft green grass to greet the indifferent cows and the roaming donkeys, all with permanent smiles on their faces. 'They look like they're laughing,' Ruby said.

'Probably are. At us, and how ridiculous we are for giving them everything, when they give us nothing in return.'

'Donkeys make me feel all warm and fuzzy, so that's something worth having.'

'True,' Milo agreed. 'I guess that's why they'll be forever in our hearts.'

The donkeys were, as expected, mostly tame and very pretty, presenting themselves in an array of muted colours of browns and greys, and as Milo offered carrots and apples, more came strolling down as if they had all the time in the world, which, to be honest, they probably had. Ruby looked around for something brightly coloured and interesting to use as a backdrop, finding a silvery-leaved lavender bush and a green, if slightly rusting, wheelbarrow that she wheeled in front of it.

She snapped away at the cows and obliging donkeys, who happily stood in front of a tree or scratched their backs on a post. Spotting a rugged and handsome farmhand wearing a checked shirt and green wellingtons, Ruby couldn't resist calling him over, and he happily posed by a tree looking laidback and chewing on a piece of straw. She took photos of Milo, and a lad who came to milk the cows, both posed in various positions, along with the donkeys. Carrot was a real character and seemed determined to snaffle the lion's share of treats.

Before too long she had forgotten her woes as Milo and she chatted about the sanctuary down the road and the farm, and that great British standby, the weather. She kept her mind resolutely away from Celestial Air and Richie. If she could make both of them vanish in one fell swoop it would be all the better, and if Milo was with her, then all was well.

'Fun facts about donkeys,' Milo said, interrupting her thoughts. 'Donkeys can see all four of their feet at the same time and can graze for sixteen hours a day.' Ruby was suitably impressed and scribbled all the info down, promising to take it all back to Jerry at the *Devon Chronicle* to see if they would use it as a promotion page — for free, of course. 'You've done a brilliant job at taking my mind off work, so thank you for that and for everything. I really don't know what I would have done otherwise.'

'Stop repeating yourself, Ruby. I wouldn't have done it for everyone. I've put your bags in the annexe, you'll be okay there. No one will bother you — unless you want to be bothered, of course,' Milo said, his hands in his pockets, shrugging a bit.

Ruby wanted to be bothered — of course she did. She didn't want to be alone with her thoughts for one second, because none of her thoughts were any good. 'I would love a bath and a freshen up, but as to being alone, no thanks — unless you're busy, of course. I don't want to be any bother. You've already done enough for me.'

Milo bowed slightly. 'Then we will have a glass of wine when you're ready and talk about either a plan of action or the weather and the cows, depending on you.'

Ruby smiled weakly. 'I don't think I'm ready for a plan of action yet.' She sighed heavily. 'Or maybe I am, I don't really know.'

Milo stopped next to a cute annexe behind a line of straggly raspberry bushes. It had a red painted door and two pots of lavender either side of it. 'Here we are. No rush to decide anything. Have a bath and enjoy the silence.'

'Thank you.' She put her hands together in a praying motion. 'I really am so grateful for this.'

Milo looked slightly befuddled. 'It's lovely to see you, even though the circumstances aren't the best.'

* * *

The night was drawing in, stars as clear as crystals among the vast unending sky. It made Ruby pensive; she had never seen a sky so clear. Complete silence cocooned them for a full minute before the hooting of an owl and the distant braying of a donkey disturbed it. If she listened very hard, she could hear animals scuffling in the fields — foxes, maybe badgers, of which there were many and a plague on the land, according to Milo.

She had cried off going out for dinner at the local pub, drooping where she stood, bone-tired with a weariness born of anxiety and too much spent adrenaline. So Milo made scrambled eggs on toast with slices of thick, salty bacon and she wolfed it down like a starving animal.

They were now sitting on plastic chairs on the hard standing that doubled up as a terrace. A half-drunk bottle of Merlot stood between them on a rickety iron table, a fat moth fluttering listlessly around the storm lamp that Milo had found in the barn.

Ruby batted the moth away as she sipped her wine and stared up at . . . nothing. A vast swathe of deep navy *nothingness* that was as beautiful as anything she'd ever seen — no more than the tops of trees and a sky that she would happily drown in keeping her company. To float away on the wisps of cloud that crossed over the moon and empty her head of bad thoughts would be bliss. Or to fill her head with the sounds of swallows and bats and lowing cows; she would be forever content.

'This is a million miles away from the bother of flying. I can't believe you give your time to Celestial when you don't have to.'

'It keeps me grounded. Farming is very insular — at least, this far down the country it is — and you can become very bogged down with it. Everyone needs more, not less of life.'

'That's a pretty good mantra actually. Must remember that. Hang on, you didn't see that online did you?'

'What?'

'Just checking. Richie, my *ex-boyfriend*—' she enunciated the word carefully — 'was fond of "inspirational quotes" that mostly came off the internet. He was always trying to *better* me.' She quite enjoyed calling Richie her ex and thought she might try it out a bit more often — convincing herself that it was true.

'How can you better perfection?'

Ruby almost guffawed at that. 'Yeah. No need to be sarcastic, I know myself well enough, thank you.'

'I don't understand.' Milo sounded genuinely puzzled by her words.

'The hair, the pale skin marred by a face full of freckles, the dumpy legs. I could go on.'

Milo sighed. 'You forgot the horns. Have they started growing yet?'

She touched the top of her head. 'Hmm, maybe I've got away with that one, but give it time.'

'Ruby, you have serious self-esteem issues, you know. You are beautiful, and I mean properly beautiful. You have smoky eyes, gorgeous hair that I long to touch, and a smile that makes me want to kiss you — all of the time.'

Ruby, shocked to the core, took a second to process what he had just said. Had he really said he wanted to kiss her? But she was so unused to compliments that she deflected it, put it out of her mind instantly. 'And you have serious vision problems. Are you wearing your drinking goggles?' She laughed as she peered into his face.

'No, and I don't think your boyfriend is good for you. There, I've said it.'

She laughed again. 'Funnily enough, I don't think he is either, and he's now an ex-boyfriend.'

'Haven't you been down this route before, though? Said you were done with each other but ended up back together?'

Ruby stared again. He was right, not that she relished admitting it. Why was he so interested in Richie, anyway? She wished she hadn't sullied the conversation with his name; he was the last person she wanted to think about. 'Let's not talk about Richie.'

'Has he phoned you, texted you to see how you are?' Milo pressed.

She shook her head. She hadn't expected him to contact her anyway. 'I'm done with him, trust me.' She paused. 'When do you think I'll hear from Celestial?' She was back on the ground with a bump. She wished she hadn't mentioned Richie or Celestial, she wanted to continue living in her navy sky listening to the night animals — and maybe hearing some more sweet words about how Milo thought she was beautiful, although she was almost certain she had been hallucinating a few minutes earlier.

'Give it until the morning. They will have caught up with themselves by then.' Milo nodded grimly.

Meaning that they would have had time to decide her fate. Ruby's stomach flipped once again. She didn't think she could bear the wait, but just like after her interview, wait she would do. It hadn't taken her long to ruin everything she had with Celestial, so maybe Richie was right, maybe Richie was who she deserved. Or maybe this was her chance to start again and see if there was something better out there.

'I can see your thought processes, you know.' Milo squinted slightly, a lopsided grin on his face.

Ruby smiled. 'Can you, now? So, you can see that I'm thinking we should at least have a goodnight kiss before you send me off to bed? A final kiss before the execution.'

'You have an imagination, all right, Ruby Hansen.' Milo leaned over her, making the rickety table rock precariously, their wine glasses sliding a good two inches.

Milo kissed her slowly, gently and sensationally. Ruby's toes curled where she was sitting and a heat she hadn't known could exist fired up her body in seconds.

'Okay, I think I would fight the execution, if there was more where that came from.'

She leaned in for another kiss, thinking that the annoying table should be removed immediately — and possibly their clothes. But Milo straightened and did something weird with the table, stopping it from sliding and making sure it was still between Ruby and himself.

Ruby half-heartedly tried to shove the table away but she knew something was brewing. Sure enough, the next words Milo uttered were, 'I think I need to take you back to Plymouth in the morning, don't you? I imagine Celestial will want to see you — they can't just text you. Whatever happens, it will need to be official.'

And that was . . . what was that? Surely not all she was getting that night? Not that he was expecting a night of passion, but surely something more than one kiss? And why did he want to take her back when he had just driven two hours each way to collect her? Her weary mind gave up the circles it was treading, around and around, and she docilely agreed. Milo took her hand, briefly giving it a squeeze before letting it go. She thought she detected sorrow in his eyes and it troubled her, but she was too weary to analyse anything else in this turbulent day of hers and gratefully climbed into her solitary bed, listened to an owl hooting, and fell wearily asleep.

* * *

The next morning she woke up, still clinging on to her phone as she slowly surfaced. Unfamiliar noises outside her window reminded her that she wasn't in her little corner of Devon, where the bins, emptied nearly every day because of the tourists, woke her up at the crack of sparrows. For a second, euphoria hit her. Milo had kissed her. She lay back on her pillow, luxuriating in being in a large bed all on her own, thinking through the night before. For a brief moment she'd wondered if she would be sharing her bed with Milo before too long, but that was just a dream — for now, anyway. She pushed herself upright to check her phone for missed calls or emails.

At that moment Lucy phoned, and she answered it with trepidation and a tiny amount of hope. Lucy confirmed that Fiona wasn't angry and was fencing questions from the newspapers, but had gone a bit quiet when she'd asked if the aircraft was back in action. When pressed, Lucy explained that someone official was coming from London to check over the damage, but they couldn't make it until after the weekend.

'Great, five days out of action at least. That will be added to my list of crimes, no doubt.'

'Well, look at it this way, you won't be called out of standby 'cos half the flights have been cancelled.'

'You think that's funny, do you?' Ruby said, a catch in her voice even though she knew Lucy was trying to jolly her along.

'Not funny, but we need to give the situation a title, don't we? So far I have *The Scorching of the Shoes* and *The Awful*

Arsonising of the Aeroplane, which is a bit of a tongue-twister and I think maybe I've made up the word *arsonising*. Either way, it'll go down in the history of Celestial Air.' There was a pause, during which Ruby suspected they were both thinking a little more about that. 'I don't suppose you'll be putting it on Instagram?'

'It would get a few hundred likes no doubt, but I'm not sure that's the look I'm aiming for, pair of charcoaled shoes and an aeroplane covered in foam.'

'I just thought I'd mention it as one of the crew is posting photos of exactly that.'

Ruby groaned. 'Oh God, one of the newspapers is bound to pick it up. Just my luck. That's the trouble with mobile phones, there's always someone ready and waiting to capture the moment. Nothing I can do about it anyway.' Her voice petered out; she was having trouble stopping her throat from closing with emotion.

'*Arsoning* maybe, rather than *arsonising*?' Lucy continued, regarding the naming of the latest drama.

Ruby couldn't be bothered. It used to be fun naming them but this one was way too serious, and too final. 'Thanks for trying,' Ruby said.

'You are smiling, aren't you?' Lucy sounded as if she was just picking up that Ruby was lacking in humour.

Ruby promised that, yes, it had brought a smile to her face.

'Lucy, have you chatted to anyone about mine and Richie's relationship?'

'Richie being a complete shit, you mean?'

'Well, yes, I suppose.'

Lucy thought a moment. 'Erm, Matthew Roberts was asking about you a while ago. I thought it was a bit odd — maybe he fancied you. Why?'

'Just something Milo said.'

'Oh, maybe Milo has dumped the beautiful Loretta and you're next on his list.' Lucy scoffed as if hell would freeze over when that happened.

Ruby froze at the mention of Loretta. How many times did she have to make a fool of herself before she got it through her thick skull that Milo was simply a kind man? Had he kissed her or did she kiss him? Either way, she had once again turned it into something it wasn't. What was a little kiss between colleagues? But she wasn't fooling herself. Colleagues didn't go around kissing each other, did they? What was the matter with her? Milo had come to her rescue in her time of need. Simple. And for that she was grateful.

She ended her call with Lucy and quickly showered and dressed. She walked outside and sat on a chair to resume staring at the view, closing her mind off to everything, apart from the blue sky and the green grass. The Devonshire moors were such a beautiful part of the country and she wondered if she could camp out there for the rest of her life, like one of those weirdos you occasionally come across who made beds out of willow twigs and tents out of discarded carrier bags, all so that she would never have to stand trial for the *Awful Arsonising of the Aeroplane*. Which was all very well, idling in the countryside, watching the clouds pass by and counting the stars, but she had to go back and face the music at some stage. She didn't want to consider how soon that would be.

She idly wondered where Milo had gone, when there was a roaring noise and a throaty revving as a motorbike came to a stop in front of her. Milo took off his crash helmet and beamed at her.

'Good grief, you nearly gave me a heart attack.'

'Got a helmet for you,' he said and reached into the top box behind him. 'Hop on,' he said, holding it out to her. 'More fun than a horse.'

'Really? Where are we going?'

'Around the country roads, so much better than a car and a godsend in the warmer weather when all the grockles are out clogging up the roads.'

Ruby's eyes widened as she sized up the beast Milo sat astride.

'Show you how to do it. Remember me suggesting that you took some lessons?' His smile was cajoling as he continued to hold out the crash helmet.

'Well, I'm hardly likely to be riding one of these,' she said as she took in the beast, which roared at her like a dragon.

'No, but something with a bit more poke to it than your moped would do you fine if you pass your bike test.'

She wanted to refuse as she took it in, knowing that she wasn't the sort to go on a scary ride at a fairground, let alone climb willingly on to this machine. It had accident written all over it. But nevertheless, she took the helmet, pushed it over her head, fastened it tightly under her chin, and with some difficulty climbed on behind him. He twisted around, grinning, clearly enjoying himself. 'Hold on tight and when I angle the bike, lean *into* the road, not away from it.' He pulled down his visor and gave her a thumbs-up. She slid her arms around him and he opened up the throttle. They sped off and she pressed her head into his back, terrified at first. Her eyes shut tight and she found herself praying *Holy Mother of Jesus* over and over that they weren't going to end up as roadkill, squashed into the tarmac and awaiting the crows.

But after a mile or so — when she'd dared to open her eyes — she found it exhilarating as they flew past fields, trees and even cars. She trusted Milo, not that that stopped her prayers.

They finally arrived back at the farm and skidded to a halt with a rattle of pebbles. Milo insisted that Ruby try out the bike on her own. It was too big for her, but she managed to pootle up and down the driveway without falling off or crashing into anything. It was amazing, she had to agree, even though her feet barely touched the ground and she hardly opened the throttle. She was smitten. Her euphoria was short-lived though as Milo suggested, a bit too casually, that they returned to the airport shortly.

Ruby's stomach dropped. 'You know something, don't you? What is it?'

Milo's mouth twisted in something like anguish. 'I'm sorry, but I spoke to Fiona earlier and she suggested that you popped in. Don't despair, it might be good news.'

'Why were you on the phone to Fiona about me?' Ruby's eyes flashed with anger, wondering if her safe world was all a charade and Milo had planned all of this tea and comfort to get to the truth.

'It was just an innocent chat. She phoned about a different matter. Look, Fiona likes you, but liking and having to do one's duty are two separate things. Fiona and me are friends. Don't read anything into it.'

But Ruby was reading a lot into the 'innocent' conversation. 'What else did she say? You must know something.'

Milo sighed. 'Why don't I take you there now?'

'You definitely know something, don't you?' But Milo didn't say a word, just went to find his brother to tell him that he was returning to the airport and would be back later.

Ruby felt betrayed. She had no rational reasoning for this, but nevertheless, the fact that Milo had been talking to Fiona, who was ultimately her boss, upset her. She couldn't help it. Silently she went to the annexe, stuffed her things into her backpack and went to find Milo's car. She stood by its side belligerently, waiting until he came out. 'I'm ready,' she said brusquely.

Milo looked bemused and slightly upset. 'Okay,' he said, just as tersely, as he opened the car door for her.

She threw her bag into the back seat and slammed the door before tugging open the passenger door and climbing in, feeling mutinous. She'd thought they were tight together and all along he was being Fiona's lackey. He might even have been sent to spy on her and report everything she'd told him; her safe haven was not so safe after all. She wanted to cry.

Ruby couldn't think of a single thing to say on the journey home, and Milo, frowning, concentrated on the road ahead. It wasn't until the city started to come alive around them that she spoke. They both gave up the pretence that everything would be okay.

'They might just suspend me for a few months. I could cope with that, couldn't I? I could get a job in Asda down the road from me — do anything for a while as long as I knew I would be returning to Celestial.'

Milo's frown deepened and his words were less than reassuring. 'Asda would be lucky to have your gentle smile cheering up the customers.'

Ruby nodded sourly as her stomach knotted. Pretty words were easy.

They were on the main road that led to the airport. In fact, they would be there in less than five minutes. Ruby prepared to thank Milo for his help as politely as she could. She was already regretting her outburst and feared she had left it too late to make amends.

Milo pulled up outside the airport looking grim.

Ruby quickly opened the car door. 'Thanks for everything, then,' she said, smiling tightly.

Milo put a hand out. 'Ruby. I'm here for you, you know that.'

'Thanks,' she said, her smile even more crooked as she struggled with threatening tears. She doubted he would be there for her. He would side with Celestial and his precious Fiona, she thought, even as she knew she was probably being unfair. 'Bye.'

'I'll wait for you — see what the outcome is. I'll have a coffee or something in the café.'

'Why do I think you already know the outcome?' Her mouth twisted with misery. 'I'll get a cab home — don't think I'll be in the mood for chatting. Thanks anyway.' And she walked, straight-backed and stiff-legged, into the airport building, praying she would not bump into any crew members she knew.

* * *

Merely fifteen minutes later Ruby exited the double doors where she had first met Milo and had the ridiculous conversation about his hands. She almost smiled at the memory but her facial muscles didn't seem to want to change expression from the grim downturned mouth and clenched jaw. She walked to the car park, head in the air, chin thrust out aggressively, remembering too late that her moped wasn't parked there as Milo had dropped her off. But anyway, Bananarama would never be parked there again because she no longer had a car park pass, because she no longer worked at Celestial Air.

Fiona, after delivering the news, had also asked, very kindly and sadly, for her ID. Ruby felt as if she were plucking her heart from her chest as she took it from around her neck and passed it to Fiona.

'Hey-ho,' she said to herself as she walked out of the car park, as if she'd done no more than miss the last bus home, but her heart was breaking into tiny pieces. Fiona had been so kind it made her want to weep, but still she'd explained that they couldn't possibly keep her on. Gross negligence, apparently. So, that's what setting a pair of shoes on fire in an aircraft oven meant. Fiona didn't need to embroider it. It was self-explanatory, if an unusual reason to be sacked. In fact, she might be the only case. Yay. That must be cause for celebration — she was finally original in something she did.

Ruby was quite sad that she had burned such gorgeous shoes, but grateful that Fiona, when requesting that she drop off her uniform at her earliest convenience, didn't mention having to pay for the ruined shoes.

Oh, and Fiona also knew that Cara had turned the oven back on before take-off, solidifying her belief that Milo had conveyed everything they had discussed to Fiona. 'Oh, Milo, why couldn't you have been on my side?' Tears seeped out of her eyes and she dashed them angrily away. She would not cry over Milo, she would not. He deserved as little regret as Richie. Peas in a pod, as it turned out, just one posher and more in tune with the world than the other — and a better kisser, but she would *not* go there.

She walked over to the bus stop and checked the timetable: a cab was a luxury she could no longer afford. Slumping on the graffiti-ridden stone seat, she waited, emptying her mind. One hour and one very bumpy ride later, she turned into her road and stopped, frankly amazed at the slime-coloured Porsche parked outside. What was Richie doing parking his stupid car in her space when it barely ever even moved from the barn? And what the hell was he even doing there? She thought she'd seen the last of him.

She put her key in the lock and let out a sigh that contained all the misery in the world and beyond. All of her hopes were gone and she was back to living in a rented flat that she couldn't afford. No car, no job and no beautiful red shoes, but apparently she still had a boyfriend, the one thing she could happily do without.

Richie appeared from the bathroom, hair tousled, skin pink, a towel around his waist, looking completely relaxed. 'You back, then?' He reached for a sweatshirt and pulled on jogging bottoms, all the time eyeballing her.

Ruby's mouth dried. She couldn't speak.

Glancing down at the coffee table, Richie swiped up his phone and thrust it into her line of vision. 'Care to tell me who these dudes are?'

For a second or two the life force drained out of her as she was confronted by her own Instagram page, showing images of Milo and the handsome farmhand. The farmhand looked lazily gorgeous, sleepy eyes half gazing at the camera, his thumb sexily hooked over his waistband, posing like a million cowboys had done throughout time. Milo looked like a proper farmer, an olive-coloured gilet slung over a flannel shirt, jeans bagging at the knees, as he forked hay into a pile for Daisy and some other cows.

At the time of posting she hadn't given much thought to her audience, so wrapped up was she with Milo, but now she couldn't help a leap of pride as the likes and hearts continued to rise into the thousands. *So, handsome men still beat yellow mopeds and blue aeroplanes*, she thought with amusement.

Ritchie had completely faded from her periphery while she was at the farm where she felt free to do what she liked.

She took a minute to process the images, nodding in satisfaction until she looked up into Richie's angry red face. He swiped to another image presenting a grinning Milo holding a large carrot complete with bright green tufty fronds, like a colourful child's painting, his hand pressed down on the half-eaten straw hat on Carrot the donkey's head. Carrot looked for all the world like she was grinning at the camera, enjoying the moment.

'It's Carrot,' Ruby said, her voice softening at the memory. That might have been the exact moment she decided that she had fallen in love with Milo.

The statement seemed to throw Richie. 'I can see it's a bloody carrot.' He looked at her like she was more idiotic than the grinning donkey.

'No, the donkey is called Carrot,' Ruby said. 'She has to wear a hat 'cos her fur has rubbed away on her face and ears and she gets burned in the sunshine.'

Richie acknowledged this with a puzzled expression and a disdainful curl of his mouth. But when he spoke, his voice was calm, mild, almost defeated. 'And when did this happen?'

Ruby sighed wearily. She didn't need this — at all. It took her a heartbeat to realise she didn't have to answer him. 'Didn't you leave me, just the other day? Didn't you say you didn't need the crap I gave off, or something like that?' Suddenly she was sick to death of his puzzled expression tinged with menace, one eyebrow cocked as he waited for an explanation into her behaviour. All fear drained away and she felt like laughing hysterically as it hit her that Richie was no longer a problem. Something akin to courage had replaced her fear. She had no appetite for the argument he was trying to provoke, as if their relationship was worth the hassle, when it really wasn't.

She took a deep breath. 'Really, Richie? Are you still trying to do this? Fuck's sake, we are *sooo* done here. I can't even pretend that I care anymore.'

Richie's head seemed to retreat into his neck and he took a step backward. That in itself was an improvement, Ruby thought, as normally he took menacing steps towards her — and usually it worked.

The life seemed to drain out of him too, as he slumped and dropped the phone to the sofa. He ran both hands through his still-damp hair. 'I feel like I don't even know you anymore.'

'I'm not sure you ever did.'

He looked up at her, his face pained.

She sat carefully on the edge of the sofa and Richie threw himself on to the armchair, looking at her, his eyes sad.

'You know when you said "if you love someone, set them free"? Does the same apply if you don't love someone?' Ruby asked.

'Rubes?' He leaned forward on the chair.

'I don't love you, Richie.'

'Erm.' He scratched his head as if trying to understand. 'The Porsche is roadworthy, did you see it outside?' His eyes lit up briefly and Ruby was glad that something made him happy at least; she clearly didn't. 'We can take time off and go on a road trip, find ourselves again.'

'I think we've gone too far down the wrong road to find our way back.' She quite liked the road trip metaphor but didn't expect Richie to get it.

He rubbed his nose, looking uncomfortable. 'Can't you just apologise and we can start again?' He wasn't used to backing down and he had never apologised to her, it would be a step too far, but he was trying.

'What? I am so sick of apologising for things that are not my fault. I think it's time we moved on — separately.'

Richie's eyes narrowed. 'Don't think you're getting the Porsche.'

Ruby snorted. She couldn't help it. 'You what? Are you serious?' His mindset was so far removed from hers that she wondered how they had stayed together for so long.

'Well . . .' Richie folded his arms and looked as if he was settling into one of his inspirational internet quotes — *My car defines me, what defines you?* or some such rubbish — but she wasn't going to give him a chance.

'See, it's not the blokes on my Instagram page that are the issue, it's the reason that they're there.'

'Eh?'

Clearly subtlety was beyond him — and possibly beyond her own understanding too. She tried again. 'Would I be taking photos of random men if things were right between us?'

Richie pondered this for a moment, clearly wondering what on earth she'd been up to, but then he spoke. 'Thing is, Ruby, I don't want to leave you, or this flat, but if one of them is beyond my control, the other one isn't.'

It was her turn to go, 'Eh?'

He spelled it out for her. 'I'm not leaving this flat. If you want to go, you go. I'm staying.'

So, a bit more serious than an inspirational quote.

He sat back, looking smug. 'I'm not going to suffer because of your incompetence. If you want to stay, you leave your crummy shoestring airline and we start again.'

This was a shock. He didn't know that she had actually been sacked? Why would he, though? He must have massively underestimated the severity of what she'd done. She could possibly have burned a whole aeroplane full of people to death, but she certainly wasn't about to explain that to him.

She hadn't expected him to want to keep the flat on, but it was fine, there were plenty of people looking for flatmates and he wasn't going to trap her again. Okay, her dream of having their own little place had ended, but a new dream would take its place, one of freedom to do what she pleased, not having to evaluate the fallout from every action she took.

'I'll need a week or two to sort myself out,' she said.

'What do you mean?'

'I'll need to find somewhere to live and it will take a week or two.' She paused. 'I tell you what, I'll go to Mum's, she won't mind.'

'No, no, that's not what I'm telling you.' He jumped up out of his seat, so surprised was he at her words.

But that word *telling* fired up Ruby's anger again. 'Telling me? You don't *tell* me *anything* ever again!' She lifted her hand, almost jabbed a finger at him.

He looked visibly shocked and sidestepped her, as if he thought she was going to lunge at him. He quickly recovered, though. 'I'll *tell* you this.' His pained face turned into a smirk. 'A newspaper reporter came around earlier and I had a nice little chat with him about your little stunt at the airline. Sorted out a few photos for him to use.'

Ruby paled. 'You did what? What have you said? What did he want?' She tried to keep the panic from her voice but failed badly.

'Thought that would get your attention.' Richie was back in control. 'I gave him a few images. One of you wearing the pink crash helmet — you know, where it flattened your fringe to your forehead and made you look like an egghead? That went down well. And I told him that I knew you would fuck up at your precious airline, 'cos — well, it was so obvious you would. You'll never amount to anything, I've always said it, and look at you now.' He looked her up and down. 'Doing just fine, aren't you? Setting out on your own? I don't think so.'

Ruby's thoughts were still on the reporter who had come snooping. Her heart rate stilled a bit when she decided it was probably Jerry hoping to find her, but that hope was soon dashed when she asked what newspaper it was.

Richie was nonplussed at her fixation on the reporter when she should have been quaking in her boots. '*Devon Chronicle*, I think. Young lanky lad, with acne.'

Ruby sighed. It wasn't Jerry but hopefully the *lad* would write a positive article about her. It surely couldn't get any worse. Only if she stayed with Richie, she decided; if she stayed with Richie things would be a whole lot worse, of that she was sure. And the arguments for and against that used to rage in her head stilled. Conversation over. 'Well, don't mind me, I'll just gather a few things together and be out of your hair.'

Without another word she turned her back on Richie and her old life. Gathering up her trinket box and personal possessions she ensured she had her driving licence, passport and bank cards. She didn't want to have to come back again, although she knew it would be inevitable at some stage as she couldn't fit everything in her overnight case. She packed as much as she could and filled a large carrier bag, which she would stuff into her top box. Annoyingly, she realised that she would have to return for her uniform the next day; there was no way she could fit that on her moped as well and she didn't want to hand it back in a crumpled state.

She marched out, trepidation setting in now. It was all very final — and scary. Also, she was used to pootling around town on her moped and yet it was a good forty minutes to her mother's house over the Tamar Bridge, and she had never driven for that long. Still, steely core and all that. She smiled at the bittersweet memories of Milo, but he was history too. She was setting out on a brave new adventure — standing on her own two feet again.

CHAPTER TWENTY-THREE

The next morning, Ruby woke with a groggy head, having had two large glasses of red wine with her mother while she recounted her sorry tale from start to finish. Her mother had said she'd never felt positive about Richie, which was about the best she could have hoped for. Her mother commiserated with her over the airline job and said she would see what she could do to help her with a new job, but in the meantime she was welcome to stay rent free. At least her imminent worries were out of the way.

Ruby had a lot on that day. She needed to go back to the flat then return her uniform, but before she did that she booked a motorcycle lesson, deciding that a bigger beast to get to work — wherever that was — would be a necessity; there was no way she could afford a car in the foreseeable future.

Milo phoned around lunchtime but she didn't take the call, couldn't face talking to him, knowing she'd been sacked. He hadn't snapped her up to be his new girlfriend, the airline had written her off and Richie had moved into her flat. She was sad that she never met Milo's Viking cows, though. She'd have loved to have petted them and taken some photos.

No good reminiscing. Instead she wandered down to the local shop for some provisions. She loaded up with healthy food and ran her gaze idly across the front page of the *Devon Chronicle* as she paid.

In horror she stared at her own face, next to a picture of Celestial's aircraft on the tarmac covered in the crazy foam stuff that the fire brigade had doused it in. She grabbed a copy, thrust some coins at the shopkeeper and rushed out of the shop, half expecting accusing fingers to point at her as she fled. She slumped against a wall, her heart going ten to the dozen, and began to read.

'Burned to a Cinder' ran the headlines. She scoffed. Talk about misleading. Her shoes were burned to a cinder, not the aircraft, but no doubt it grabbed everyone's attention. Maybe the lanky, acne-ridden kid knew what he was doing after all. The photos were mortifying, though. The junior reporter had got hold of the photo that Jerry took, where she was thrusting out her boobs on her moped, looking like some kind of hooker. The other one was the unfortunate image of her pulling a weird face with a bright pink crash helmet pulled down over her head. Thanks, Richie.

This woman could have killed 120 people, the lead said. 'Oh fuck off, could I,' she said out loud, but actually it had been a possibility. It continued, *Crew from Celestial Air — whose motto is 'We show that we care'* (a dreadful slogan Ruby herself had made up on the spur of the moment and put on their Instagram feed) — *carried out an immediate emergency landing yesterday to ensure that a disaster was averted due to the recklessness of one crew member.* Clearly it was the one with a pink crash helmet who looked like a space-age Neanderthal pictured next to the aircraft covered with crazy foam flame retardant. It didn't need the big red arrow pointing to her face. She gawked at one of the worst photos she had *ever* seen of herself.

Ruby retrieved her purse and flicked through her cards until she found the one she was looking for: *Jerry Millet, senior editor.* He could redeem her reputation surely — or at least salvage the bits that were worth saving? She was a good person, she had loved her job and her passengers, was that not worth something? She had set up Instagram and Twitter for

Celestial and had tried *so* hard to make it work and it was just beginning to take off. She smiled at the pun. Maybe that would have been a better slogan. She considered, for a nanosecond, running it by Fiona — *Celestial Air, taking off near you* — before she pulled up short and remembered that she no longer worked for them.

She dialled the number. 'Jerry, it's Ruby Hansen, I don't know if you remember me?'

He cut across her. 'Ruby, I've been trying to contact you. Are you okay?'

She laughed. 'Yes, and I'm glad someone cares I'm alive. I'm just reading that article by one of your lads. It doesn't show me in the best light, does it? I look alternatively like a tart thrusting my boobs out on my moped and an ugly alien with a pink egg for a head.'

It was Jerry's turn to laugh. 'I'm so sorry, my boss asked the lad to write an article — didn't know that I'd met you, and I guess he thought the editor wanted a hit job. Currently we're interviewing John, he'll be in the paper tomorrow. Sorry to say, it's turning into a pretty big scene. Nothing much happens around here, so the boss is keen to make the most of it.'

Ruby sighed. Her chances of it all dying down were negligible to nil, then. 'Who's John when he's at home, and why are you interviewing him?' Ruby couldn't think of any crew member named John. There were three Jasons, one of them being the coward who escaped first off the aircraft and then said he was helping the people at the bottom of the slide, and the other two had been nowhere near the aircraft that day.

'The fireman, you remember? John, the trainer? He's retiring at the end of the month and had never put an actual aircraft fire out until three days ago. It was his life's dream to actually put out an aircraft fire.'

Ruby laughed out loud at that. 'Ahh, that John.' She paused. 'You are joking, he never put out an aircraft fire? Is that why you're interviewing him? I've actually helped someone to fulfil their dream by setting my shoes on fire?'

'Yep, looks that way.'

'Well, there you go then, every cloud and all that. Good one, John, hope you had a blast.' There was silence as Ruby hoped Jerry would offer to help redeem her reputation.

Luckily he said, 'Look, I can try and make things better. Email me your side of the story and I'll see what I can do.'

Ruby readily agreed, although she didn't think it would help, as her side of the story was just as damaging as the young journalist's story, but without the pink egghead and boob-thrusting photos. Smiling, she considered adding *The Titillating Tits* to her and Lucy's list of accolades, but she really didn't have the heart for it.

She wondered briefly about Milo, who hadn't phoned back since she'd ignored his call. He didn't know where her mother lived, so there would be no fetching up with a bunch of flowers and an apology — although she did think she probably owed him one, rather than the other way around. She would leave him to Loretta, she decided with a pang of heartache; some things were just not meant to be.

She dropped off her shopping and once again climbed on her moped, dreading the journey back to the apartment she used to call home, but she had to hand in her uniform and wanted to get it over with. She was dreading that part too, unsurprisingly: handing back the uniform she had been so proud to wear. She tried to picture the sense of exhilaration and freedom she might have, once she had severed all ties with her old life, but really, who was she fooling? She would miss Celestial Air desperately.

She was at least reassured that the mould-coloured Porsche wasn't outside the flat as she dismounted from her moped and ventured inside for what might be the last time. Taking a quick look around, she wasn't sure if she was gratified or sad to see dirty dishes piled up near the sink and a sad pile of dirty clothes on the floor by the washing machine. She sped up a bit, not wanting to push her luck and have to confront Richie coming through the front door.

She walked into the bedroom and gasped at the sight on the bed. Her pink silk nightdress, the one with the split up the side — the one Richie loved so much — was laid out, full length on her side of the bed. She put her hand to her mouth, stifling a scream, imagining for one second that it was a dead body. What was Richie trying to do, make her weak at the knees, or scare the very life out of her?

A red heart-shaped note placed by the cleavage read, *I miss you*. It was *so* not Richie that she wondered if he had actually pinched the idea off the internet. She certainly couldn't imagine what he expected from such a gesture. What it actually did was turn her stomach and piss her off. She'd always hated that nightdress, which she equated with sex — when Richie wanted it, rather than when a mutual desire kicked in.

Marching into the kitchen she pulled out the scissors and headed back to the bedroom. The anger that had been slowly burning the whole time she knew Richie was finally being released and it was cathartic. She picked up the flimsy silk and hacked at it, stabbing it with the scissors until the fabric gave way. Breathing heavily with exertion she cut it into as many pieces as she could, working like a woman possessed. Finally she stood back and surveyed her handiwork. It would do — at least it would let Richie know that they were well and truly over, and he might want to keep away from her in case she still had the scissors in her possession. She picked up the heart-shaped note, cut it in half and placed it on top of the ripped pieces of nightdress, which she'd straightened and laid on the pillow in a neat pile. Too much maybe? She shook her head. No, not enough really. But she would call it a day and chalk Richie down to one bad experience she didn't intend to repeat.

She rode to the airport, feeling calm and cleansed, and almost forgiving. Parking her moped by the bus stop she pulled out her precious uniform from the top box, stroking it as she shook the creases out and hung it upright by the gold Ted Baker coat hanger she'd always used to show that it was something special in her wardrobe. She would leave it on the hanger as she couldn't see it being needed ever again.

She faltered in her stride as she neared the airport building; maybe another day or two might help to summon the courage up. She couldn't bear to give her uniform back, couldn't bear to see Fiona again and couldn't bear to leave the Celestial building for the last time.

How could she do the walk of shame for everyone to see? Maybe she could post it instead, she thought, before rejecting the idea, as apart from it being completely unsuitable, it would cost her a fortune and she had no spare money.

She elected to go into the building with all of her bike gear on: boots, waterproof jacket and trousers, helmet and all. No one would dare challenge her. She walked wide-legged to stop the friction on her legs and suddenly felt like Darth Vader. It was a long walk.

'Ruby, is it you under all that armour?'

No, no, no, she thought, catching sight of Milo walking towards her, his gentle but perplexed eyes fixed on hers, bringing the memories flooding back. She wanted to pretend that she hadn't seen him, hadn't heard him. She pulled her visor down and tried to keep walking, pretending she really was Darth Vader. But he walked straight up to her, took hold of her shoulders and turned her to face him. 'Ruby, stop it. Whatever it is you're thinking, none of this is my fault.'

'This is not me, I've come to audition for the part of, err, monster for the burnt-out aircraft challenge.' She said it in a gruff monster-like voice and actually hoped Milo would believe her and walk away.

Instead, he burst out laughing. 'I've heard mewling kittens sound fiercer than that.'

She was quiet for a moment, knowing she was rumbled, before bursting out: 'You colluded with Fiona.' She wanted to stamp her foot with frustration.

'I did not. I've known her half of my life. We just had a chat. She told me you were coming in today and I've been hanging around all morning, waiting.' He let go of her shoulders and she considered making a dash for it, but the cartoon image she knew she'd make stopped her in her tracks: an egg-headed alien running stiffly on wide legs, gripping on to a Celestial Air uniform hanging off a gold hanger. Any vestige of credibility she had left would be gone, her image forever stamped on the retina of anyone who saw her trying to leg it.

She remained mutely where she was, visor still pulled down, regretting not trying harder to be a credible monster.

Milo sighed. 'If you must know, I tried to convince Fiona to find some way to keep you on, but the board would have none of it.'

'How hard did you try?' Her voice was muffled under the helmet but she liked it fine that way because it hid the tears sliding down her cheeks.

'You set fire to one of their aeroplanes, and unfortunately that's likely to cancel out any Instagram and Twitter likes. Your lovely personality goes a long way to evening out the odds, but even that wouldn't cut it.'

She glowered at him. 'Don't start that soft-soaping stuff again. I nearly fell for it once, not again.'

'Oh, Ruby.' He closed the gap between them. 'Will you lift that bloody visor up or take off the helmet, for God's sake?'

Mutinously, she did as she was told and her hair tumbled out.

'There she is, my *heilan' coo*.' He stroked her hair automatically, static making it stand on end, and gathered it together in his hands to tame it, twisting it into one long snake over her shoulder. He gazed at her as if he was drinking in all the water in a crystal-clear pool after a drought. He sighed and shook his head and without a word lowered his lips towards hers in a brief, chaste kiss. 'I'm still on your side, you know,' he whispered into her ear as he let her go, stray strands clinging to his shirt.

'Then maybe you can do me a favour.' She thrust her uniform at him. 'Give this to Fiona, will you, with my best regards?' And without another word she turned on her heel and headed back the way she came, waterproof leggings rustling with each step.

More determined than ever, Ruby rode back to her mother's house, indignation and righteous anger fuelling the way. If she'd run out of petrol she would swear the adrenaline coming off her body would have carried her back. But it all dissipated once she'd reached her destination and reality hit home; her loss washed over her again and again until she put her head in her hands and wept.

Not knowing what to do with herself, she filled a hot water bottle, climbed the stairs and changed into her pyjamas, the ones she bought for the life-saving day: pure linen, why had no one told her how cool and comfortable linen pyjamas were? She crawled into her bed, curled around the hot water bottle and closed her eyes, imagining she was cocooned in Milo's arms, shielded from all the wrongs in her life as he stroked her hair and told her everything would be fine.

She must have slept as she awoke with a start to her mother shaking her. 'Ruby, your airline is on the telly, come down.'

Bleary-eyed and slightly out of sorts, she staggered down the stairs. Rubbing her eyes, she plonked down on the battered sofa that was permanently covered in cat hairs.

Her mother indicated a cup of tea, flicking on the kettle, and Ruby nodded. 'Yes, please.' Minka, a Siamese-cross, snuck up to Ruby, purring her throaty bass note, sounding like a distant lawnmower, pawing at Ruby tentatively and padding down on her lap. Ruby stroked her absently as she was confronted by John the firefighter's animated face on the local news. He was giving everyone grief by the sounds of it, about why no one should put their shoes in a hot oven. Why was he labouring the point as if it was what people generally did? No normal person would ever do that — but Ruby had, and it silenced her inner criticism of him.

She cheered herself up by shouting insults at the television presenter, who was determined to paint her in a bad light, and watched in mortification when they mentioned the dreaded shoes, anticipating a picture of her pink egghead and goofy smile flashing up on the screen at any second.

She was shocked into silence though as the camera panned over to their other guest. Milo, resplendent in his pilot's uniform, sat opposite John on a squashy sofa sipping posh water that he poured from a green bottle. The little frown line between his eyes was going into overdrive as he listened, lips flattened, fingers white as he gripped the glass in his hand.

As soon as he came on to the screen, the ticker tape that flashed up showing the viewers' texts went into overdrive too. *Who's the fittie?* and *Cor, wouldn't mind him landing on me.* Ruby laughed even as she had the irrational urge to shout, *He's mine, back off!*

Her mother, too, seemed glued to the television. 'Do all your pilots look like him? I might be applying for a job soon.' She grinned.

'Good grief, Mother, that's Milo.'

'Oh.' Her mother sat down on the sofa. 'This is good news. I thought you said he was a farmer, and you'd been to his farm?' Her mother glanced briefly at Ruby before returning her focus to the screen.

'He's a pilot too.'

'Well . . .' was all her mother said, eyebrows raised.

For which Ruby was grateful because she wanted to hear what Milo was saying. He was defending her, saying that such a thing could have happened to anyone. Yeah, anyone who drove to work on a moped and was daft enough to put their shoes in an oven, Ruby thought. He went on to tell the story of how Ruby had saved someone's life in the swimming pool. She didn't know Milo knew about Abbey and the *Splendid Saving* but she loved that he told the world about it, just so she didn't look like a complete numpty. She drank him in: the tiny crease on the left side of his smile, the frown line when he concentrated, the way he ran his fingers through his hair when he was exasperated. She wanted to weep for what she had lost. Had he ever been hers, though? No, was the sad answer.

She leaned forward as if to reach out to him and inadvertently deposited Minka off her lap and on to the floor. Affronted, Minka meowed and showed her displeasure by sticking her tail in the air and flouncing off. Ruby didn't even notice, she was too engrossed in the conversation on the television.

Milo had moved on to the future of the airline and agreed that, yes, it was an unfortunate incident, but it was also a great opportunity to evaluate and discover. It proved the safety of Celestial Air would never be compromised and airlines all over the world should take what they could from the incident. It was, overall, a good thing.

Apart from one of the crew being sacked, Ruby thought, wryly.

She knew he was putting a spin on what happened, bigging up Ruby's better traits as an ambassador to Celestial, her good nature with the crew and expertise with handling passengers. *Blah, blah, blah,* she thought, wishing he would tell them all about how he loved her Viking hair and the dance of freckles across her nose. Probably best not to mention the horns, she thought, smiling against the odds.

'So, tomorrow we're hoping to hear Ruby's side of it — stay tuned to *West Side Stories*, bringing you all the local gossip in one fabulous show.'

'As if,' Ruby huffed out, just as her phone started buzzing. She picked it up, still in a Milo-filled world.

'Hi, it's Natalie here, from *West Side Stories*, local TV breakfast show. Heard of us?'

Ruby nearly dropped her phone. 'Yes, I was just watching your programme.'

'Great, so I don't need to explain myself. We're sending a car over tomorrow at nine thirty to bring you into the studio to hear your side of the story. This is going nationwide, you know, we're all very excited about it. More importantly for you, it's your chance to defend yourself, explain what happened.'

Ruby was too taken aback to think straight. 'How did you get my number?'

'Oh, a friend on the *Devon Chronicle* put me on to your story. Jerry, is it?'

'Brilliant,' Ruby said, heart sinking. She was sure he had her best interests at heart, but this was not the way she had hoped to redeem herself.

'You'll shine, I know it. Now, don't wear jazzy colours because it makes the screen dance — or anything black and white. Do your own make-up as we might not have time, but we'll touch it up if you look shiny.'

Shellshocked Ruby goggled at her mother, who was making frantic *who is it* motions, waving her hands around. Ruby pointed at the television and ended the call. 'They want me on the programme. Do you think it's to make fun of me, make me look like some kind of pyromaniac — with a shoe fetish?'

'Oh, love, I don't know, but you'll do well, I know it.'

Ruby groaned. Sometimes her mother's unswerving faith in her daughter was a little dispiriting. 'What have I agreed to?'

'You'll soon find out. Actually, why don't you call that nice young pilot and ask him what's going on?' Her mother winked at Ruby and, standing up, performed a little bottom wiggle on her way to the kitchen, grinning, before turning her attention to the kettle.

CHAPTER TWENTY-FOUR

There was one last thing to do before she went live on television. Her story would be out there before the day was done and she needed to let her Instagram family know the sun had prematurely set on her career. A little bit overdramatic maybe, but she had some wonderful sunset pictures she hadn't yet used and was not one to let an opportunity pass her by. She described what had happened with tears in her eyes, finally pressing *send* as she slumped in the back of the Mercedes ferrying her to the television studio. It felt a bit like she was being driven to her place of execution.

She had decided that she wouldn't ever fly again, didn't feel that she could and she wished she hadn't agreed to take part in the programme, but there'd been mention of Jerry, and Natalie on the other end of the phone had been so friendly, made her think that justice was a thing and the way forward was to appear on the breakfast show to make it happen.

The car crawled through the narrow streets and Ruby tried not to sweat with anxiety. She was clearly losing the battle, as she had to keep wiping her palms down her jeans. She didn't have the heart to wave like the Queen (God rest her soul) as she would normally have done in a posh car, didn't really have the inclination to take a snap or two of the luxurious interior, although she did it anyway — some prehensile actions are not worth fighting, but it was a lacklustre effort. She ran her hands over the soft, cream leather seats wondering if there was a hidden bar somewhere full of champagne. There was always a bar in the back of these chauffeur-driven cars on the television programmes, especially when the prom girls were let loose for the evening. Not that she wanted a drink: it was nine thirty in the morning, but it would have been nice to tell her friends that she'd had champagne on tap.

When she arrived she was almost immediately ushered into the studio before they went live, which Ruby decided was intentional, to stop her from running out of the door when she found out what was in store for her. Someone had obviously been digging the dirt, as they knew everything about her, knew that she rode to work, come rain or shine, on a yellow moped called Bananarama, and knew about the *boom* knickers, which turned out to be a great talking point for the phone-ins. Endless people called in with their ghastly or funny underwear stories, which Ruby found only mildly amusing. Surely everyone had a story about their dress being tucked into their knickers after coming out of the loo in a busy pub, or going swimming and forgetting to pack underwear? But the stories were relentless, and by the end of it Ruby half expected an advert to flash up to say where her *boom* knickers could be purchased. Surely there was a point to all these strangers rambling on about their undies — or lack of?

They didn't seem to be very interested in Ruby at all, although she briefly had a moment to explain that she actually loved Bananarama and was taking lessons with a view to buying a motorbike, and yes, it was true that she rescued one of her colleagues from drowning.

Natalie's *who gives a flying fuck* expression said it all.

So she sat, mute, trying to smile as everyone talked over her and around her. She felt like part of the furniture, and her only hope was that they had finished with her, or had forgotten why she was there. She didn't herself know why she was there; it wasn't as if she was going to plead for her job back. Been there, done that, and it was time to move on.

They asked her a few more desultory questions and then introduced to the audience an up-and-coming blue-haired comedian who she'd never heard of. She hoped the comedian, who she decided was trying to be louche and cool but only succeeded in being irritating, was the star of the show and that her time was over.

She got the distinct whiff of weed off his tee shirt, which stated *I'm not as weird as this one* — with an arrow pointing to the left, where Ruby sat. *Charming*, she thought, as he launched into a silly story that she couldn't even be bothered to follow. Belatedly, she realised that she wasn't there for a ten-minute chat followed by a handclap out of the studio, she was expected to sit through the whole hour of the show.

Her phone was buzzing frantically. It was Instagram, of that she was certain, and she was desperate to see her messages, but her phone was in her back pocket and no way was she brave enough to pull it out, even for a brief glance.

However, she was completely discombobulated when, still thinking about Instagram, the conversation unexpectedly turned back to Celestial Air and Ruby's part in their downfall, or otherwise. The comedian was looking at her belligerently as if she had stolen his thunder. The presenter, with shuffling notes, looked at Ruby sorrowfully as the background music stopped and the whole studio went completely silent.

What the hell? thought Ruby, half expecting a hooded executioner with a huge axe to appear, to a deathly drum roll.

'So, Ruby Hansen, how would you feel if we told you that just this minute, you'd had the offer of a job in a major airline? One that wears a uniform similar to Celestial's — maybe the one you'd always set your sights on?'

Ruby shuffled in her seat uncomfortably. What were they talking about? Surely not? She wasn't going to give them the satisfaction of looking excited only to be shot down. In flames. Watching them all guffaw at the hilarious prank. *Well, they were interested until they found out you set an aeroplane on fire.* Cue for laughter all around.

She stopped shuffling and began eyeing up the exit door.

The presenter went on. 'Or you might hope for your old job back? You might be interested to hear that we have been running a little poll as you were sitting here. Yesterday, one of your work colleagues, Milo Fraser, appeared on the programme, and according to him most people at Celestial Air love you. They love Milo more, and I can see why—' she grinned cheekily — 'but today is not about him.'

Keep your orange-tanned hands and hawkish hooded eyes off him, she thought indignantly. And only *most* people loved her? But then she remembered the Horrid Hostie Vanessa on the fateful Scottish night stop and she had to concur it was a strong possibility.

Her infernal Instagram was going like the clappers, vibrating ten to the dozen. It was probably a bad move to post her *au revoir* just before coming on live television. She tried to ignore it; she needed to concentrate on what the presenter was saying.

'The poll was a simple yes or no as to whether you should be reinstated, given the boost to the airline's fortunes, mostly caused by you setting fire to the aircraft.'

Ruby gritted her teeth. *If I hear that one more time . . .* she thought, as Natalie faced the camera, another fake smile on her face.

Ruby wanted to punch her.

The silence grew, and Ruby, convinced she was hyperventilating — she knew all the signs — began to take slow, measured breaths to stop it.

She didn't, not for one minute, think they were still waiting for a response from Celestial, they were just sensationalising the whole programme at Ruby's expense.

Right then, in front of half a dozen cameras and God knew how many people sitting in the audience, she decided that setting an aeroplane on fire was preferable to being on telly, but unless she stood up and swept out of the studio, which she was indeed tempted to do, she would have to sit through this farce of a programme and pretend to be excited about a stupid poll. She knew they wouldn't take her back and she wouldn't go anyway, even if they presented her with her own gold-plated aeroplane. Stuff Milo, and Fiona, and John, and Vanessa, and the whole bloody lot of them.

She was definitely over-breathing; she needed to calm down.

The ticker tape kept tickering, or whatever it was the stupid thing did: percentages shooting up in blue and down in red. Talk about trial by text message. Twitter had nothing on this cheerful daytime programme for bias. She saw movement to the left of the audience and to her horror Milo sat down in the front row.

'I think I saw a little sparkle in your eyes then, didn't I?' Natalie turned to the camera and winked. The camera lights slowly swivelled to Milo, lighting up his face. He looked pale and drawn and refused to smile even though the camera clearly zoomed in on his face.

'Can I go now?' Ruby asked in a loud voice. She stood up and then sat down again as Natalie continued to speak. Ruby thought she might puke. Was Milo part of the set-up too?

She glared at Milo and said, rather too aggressively, 'What are you doing here?'

Milo looked most uncomfortable even in all of his gorgeousness. His smile was weak and his hands fluttered ineffectually as he gazed around the studio, lights burning in his face.

She had been played again and had fallen for it all. It was just titillating television nonsense, and she wanted no part of it.

Ice cold lips pressed together, she said to him, 'I can't believe you've been duped into this, making a disaster into some kind of circus show.'

'I haven't, really I haven't. I've come to . . . to support you.'

Ruby narrowed her eyes, anger rising within her. It was a bit late for support: in her eyes he'd betrayed her when she needed him most.

Once again the studio stilled; you could have heard a pin drop. Ruby looked at Natalie and then at Milo, and then at the camera. 'I'm not up for discussion anymore, and I don't need supporting, thank you. Now, if you'll excuse me, I have some Instagram messages to answer.' She took out her phone, nodded to the comedian, good manners prevailing, and strode off the stage. She could hear thunderous applause as she left.

You got your pound of flesh, she thought, and the audience had clearly enjoyed the show. She exited through the back door to where the Mercedes was still waiting for her. The chauffeur jumped to attention but Ruby waved him away. 'Thank you, but I'd rather walk. I need to burn off—'

'Some steam?' He nodded. 'I've heard it all before, girl.'

Ruby stopped. 'I don't suppose you have any champagne in that car of yours?' she asked.

'Yes, ma'am,' he said. 'Give me one moment.' He disappeared into the depths of the back seat, his large bottom poking out as he rummaged and reappeared, producing two mini bottles of champagne, one in each hand.

'Which one?' he mocked, holding them behind his back.

She glared at him.

'Oh, both, okay.' He feigned surprise. 'Well, there you go. Can't say that's a first either.' He untwisted the metal cage on top of one, popped the cork and presented her with it. She was pleased to see it wasn't a screw cap and was therefore more likely to be very quaffable. She would have drunk it either way: desperate times called for desperate measures.

She grasped the stubby bottle as if it was a life raft. 'Cheers.' She raised the bottle in the air and he waited while she took a long swig.

'Enjoy.'

'I will.'

'You'll be fine,' he said as he climbed back into the Mercedes, saluting her briefly.

'Thank you.' She blew him a kiss; it wasn't his fault that she felt humiliated.

She set off briskly, not having the first clue how to get home. As she turned the corner she literally bumped into Milo.

'Ah, there you are,' he said as if she'd just returned from popping out for a pint of milk.

She glowered at him and took another long pull on the bottle.

'Oh, champagne, lovely.' He wrenched the other bottle from out of her unwilling hand, uncaged and popped the cork in one swift movement, like a pro, and took a long swallow. He actually smacked his lips while Ruby glared at him.

'Now we're on an even playing field.' He took another swig.

'Really?' She put her hand on her hip and tried to look fierce but actually she wanted to laugh, and the relief that he'd come to find her was meltingly marvellous. Never had she felt so alone sitting on that sofa, and now she had Milo again.

She looked at him, smart but incongruous in his uniform, his smile wavering, his eyes beseeching, and she admitted to herself that she wanted to be wherever he was. She loved Milo and anything else could go hang. Her dream wasn't to work for a huge airline, or any airline, ever again; her dream was to stay in Devon with Milo. And Daisy the cow and Carrot the donkey, seeing their beautiful eyelashes flutter as they accepted apples, with a flash of huge teeth. Maybe she could help bees grow honey, or whatever bees did in a beehive. And she could take pictures. She loved taking photographs. How much would she love doing that?

'You missed the best bit,' Milo said, starting to stroll along the road. She followed him and fell into step, both of them tipping back champagne into their mouths.

'Don't tell me, you slugged the patronising comedian a good one, and told Natalie that she was so orange she looked like an orangutan?'

He smiled. 'Close.' He waggled his head from side to side. 'Actually, not close at all, I'm far too polite.'

'Go on, then. I can see you're dying to tell me.' She shook her mini bottle as she peered down the neck of it and grimaced with sadness at its emptiness.

'Well, you weren't invited back to Celestial Air, but you had an offer from Kawasaki to be the cover girl for their women's bikes.'

That took her by surprise. 'Really? But I only have a moped. Wow.' She thought about it for a minute. 'Yes, that would be good, I could make something out of that.'

She didn't like the sound of flying out of Heathrow for the airline of her dreams anymore, but she did like the sound of a bigger bike. 'That would be cool,' she added, grinning as the idea took hold.

'They loved that you were determined to pass your test and get a motorbike. Everyone likes a woman with a bit of courage.'

'I thought everyone liked a loser — at least they did when I was sitting on that stage.'

'Oh, Ruby, everyone loves you. At least I do.' Milo widened his eyes as if he'd let the cat out of the bag.

'Oh.' Her own eyes grew wide and round. 'Okay,' she said, lost for words. 'Thank you for letting me know.' Then with a rush she asked, 'Do you really?' She was doubtful, thought it was all a bit one-sided. She loved him and he loved someone gorgeous, someone who was not her.

He turned her to face him. 'Yes, I definitely love you.'

'Wow.'

He peered into her eyes. 'This is the part where you say you love me too.'

'Oh Milo, yes.'

'Yes?'

'Yes, I really do love you. Wait, you don't have a camera pointed on me, do you — the last laugh?' She swivelled her head wildly.

'No, Ruby.' He sighed, but he was smiling.

'Well, then.' She smiled suddenly, buoyed up — a different person. 'Bit of a let-down that we've already had the champagne celebration, though.' She took the bottle from his hand and shook it, necking the last two gulps.

Milo took her hand. 'Would you like to come home with me?'

Ruby spluttered out the mouthful of champagne. 'Blimey, you don't waste any time.'

He laughed. 'You know I don't mean it like that.'

'Oh, that's a shame, 'cos if you're asking . . .'

'Oh, well then . . .' He ran his hand through his hair, confused. 'But I don't want to presume.'

'Relax, we're cool.' She laughed as he floundered.

They both stopped and took stock of each other. Ruby gravitated towards him and he took her in his arms and they kissed right there in the street. Truly and properly. A longed-for kiss that Ruby had dreamed of; it was finally here.

'I know somewhere that has champagne and we could continue the celebrations?'

'Where is this place?' she demanded.

Milo put his arm around her shoulder and steered her in the direction of his car. 'Come with me. I know a secluded farm where the navy sky is full of stars that twinkle at night and there's a donkey that talks to you . . .'

'Yeah, right.'

'No, he really does.'

Ruby laughed. 'Take me to this talking donkey.'

'Walk this way, ma'am.' He kept his arm steady around her shoulder and ushered her into his car, opening the passenger door and making sure she was settled in.

He walked around to the driver's seat and sat down heavily, deflating, as if all the air in his body had escaped. For a moment he held on to the steering wheel, staring out of the window. He exhaled loudly. 'I think we've done it, Ruby Hansen.'

'Done what?'

'Managed to wind up together without too much fall-out, apart from . . .'

She twisted towards him and held up her hand as a warning. 'Do *not* mention the burning aeroplane. I never want to hear about it again.'

'I was on about the parking ticket.' He gestured to the yellow plastic envelope stuck to his windscreen.

She smiled in relief. 'You were *so* going to mention the aeroplane incident.'

'Never again. It's all history and we, my love, have a future to discuss.' He patted her thigh and turned on the engine. 'Over champagne and bacon sarnies.'

It sounded like the best feast ever.

* * *

Ruby amazed herself by falling asleep on the journey down to the farm. It was as if a switch had been flicked, releasing her pent-up adrenaline and eliminating her fears. She finally had permission to relax.

She grasped Milo's hand and held it in her lap as she drifted off, which must have made for an interesting driving experience for Milo, but she was scared that if she let go she would wake up and find it was all a dream.

She awoke as Milo pulled up outside the farm. Blinking, she pushed herself upright and gazed around. The skies were as blue and as vast as she thought, the grass was fresh and green, and the trees waved at her in welcome. She fought back unexpected tears. Was the nightmare truly over? Could she finally move on?

But even as she gazed around in gratitude, she knew this could only be a temporary respite. She had no home and she had no job. She couldn't fly anymore, and she would always be remembered as Ruby who burned the shoes. She had brought to life the red shoes she'd longed to wear, only to burn them to a crisp. But she wouldn't beat herself up about it anymore. No one died, as her mother would say when Ruby moaned about something trivial. She now had a blank canvas and the opportunity to start afresh with Milo by her side.

'Wake up, sleepyhead, we're here.' Milo kissed the top of her head and shook her arm gently.

'I'm awake. Give me a moment.' She ran a hand through her hair, a foolish move if ever there was one, but she needed a minute to compose herself. She rummaged in her bag, found a small compact and checked her face; she would do.

Milo's brother, his wife and the dog — Loki, if she remembered correctly — were standing outside by the door waiting to greet them.

Milo clapped his brother on the back, gave his wife a hug and tussled with Loki. He turned to Ruby. 'You remember Gabriel, right? And this is Merry, his wife.'

'Hi, yes.' Ruby gave a shy wave, taking in the plump lady with twinkling eyes and a ready smile. Loki's tail wagged and he barked briefly, chomping at the bit to greet Ruby, but Merry had a firm hold on him and he finally sat down obediently, tail thumping the ground.

'Lovely to meet you,' Merry said, striding towards Ruby, inadvertently loosening her hold on Loki, who launched himself at their guest.

Pleased to be remembered by Loki, but not so pleased when he nearly knocked her off her feet, she pushed him away. 'Hey boy, down.' And he sat down. She grinned, proud of herself.

'Dog knows a good 'un, but I'm sure you promised us a buxom wench,' Gabriel said, folding his arms.

Ruby, hearing this, faltered in her stride. She carried on fondling Loki's ears but glanced warily at Milo.

'I suppose she'll do for now,' Gabriel continued. 'She might be stronger than she looks. She can be the cowgirl and the parlour maid.'

'What about the beehives?' Milo asked.

A look of confusion crossed Ruby's face. 'I do like bees,' she stammered, 'but I know nothing about them. I'm not sure I understand. Are you suggesting that I stay here, what? As a helper?'

She bit her lip. What was happening? Had Milo meant something completely different from what she'd thought? A job vacancy filled, not a lover?

'I've put her in the annexe,' Gabriel added. 'She'll be comfortable enough in there.'

She threw Milo a panicked look. 'Don't you want me to stay with you, Milo?'

'The annexe is cosy,' he said.

Ruby swallowed and felt her face going red. Milo immediately rushed over to her, folded her into his arms and whispered into her ear. 'I'm just saying that for my brother's benefit. He's winding you up.'

'I heard that.' His brother chortled.

'You poor girl. Gabriel is only messing with you,' Merry said, shaking her head at him. 'He thinks he's funny. I'll fetch your bag out of the car and you can freshen up.'

'I don't have a bag. I don't have anything.' Ruby tried not to sound sorry for herself, but she was so confused by the conversation and had no idea whether she was welcome or not. Tears spilled over her eyelashes. 'I'm sorry, I think I should leave.'

'Not happening. You need tea and cake. Come on, I'll put the kettle on.' Merry linked Ruby's arm and walked her into the farmhouse. 'You need fattening up a bit too,' she said. 'Give it a week or two.'

Ruby had never been called thin in her life, but looking down at herself she realised that her clothes were hanging off her. Not the way she would have chosen to lose weight, but every cloud and all that.

And Gabriel was joking? She was finally absorbing Merry and Milo's words. Relief flooded her and she began to relax once more.

Milo followed them inside and she threw him an evil look through her tears but couldn't help smiling. 'Not funny,' she said.

He threw his hands up in the air. 'I just went with the flow.' Gently he said, 'I didn't mean to upset you.'

Ruby shook her head and grinned.

Milo grinned back. 'I'll make it up to you as soon as we're on our own,' he whispered in her ear, rubbing her arm and sending a delicious shiver down her spine. Out loud he said, 'Anyway, what's ours is yours. I'll get you a frying pan.'

'You're doing it again, Milo,' Merry warned. 'Don't make her think she's here as a paid hand.'

'Sorry, but I'm really not. I promised her a bacon sandwich.'

'Which she should not be expected to make herself.'

'It's okay, I make a mean bacon sarnie,' Ruby said.

'You see? I don't know how we managed without you already,' Milo said as he pulled out a pack of bacon from the fridge.

'I am starving, actually. I haven't eaten properly in weeks.'

'We'll eat, and then we'll go and see the talking donkey. Champagne is already chilling. We'll take it with us,' Milo added, giving her a huge wink as he angled his head towards someplace else.

Merry raised her eyebrows at this statement but refrained from commenting.

'What does this talking donkey say, then?' Ruby asked.

'Gottle of geer, mostly,' Milo said, doing the rictus ventriloquist face again.

'Bottle of beer? Why does he say that?'

''Cos he's a very thirsty donkey.' He passed her a greaseproof packet of bacon. 'Now stop asking daft questions and get that bacon on.'

'Already at home.' She laughed, shaking her head. 'I'm feeling the *lurrve*.'

'So you should, because I have nothing but love for you.'

'And a talking donkey.'

'There is that,' he agreed.

CHAPTER TWENTY-FIVE

Six months later, Ruby was racing through the winding roads from Milo's farm in Dartmoor on her Kawasaki Ninja 300 motorbike. She now took care of the social media sites for the *Devon Chronicle* and a couple of small businesses, and was fast gaining a reputation as a social media guru. The rest of the time she helped out with the new beehives set up in Milo's field and was learning how to round up sheep with the help of a new sheepdog. The sheep travelled far and wide on the hillside and it could be a good half day's trek to find a flock that had ventured out too far. It was knackering but she loved it.

Her other hobby, photography, had taken off rather better than she had imagined. Her photographs of *heilan' coos* had been made into celebration cards, and her close-ups of bees sold consistently well in framed prints at the local nature reserve shop.

She wore sturdy boots when she ventured out on her motorbike and a top-of-the-range crash helmet that was replaced every time Kawasaki upgraded their range, Ruby being an ambassador for the brand. That took up some time too, with photo shoots as she raced around bike tracks, a camera focused on her. So, all in all, she didn't miss flying, and Milo and Lucy kept her up to speed on the shenanigans the crew got up to. She never did discover if Virgin had really offered her a job but was glad that it was mooted as it made her realise that all she wanted was to be with Milo and stay in Devon.

On this particular day she was going into town to meet Lucy for coffee. The traffic slowed and, as Ruby guessed, a car had broken down on the side of the road. It was always a problem on the single carriageways, especially in the tourist season. At least it wasn't a camper van taking up the whole of the road, she thought, and the driver had the courtesy to pull into the verge as much as he could. Still, it was causing a considerable backlog.

Ruby slowed down and pulled over in case it was a tourist. She always helped them out, almost saw it as a duty to look after them, as they'd bothered to drive from God knows where just to see the views she took for granted every day. As she parked her bike safely and dismounted, she saw that it was a dull-green Porsche, looking like a squat old toad.

No, it couldn't be, could it?

Keeping her helmet on as she headed towards Richie, she slowed, all of her nerve ends tingling with the urge to run back to her bike and speed away.

'Hi, mate, thanks for stopping. I could really do with a bit of help.' Richie took a few steps towards her.

'What's the problem?' She tried to keep her voice deep and neutral. The helmet helped disguise her voice and, knowing Richie, it would never in a million years cross his mind that it could be a woman on the motorbike.

'Thing's a piece of shit, to be honest. Wish I'd never bought it.' He thrust out his chin towards the car in a show of contempt, a move she knew well.

'Can I borrow your phone? Mine's died on me. Do you mind? I'll be quick.' He held out his hand as she dug for her mobile and passed it to him.

He went to punch in a number but suddenly stopped, his hand hovering. He stared, took a moment to try and understand what he was looking at, glancing up at Ruby in confusion. 'Whose is this phone? I know this person . . . I don't understand.'

The screen saver was a picture of Ruby on Dartmoor in the height of summer, her hair highlighted by the sunlight slanting down on her, as she fed a lamb milk from a bottle. She was laughing up into the face of an unknown person, but her happiness was clear to see.

Richie stared, took a step backwards, ran a hand through his hair and finally stared at the woman in the crash helmet as if coming to an impossible but irrefutable conclusion. 'Ruby?' He shook his head as if his eyes deceived him, but could not stop staring down at the phone and then back up at the woman standing in front of him.

She let him sweat until, finally, she pulled off her helmet and shook her hair free.

He gawped, transfixed by her glossy red hair, permanently lightened by the sunshine. Her freckles, which Richie had taught her to hate, were even more pronounced across her nose. Milo adored them. The grey eyes that Richie had once found flat and uninteresting now sparkled with the joys of living as she looked with detached interest at the man she'd once loved wholeheartedly.

He shook his head in awe. 'You look so beautiful. Your hair . . .' His voice held a note of disbelief and she wondered which one was the greater surprise: her being a biker girl or looking beautiful.

'What, this ol' *Labradoodle* hair?' She flicked it over her shoulder pointedly, letting it cascade down her back.

'I've seen you on the telly — the adverts — NinjaGirl, yeah?' His voice held a note of wonder. 'You have a motorbike? Of course you do, that's why you're NinjaGirl.' He sounded regretful as if he finally put two and two together and realised what he'd lost.

Ruby didn't care enough to have the conversation, to tell him that yes, she was the cover girl for Ninja bikes and they gave her motorbikes for free, to try out and to review.

She would never forgive Richie for making her feel worthless, never. She stared at him. 'Make your call — no rush.'

Richie looked down at the phone again and up at Ruby, as if he was still processing this new revelation. He lifted the phone, and then he stopped, glanced askance at Ruby and said, 'So really, it's all down to me, that you're where you are now. I bought you the moped, don't forget.'

'Make your call, Richie.' Ruby's voice held a note of menace. How bloody dare he?

He took a step forward as if to embrace her. 'It's so lovely to see you.' His voice was gentle, loving almost, as if they hadn't split up in a whirl of anger and recriminations. 'Bloody hell, I never thought . . .' he continued, faltering.

'That was your problem: you never thought I was up to much, did you?' She paused, wondering whether to bother continuing. No, nothing more to say. 'I guess it's best to just remember the good times — I think there were one or two.'

'We had good times.' Richie began stepping towards her, hands beseeching. 'It was sweet, Ruby, you know it was.'

'Maybe it was.' *Until it wasn't*, Ruby thought, raising her eyebrows as if to dispute the comment. Nope, she didn't intend to go there. 'So, your car, it just stopped, did it, as you were driving? Shall I take a look? Pop the bonnet, will you?'

'What?' Richie almost scoffed. 'This thing is ancient. It would be easier to rebuild the pyramids than understand the workings of a Porsche engine.'

'True. Today's engines are just plugged into a computer to find the faults, but I don't think it would help this one.'

Richie looked more confused than ever.

'I took a car mechanics course when I passed my motorbike test.' Her pointed barb, as she suspected, went straight over the top of Richie's head. 'Don't want to be left on the roadside like some *girl*, do I?'

He shook his head, still looking confused, but he followed her over to half-heartedly peer inside the engine.

She spotted the loose battery cable instantly and pushed it back on, spending the next five minutes under the hood cleaning the spark plugs, just so that Richie thought she was doing something clever. 'I thought you spent all that time out in the barn learning about your car — as you were doing it up,' she asked, slightly vexed that it was such an easy fix and Richie couldn't even do that.

Looking sheepish, he said, 'Trouble is, they had a pool table and a darts board there.' He actually grinned. 'Good times,' he added, trailing off when he saw Ruby's thunderous face.

The one chance he had to learn a trade and he couldn't even be arsed to do that. And he was the one who had the nerve to say *she* would never amount to much.

Eventually, when she was bored of cleaning off blobs of oil from the engine and watching Richie fight with himself on how to deal with this turn of events, she slammed down the bonnet. 'Turn it over.' She waved her hand in a circular motion.

Richie looked blank.

She sighed theatrically. 'Start the engine.'

'Oh, right.' Obligingly, he turned the key in the ignition and the car started with a satisfying purr.

She nodded and without another word picked up her helmet and walked over to her motorbike.

Richie waved his arms around and, sounding panicked, jogged over to her. 'Wait, wait!' he shouted.

She waited but didn't make a move towards him.

He drew level with her. 'Can we meet up for a coffee or a drink?' His tone was pleading, but it didn't give her any satisfaction.

'Hmm. Well, I'm flying up to Inverness in my boyfriend's aeroplane tonight. We're staying in his father's castle for a couple of weeks, so probably not. It's a really small aeroplane.' She did that thing with her fingers that Milo always did when he was describing his aeroplane. 'But it does the job, know what I mean?'

Richie's jaw dropped and his mouth fell open. She wasn't sure she'd ever seen anyone actually do that before and it was interesting to watch. His mouth puckered as if he'd been sucking a lemon, he inhaled loudly, and his cheeks reddened. She didn't know if it was humiliation or anger, and the beautiful thing was, she didn't need to know, and she certainly didn't care.

'If it helps, I'm sorry about everything.' He actually hung his head.

'Good, because you should be.' She looked at the sad state before her and wondered what she'd ever seen in him. He deserved nothing from her. 'You could always follow me on Instagram, if you want. I'm sure you'll find me, you were always good at tracking me down. Take care now.' For a millisecond she felt sorry for him, but it was a fleeting thought as she watched him climb back into the manky Porsche, his head hung low. She waited as he started up the engine again and then turned away.

Her world had certainly come a long way since the pink alien crash helmet and dear old Bananarama, which now languished in one of Milo's outhouses, occasionally used for pottering around the village. She picked up her top-of-the-range crash helmet, the one with interior padding, noise insulation and optimum air flow, pushed it on her head and climbed back on her bike. She had intended to wait until Richie had left, just to make sure the car was okay, but instead, in a moment of *fuck you*, she opened the throttle and, with a good throaty roar, sped past Richie, showering him with gravel.

EPILOGUE

Ruby looked down at the ground far below as the aircraft hit 30,000 feet, the twinkling lights fading as it soared up into the sky and levelled out. She smiled, remembering the first time she had seen such a sight, almost three years before when she was a rookie hostie. Not for one moment could she have foreseen the about-turn her life would take, but she thanked heaven every day for Milo and the true love she had found with him.

They weren't flying in Doris, as Milo fondly called his two-and-a-bit-seater aircraft. This time they were on a proper aircraft with gold-tipped wings, and 'Celestial Air' written on the side in a fancy, flowing font. One of six aircraft Celestial now owned, and the flight was satisfyingly full. Even though Ruby no longer flew for Celestial she was still friends with Fiona and there were no hard feelings.

Ruby and Milo were heading to Scotland, their end destination being the large house with a turret that was not a castle but near as damn it. The Destination would hopefully by now have a large marquee erected in the grounds, connected to a long archway covered with climbing white jasmine flowers, small and waxy, and purple wisteria hanging low in thick bunches. Large trestle tables would be waiting to take the weight of food for two hundred people — friends, family, all of the staff and most of the village would be there. Champagne would flow and Scottish reels would be danced — Loretta would damn well make sure of it.

Milo and Ruby were now both minor celebrities. Ruby, with her work as NinjaGirl, had been interviewed in countless magazines and periphery productions, and Milo, now a captain, was an instant hit when the series about the Destination, produced and presented by Promo Live, was televised. People swooned over his posh Scottish accent, and his good looks — think early Hugh Grant, a presenter had said when describing him — made him one of the most googled celebrities of the moment.

Loretta, Promo's PR supreme, ensured everything ran smoothly for Ruby and Milo, just as she would ensure the forthcoming nuptials in the grounds would run as close to perfect as was possible. She was in her element when bossing people around and Ruby had become quite fond of her, and wondered why she had ever thought she was a threat. It went without saying that Milo only had eyes for Ruby — and vice versa.

* * *

The captain's voice boomed over the PA. 'We'd like to congratulate the happy couple, Captain Milo Fraser and the soon-to-be Mrs Fraser, on their forthcoming marriage. Some of you might have heard of Ruby, once famous for her flaming-hot footwear.'

A rumble of laughter set up from most of the passengers, who were frequent flyers with Celestial and knew all about the emergency Ruby had caused.

'Just say that one more time,' Ruby grumbled under her breath. For all her fame, she would forever be known as the lady who set the Celestial Air aircraft on fire, but she had got used to it and accepted her fate with a smile. She forced one on her face now.

'And just for your information, to keep this flight a safe one, she's not allowed anywhere near the ovens.'

The passengers laughed and someone started clapping.

Passengers just loved clapping. Ruby had discovered that early on when she was still a member of Celestial Air. She smiled at the ones who had turned around to congratulate her and Milo, always aware that smiling was the only response to give.

One of the crew cleared her throat on the PA and started crooning, 'Going to the chapel and they're going to get married . . .' A steward ceremoniously walked up the aisle in a slow march with two glasses of champagne and two cupcakes on a tray, one with pink icing and one with blue.

This time everyone began to clap and a few people cheered.

Ruby blushed and Milo stood up.

'Please don't tell them the story of how we met, or about the Venus de Milo,' she begged, as he looked for all the world as if he was about to launch into a speech.

'I'm just taking a bow.' He waved politely to the passengers, smiled and sat down again. 'See?'

'You were *so* going to launch into your story.'

'I was indeed. It's a good job I have you to keep me in line.'

'Mind you, your story worked on me, *Milo with the hands.*' She smiled indulgently.

'Ruby, I hereby promise the jazz hands and the Venus de Milo story dies today, here and now.' He put his hand on his heart.

'Thanks. Even though you already told the whole world the story on Promo Live — and your mum was mortified.' She smiled again, took one of the glasses, passed it to Milo and picked up the other. Holding their drinks in the air, they thanked the passengers and the crew and then clinked glasses. 'To Celestial Air and the Destination, may we all be forever homeward bound.'

The captain's voice came over the PA again. 'If you look to the left of you, you can see the beginning of the Aurora

Borealis, which, as you all probably know, is a spectacle to behold and is often on display in the best parts of Scotland.'

Ruby peered out of the window, squinting. 'Yes! That's another thing ticked off my wish list.' She paused. 'Can't wait to say hello to the *heilan' coos* again, I'll bet they've missed me.'

'Aye, you do seem to have an affinity with my *coos*, but I'm still waiting for your horns to grow.' Milo stroked her hair, shaking his head in dismay. 'You do know the only reason I'm marrying you is for your Viking blood. I'm planning on starting a whole new line of Vikings in Scotland, so I do need for your horns to grow.' He tapped his fingers impatiently.

She patted his arm. 'Be patient. I've told you, they take a long time.'

They both grinned at their foolishness, so in tune and so in love.

Milo sighed and leaned back in his chair. 'I guess we have all the time in the world.'

'I'll drink to that.' She leaned over and kissed him.

He caught her as she pulled back and deepened the kiss. 'You certainly will, Mrs Fraser to be.'

She grinned. 'I like the sound of that.' They clinked glasses and watched the sky dancing with vibrant colours of green and purple as the aircraft slowed and came in to land in Inverness, the place Ruby and Milo would eventually call home.

THE END

ACKNOWLEDGEMENTS

I would like to extend a huge thank you to Sarah my editor for vastly improving my novel and to Choc Lit for having faith in me and my writing. Also, a big thank you goes to my airline friends for the anecdotes and reminders of fun days.

ABOUT THE AUTHOR

Jackie Ladbury writes heart-warming contemporary and historical women's fiction that is nearly always guaranteed a happy ever after. From spending many years as an air-stewardess and seeing first-hand that it really is love that makes the world go around, she determined to put the same sparkle and emotion into her stories. Her life is no longer as exotic (or chaotic) as it was in those heady days of flying, and she now lives a quiet life in Hertfordshire with her family and two cats, spending most of her time making up stories and thinking up reasons not to go to the gym.

For more information on Jackie visit:
www.twitter.com/jackieladbury
www.facebook.com/jackie.ladbury

THE CHOC LIT STORY

Established in 2009, Choc Lit is an independent, award-winning publisher dedicated to creating a delicious selection of quality women's fiction.

We have won 18 awards, including Publisher of the Year and the Romantic Novel of the Year, and have been shortlisted for countless others. In 2023, we were shortlisted for Publisher of the Year by the Romantic Novelists' Association.

All our novels are selected by genuine readers. We are proud to publish talented first-time authors, as well as established writers whose books we love introducing to a new generation of readers.

In 2023, we became a Joffe Books company. Best known for publishing a wide range of commercial fiction, Joffe Books has its roots in women's fiction. Today it is one of the largest independent publishers in the UK.

We love to hear from you, so please email us about absolutely anything bookish at choc-lit@joffebooks.com.

If you want to hear about all our bargain new releases, join our mailing list: www.choc-lit.com/contact